5/29/08

Pat,

THE ATKINSEN TICKET

Hope you enjoy the
political intrigue.

By

Ken Gorman

Ken Gorman

Published and distributed by:
High-Pitched Hum Publishing
321 15th Street North
Jacksonville Beach, Florida 32250

Contact High-Pitched Hum Publishing at www.highpitchedhum.net

Visit justiceonamission@comcast.net to contact the author.

The Atkinsen Ticket

Prologue

"Who the hell are you?" the middle-aged office manager growled, looking over the top of his glasses at the well-built man.

"Take it easy, boss," the man answered, pointing at his badge. "I'm Justin Morse and I switched with Big Paddy today so he could work opening day in the grandstand concession office."

Morse's breathing was back to normal after passing through the employee entrance at Yankee Stadium surrounded by New York City's finest and a second security gate to the bleachers.

"I don't see his name on this list," the secret service agent grumbled to a stadium supervisor at the access to the bleachers from the grandstands.

"There it is, sir." Morse pointed to a handwritten notation indicating he replaced Patrick Estess. "Thank you," he said to the agent, who waved him on.

The manager eyed Morse suspiciously while fussing with his ledger pad.

Morse added, "You can check with—"

"Those big-shot supervisors never tell me nothing," the manager mumbled. "Here's the way things work here, Morse. I've been doing this on opening day for sixteen years so you just follow my instructions and everything will be okay."

"Yes, sir," he replied, "anything you say," which seemed to please the old guy's ego.

"I take care of signing out the boys with their refreshments and check in all the money when they return. You fill up the trays and let the older guys with seniority get the beer. Got that?"

"No problem, boss." *I can get rid of this runt anytime I want.*

"Get your coat off and find a jacket behind the door over there," the manager ordered. "Then take two boxes of hot dog rolls to the bleacher refreshment stands. We've gotta get organized."

Morse selected a large size and, while the manager was distracted with new boys, he changed from his leather jacket into the white concessionaire's jacket covering his black turtle-neck shirt.

Once the bleacher gates to the stadium were open, work became hectic with the vendors running in and out of the office to hawk their products to baseball-starved fans.

Morse knew what he had to do in order to gain free access to the large walk-in refrigerator.

At last there was a lull in activity. The manager, no longer under stress, told Morse, "Once the game starts, we can have a beer and relax."

"Fine with me, boss. I can't wait." Grinning at his double entendre, he decided *I'll take him down right now.*

"I think I'd like that beer now, boss."

"Bullshit, just wait a few more minutes."

Morse approached the counter as the manager recorded entries in the ledger.

"Whaddya doing to …Aahg."

In a split second Morse had grabbed him around the neck and jammed his thumbs into the short man's throat. He lowered the manager to the floor in slow motion.

Morse stepped over the body and locked the door to the concession office. The dead man's congested face was pale and contorted from strangulation. His bulging eyes were fixed on the ceiling as if he were searching for his killer.

Checking his watch, Morse grimaced at the tight schedule. *Christ, it's only fifteen minutes to game time.*

Removing his concessionaire's jacket, he moved rapidly to the walk-in refrigerator. Rubbing his nose at the meaty smell of hot dogs, he easily spotted the two boxes of rolls with the initials JWB printed on the side. It would take less than a minute to assemble the weapon, but no more screw-ups could be tolerated.

As he sensed the seconds ticking away, Morse ripped open the Stadium Bakery Company boxes and removed the semi-automatic rifle from one and the magazine clip from the other.

Butch did his job well, he thought.

After snapping the folding stock in place, he inserted the magazine with ten 5.56 mm rounds. He retrieved the black ski mask from his jacket inside pocket. After dragging the dead body, with its bulging eyes now staring at him, into the smaller ice cream refrigerator, he closed the door and left the office into the under-belly of the bleachers.

The long, wide arching corridor, stretching from the old bullpens in right and left field, was dimly lit. The six month off-season could not expel a stale odor. It was common knowledge that this legendary stadium, "the house that Ruth built", would be demolished and replaced by a new ballpark across 161st Street.

The office adjoined the first ramp to the stands in dead center field. It had been many years since fans were permitted to sit in this specific fenced-off section of the bleachers where the benches were painted black.

Approaching footsteps momentarily paralyzed Morse. He fell to the ground and rolled into the dark crawlspace created by the high ceiling running downward from the back bleacher wall toward the playing field parallel to the bleacher seats—forming an oblique triangle. He gasped for air as he lay flat amidst cable and electrical supplies. A claustrophobic feeling gripped him as he waited, his sticky finger caressing the trigger. He watched, wide-eyed, as four highly-polished shoes stopped for a moment in front of his hiding place, answering a call, and then took off in a trot.

Cops are heading to the concession office, he presumed. *I have to move fast.*

"Oh, say can you see, by the dawn's early light ..." arose a tenor's voice from the field.

Although the April air was cool, Morse was perspiring and uncomfortable from hiding in the dirty crawlspace as he moved in a crouch to find the right location for his task.

He had a choice of three ramps, but the first two each had two policemen standing at attention and saluting during the National Anthem. His escape route to the street was a roll-up metal door directly opposite the third ramp.

"I've gotta make my move at the next ramp, no matter what," he grumbled. *No sweat to get to my exit.*

"O'er the land of the free ..." The fans had joined in the singing, off-key to be sure.

Great. There's only one of them. Morse placed his weapon down and tiptoed up the ramp.

"And the home of the brave."

He grabbed the policeman around the neck and twisted in a jerky motion, which he had been trained to do in the military. He heard the man's neck snap.

The crowd cheered as four Air Force F-16 jets performed an ear-splitting fly-over, which added to the excitement of the official start of another baseball season.

Morse held the policeman's body upright. Backing half way down the ramp, he shoved the body off into the crawlspace. He fetched his weapon and returned to the top of the ramp. On hands and knees he crept to a vantage point to carry out his mission. He set the rifle against his shoulder blade and focused the telescopic sight toward the infield; and he waited in a prone position, blending in with the black background of the center field bleachers.

For the first time since the day started, he felt at ease, consoled by a perfect view of his target—the pitcher's mound. His heart rate slowed as he took deep breaths.

The stadium was packed to capacity, over 56,000 fans. As he scanned the crowd, Morse could see the sign in the first row of the upper deck behind home plate—John 3:16. He smirked at the reminder that this was Good Friday.

The voice of the public address announcer blared out on the loudspeaker, "Welcome to the opening day game between the New York Yankees and the Washington Nationals. Here to throw out the first ball is the President of the United States, Herbert Quinton Atkinsen."

Morse sensed an eerie silence as he caught sight of the President emerge from the Yankee dugout on the first base side of the field, waving at the crowd. The applause was boisterous but couldn't drown out the jeers.

Chapter One

FOUR MONTHS EARLIER

"The National Committee would like to know when you're going to commit you will run for a second term," Steve Wagner informed President Atkinsen.

Wagner, the White House Chief of Staff, had already covered the routine topics at their early morning meeting, saving two items for discussion. These sessions had been standard practice for close to three years, whether in the Oval Office or on Air Force One.

The penultimate subject concerned Atkinsen's plans for the future. Party officials, led by Chairman Oscar Jackman, assumed the President would run for a second term, and be unopposed, but were pushing Wagner for a formal announcement from the President.

"I think I'll keep them in suspense a little longer," Atkinsen answered without emotion as he handed several files back to his Chief of Staff. "There's plenty of time before the primaries and the convention next August."

"Mr. President, they insist time is getting short for raising the necessary funds," Wagner said. "Jackman is concerned that Senator Robinson has been getting all the publicity and his popularity has risen in the polls despite the rumor that House Minority Leader Granger may challenge him in their primaries. It's his job to worry and—"

The President raised his hand to interrupt, saying, "Of course, I'm aware of all that. Jackman has done good work for the party …and he's a good fundraiser. There's just something about the guy I don't …I can't figure out."

Atkinsen spun his chair around to look out at the Christmas tree on the lawn. He wondered how many answers to issues in the past seem to come from this scene, no matter what season of the year or who was president.

"Let them know I'll decide right after the holidays," the President said. "Put a meeting with Jackman on the calendar for the second week in January and invite House Speaker Allcott and Senate Majority Leader Lewis. I'll deal with my State of the Union address as well. Oh, don't forget Clark Styles."

"If that's what you'd like," Wagner said.

Atkinsen turned away from Wagner again, acting preoccupied with the photo on his desk of his youthful-looking wife on their honeymoon, when her hazel hair hung down below her shoulders. He knew full well that the Chief of Staff worried about his disenchantment with the thriving bickering and badgering in Washington in advance of a presidential election year.

Wagner squirmed in his chair as he raised the last agenda item. "Mr. President, do you need anything further for your meeting with Secretary Brown?"

Atkinsen checked his watch and said, "No, I'm all set." He nodded at Wagner. "Jordan is due here in five minutes."

"Thank you, sir. I'll be in my office until three o'clock," he said. "Then I'm leaving for Florida for the holidays."

"Merry Christmas, Steve, to you and your family."

"Merry Christmas, Mr. President." Wagner lingered for a moment at the door as if to add another holiday wish, but no words were spoken.

Based on Wagner's strong recommendation, Atkinsen had to consider the dismissal of Jordan Brown, Secretary of the Interior. Brown could become the first change in the cabinet, the unity of which had been a source of pride to Atkinsen. He was dismayed as he recalled the conversation with Wagner one week earlier.

"To be blunt, Mr. President, Secretary Brown has not implemented your policies … always giving excuses for delays," Wagner had reminded him.

"I'm really disappointed," Atkinsen acknowledged, as he reviewed the dossier of Brown's past experience and reputation as a former CEO of an Oklahoma utility company.

Wagner continued, "He seems so concerned with environmental issues in Colorado that he's falling far short of our oil and gas lease sale goals."

"Has he explained his position any better?" asked the President, shaking his head at a needless problem.

"Brown says we face delays and legal action if industry doesn't follow best practices to reduce the environmental impact. The—"

"I can't argue with him on that," Atkinsen stated.

"The fact is, sir, Secretary Simon and the DOE have based their projections on Brown achieving his goals on land management. Simon is upset with Brown's procrastination and—"

"Let me talk to him … and we'll see."

"But—"

"Enough, Steve! I said I'll discuss the issue with Brown next week. So back off."

The President removed his reading glasses and cast a disapproving glance at his Chief of Staff. "Let's table a final decision until after the State of the Union address."

"Yes, Mr. President," was the clipped response.

* * *

"Good to see you, Jordan. I'll keep this meeting short so you can get home with your family."

"Thank you, Mr. President," said Jordan Brown, who looked about the office as if he expected others to be present.

Atkinsen's demeanor was stern, as he motioned to Brown to sit in front of his desk. "Take a minute to read this summary report prepared by my Chief of Staff."

Atkinsen observed Brown's reaction as pages of the report were turned, noting the placid look change to agitation.

"Mr. President, this is uncalled for," Brown stammered. "I'm following procedures to avoid environmental delays. We're working hard to achieve our expectations."

"Okay, but—"

"Pardon the interruption, sir, but my team has significant lease sales planned for the first quarter next year."

"Jordan, that's what I want to know. Can I expect then that you will meet the original plan you proposed?"

Brown hesitated and replied, "I believe we will by the end of June, Mr. President."

"Fine," the President said. "We'll see how that impacts the requirements of the DOE and Frank Simon."

Brown's face turned red with anger. He stood and said in a loud voice, "Simon has a grudge against me and my staff. I don't deserve any criticism from him and you shouldn't—"

"Excuse me, Mr. Brown, please sit down!"

The President's eyes fixed on Brown like a laser beam.

"I'll decide who's to blame and I expect the cabinet members to work together." He ran his hand across the corner of his mouth to wipe away a trace of saliva. "Is there anything else you wish to say about the report?"

Atkinsen wondered if Brown was infuriated with or simply embarrassed by the charges against his performance. In either case Brown's defensive behavior bordered on disrespect.

Brown was tight-lipped for a moment, and then answered, "I hope you consider all the facts."

"Fair enough," the President said, taking no further umbrage at Brown's tone. "Good afternoon and have a Merry Christmas."

"Thank you, sir. Same to you."

For several minutes after Brown left the Oval Office, Atkinsen reflected on Wagner's analysis and Brown's reaction. He was ambivalent about a cabinet change at the Department of the Interior at this time.

He jotted notations on the margins of the file and left it for his Chief of Staff with instructions to follow-up on the problem, including the Energy Department's status. At the top of the cover page his note read, *diary for February 1st*.

"Anyway, I would never fire someone on Christmas Eve," he said to himself.

Chapter Two

Before going to bed that evening, Atkinsen had a faraway look, mesmerized, at the lighted Christmas tree on the lawn. The Brown affair no longer held his attention, but he still felt distraught. The thought of another Christmas alone left an emptiness that permeated his body.

With an unpremeditated impulse, he picked up the phone on the night stand and said, "Agent Williams, I think it's a good idea if we all go to church on Christmas."

"Yes, sir, Mr. President," replied Ashton Williams, the Agent in Charge of the Secret Service President Protection Detail.

Arrangements were made to attend nine a.m. services at St. John's Episcopal Church, known as the Church of Presidents. It was built in 1815, and President James Madison was first to attend services regularly. The classical Greek structure shaped like a cross was later adorned with a Roman portico entrance, which added to the yellow exterior.

The President was escorted to pew 54, which by tradition was reserved for presidents.

On behalf of the congregation Rector Guzman welcomed Atkinsen. "Good morning, Mr. President and Merry Christmas. We are pleased to share with you this service on the birth of our Lord, Jesus Christ."

Atkinsen nodded to the Rector and paged through the Book of Prayer. He hoped that a spiritual reflection on this day would be helpful to his frame of mind. Since he was an infrequent churchgoer, he felt uneasy at the outset of the liturgy as if he were imposing. Absentmindedly, he gazed around the church interior. The memorial stained glass windows and marble surrounding the altar were more stirring than he recalled. The scent of evergreen and numerous wreaths on the altar pleased his senses, as he raised his head and inhaled.

Although Atkinsen tried to concentrate on the Rector's words, his mind wandered. He was rambling in the shadowy world of politics.

How does Jordan Brown live with himself? He's ready to blame others for the inaction of his department. When Wagner gets an idea in his head, he loses all sense of fairness.

Atkinsen caught the Rector refer to, "we all have a free will so …" The words drifted away.

Some people spend their lives ridding the schools of prayer or even the mention of God. Society seems to emphasize personal freedoms, but at what cost.

Organ music reached his ears as a soprano sang *Amazing Grace*. He stood and visualized the words. *How Ellen loved that hymn.*

The congregation sat to listen to Rector Guzman's sermon, but Atkinsen continued day-dreaming.

Even God Almighty would have a problem resolving the status of illegal immigrants. How can I cut spending if the Congress doesn't give me line item veto power? There's so much I wanted to accomplish. It's time to consider my legacy.

The President buried his head in his hands as he bent over in the pew, seemingly in prayerful reflection. *I don't have the stomach for this anymore, especially without Ellen by my side. Phony dinners and photo ops with congressmen and foreign dignitaries; all trying to outdo one another. And I'm no better than any of them.*

The Rector had begun the Eucharistic Celebration. Atkinsen hesitated for a moment, and then received communion. He sat down, lost in his thoughts.

"Let us pray for the deceased," announced the Reader.

He covered his face with his hands as he thought of Ellen. *I can't let anyone notice me like this.*

He bowed his head to say the Lord's Prayer. *Concentrate …* "Our Father, who art in heaven…"

How can I run for reelection? Same old ego trip. Shaking hands, reciting the same speech over and over again. Raising money! My opponent is ruthless. I can't sink to Robinson's level.

Atkinsen's face turned blank, terrified by scenes that no one else could see.

Suppose Robinson or reporters dig up that stupid one night stand with Mary Stevens. Jesus Christ! What if they check on Ellen's background and her depressive illness?

"Have a wonderful Christmas day, Mr. President," the Rector said, as he shook the President's hand after the service.

"Thank you and Merry Christmas to you. It was a meaningful service." He felt deceitful for pretending active participation.

These mood swings have got to stop.

As Atkinsen was about to climb into the waiting limo, he looked back at the church and realized he had not asked God for help. He wasted one hour and failed to pray for guidance.

Chapter Three

After lunch, Atkinsen spent a quiet Christmas day reading in front of a crackling fire in the fireplace of his upstairs residence at the White House. He loved this room for its simplicity, a credit to his wife's choice of décor. *She felt humbled by the aura of this room and exploring the House, always referring to it as our temporary home.*

Despite dozing several times, he made some progress reading *Team of Rivals, the Political Genius of Abraham Lincoln,* by historian and baseball lover, Doris Kearns Goodwin, as the music of the Broadway play *Show Boat* added to the serenity.

Sipping a diet Coke and standing to stretch, his vigor revived to face reality and his responsibilities. Decisions had to be made.

His conflicted mind had eased. He rationalized, "The people spoke with their vote. So far, I haven't let them down." He had mouthed these words staring into a mirror above the antique credenza.

Gazing at a framed picture of his pious wife, the President reflected on the rigors of a potential second term, as a widower for the past two years. If reelected, he knew the recent scene with the likes of Jordan Brown might be repeated any number of times.

"I hate that part of the job." He clapped his hands together; the sound echoed throughout the high-ceiling room.

They're all taking for granted I'll run again.

"Are they forgetting I was virtually drafted at the party convention four years ago?" he muttered aloud, staring at his wife's picture for affirmation. He recalled her words, "Only in America could something so unexpected happen."

He leaned back in his chair, eyes half closed, as he relived those unforgettable events.

"Herb, the California delegation will throw all their votes to you on the second ballot," announced his excited campaign manager, Bill Frick. Frick had just left the convention floor and rushed to the candidate's sixth floor hotel room. "They're upset with Washburn's domestic spending programs and the budget deficit."

"I can't believe the party would reject a sitting President," Atkinsen said, stunned at the turn of events. "Perhaps President Washburn's health is worse than reported."

"Everyone's talking about your interview on *Sixty Minutes*," Frick added, out of breath from his dash to the room. "Let's face facts, Herb. The reason Georgia pushed your candidacy in the primaries as favorite son was your reputation in law enforcement. Now you've gained national prominence."

Morley Safir of *Sixty Minutes* had asked Atkinsen how he would handle the responsibilities and pressure of a national figure.

Atkinsen answered, "I believe my background has prepared me to know and support the constitution of the United States and value our position in the world with friends and those with whom we disagree. As for the pressure, I can't say for sure how I will cope with the gravity of each circumstance. But, I will surround myself with the best, most experienced advisors in diplomacy, monetary policy, and defense to reach the right decisions."

"The response to your honesty was extraordinary," Frick added. "And, whether you like it or not, the sympathy factor for your wife's condition helped your popularity."

Herb Atkinsen was a Federal prosecutor in Georgia who had received laudable press endorsements and national attention for successfully "cleaning up" a crime ring in Atlanta and an internet child porn operation in a suburb of Macon.

In a vulnerable period of his married life, and despite his initial objections, he agreed to run for president in the primaries. His wife's encouragement was the overriding factor. A scant three months prior to the decision, it was discovered she had breast cancer.

"Herbert, I think it would be wonderful for you to get involved in politics," Ellen Atkinsen had said. "You deserve the chance to accomplish all the things we've talked about," she said in a convincing tone. "I'm not the only one who believes you're a born leader." She gave him a hug and added, "My sister is available to spend more time with me, so don't worry about me being alone, and you know I have wonderful care with Dr. Murphy."

The second ballot at the convention produced a stunning groundswell of support for Atkinsen. Frick told him, "It was the compelling case made by your old friend, Harry Grant, in the party caucus that initiated the momentum toward you, in spite of a last minute protest from Governor Bliss of Missouri."

"I'm uncomfortable about this rebuke to the President," Atkinsen said, feeling a heavy heart in the face of victory.

"Wait a second, Herb. There are persistent rumors that Washburn's physical vitality is deteriorating, so that probably explains it," Frick replied to placate his friend.

Atkinsen, the unlikely nominee, seemed a long-shot at best to run against a tough opposition candidate, Senator John Bartholomew Robinson from Kentucky. Even his acceptance speech lacked the conviction of a vision, despite an energetic promise that, "I will campaign hard and long. My opponent will set the country back on a path to isolationism. That cannot happen. The election of our party is in the best interest of the country."

President Washburn sent a congratulatory telegram to Atkinsen promising his full support.

The headline in the *Atlanta Journal Constitution* ran:

Underdog Atkinsen Wins Party Nomination

The small print declared: *Uphill Battle Faced by Little Known Prosecutor.*

Steve Wagner came on board to direct the national campaign, replacing Bill Frick. Harry Grant had convinced Atkinsen that a change was required.

"Herb, Frick couldn't get a word in edgewise in the caucus and his suggestions were weak," Grant informed Atkinsen. "Sure he ran a smart campaign for the Georgia delegation, but the national politicos ate him up. I've told you about a labor lawyer in D.C. who would make a great campaign manager."

"Okay, I've heard enough," a frustrated Atkinsen announced. "I'll tell my friend he's out, but Wagner's got to operate under my guidelines. No negative crap! Frick and I already had that agreement."

While their initial relationship was lukewarm, Atkinsen and Wagner became the perfect team. They were similar in physical appearance—about six feet tall, 185 pounds more or less, and blue eyes. The resemblance ended there. Atkinsen had a clean, youthful face with dirty blonde hair, graying at the sides. The younger Wagner was rugged-looking with a widows-peak hairline, which had fit his image as the stereotype US Marine. A heavy beard gave the impression he was always unshaven.

The contrast was equally evident in their temperament. The future president was mild-mannered and sincere, thoughtful and clever, and a gifted public speaker. Wagner was a shrewd problem-solver, a methodical quick study. A low boiling point was contained as quickly as it flared up. His character was formed during his years at the University of Chicago, as well as four years of service in the marines.

Wagner's campaign strategy was to focus on twelve key states and hire a Wall Street investment banker to handle fundraising. He informed the headquarters staff, "I want a grass-roots blitz in those twelve states and let the National Committee allocate extra funds to the others. We'll provide detailed releases of the candidate's positions on a daily basis and prepare television ads emphasizing his character."

A staffer raised his hand and said, "Steve, we know that Senator Robinson is a vigorous campaigner and is not above using any information or dirty tricks to win. Will Mr. Atkinsen respond to personal attacks?"

"Let me say this." Wagner replied after a brief pause, "Our candidate intends to frame his policies and point out specific differences with Robinson that are a matter of record. We do not intend to get down in the gutter with, well let's say, innuendos or rumors, and certainly not lies, to defeat him."

The turning point in the campaign came during their final television debate in Chicago's convention hall. Robinson had taken pride in his achievements as a three-term senator, emphasizing his experience. Most notably, he had co-sponsored successful legislation to restrict the sale of electronic parts to China. He got caught up in the drama of the long evening and confidently declared, "I will be the next president of the United States."

In a calculated response to Robinson's gaffe, Atkinsen said, "You're right about one thing, Senator, the public cries out for new ideas." Facing away from the camera and directly at his opponent, he asked, "If you're so sure you are the leader the country wants, why don't you give up your seat in the Senate before the election? Is—"

"Hold on," Robinson interrupted, with a deriding grin.

Atkinsen seized the moment. "Is that your fall back position? Is that your contingency plan if you lose?"

"There is no requirement I do that. You're digressing from the issues," Robinson bellowed, his eyes shifting back and forth between the moderator and his rival.

The moderator posed a new question, but Atkinsen's barely audible last words were, "Doesn't sound like you're too confident to me."

The press and TV analysts picked up that exchange and gave it traction in the final week of the campaign. The headline on the Editorial page of the *Chicago Sun Times* read:

Opponent's Whisper Gives Robinson an Earache

While Robinson fought back in subsequent speeches, a dramatic sea change was underway toward Atkinsen and his running mate, Clark Styles, the senior US Senator from New York.

On election night Atkinsen, Grant and Wagner watched the returns in an Atlanta hotel. Ellen went to bed at 10:30. Just after midnight, Bret Hume of Fox News reported that Robinson was the projected winner of Michigan's seventeen electoral votes. "According to our tally, Senator Robinson now leads by four electoral votes. How close is that?"

Grant said, "That leaves Missouri and New York as the only undecided states."

"Let's hope Governor Bliss got out the vote in the big cities," Wagner said; it sounded like a prayer.

Hume was back with another result. "We are projecting that

Missouri will go to John Robinson. That puts him ahead by fifteen votes."

A sly smile seemed chiseled on Grant's face. He winked at Atkinsen, who was sitting with shirtsleeves rolled up and relaxing on a couch, and judged, "It's up to Clark Styles' strength and patronage, particularly downstate."

At ten minutes to one, an excited Hume reappeared on the screen. "Fox is prepared to predict who the next President of the United States will be." He checked the notes the staff had handed him. "Based on New York's thirty-one electoral votes going for Atkinsen, we project him the winner by only sixteen votes, although it looks like Robinson has fifty-point-three percent of the popular vote. The electoral vote tally works out as two-seven-seven for Atkinsen and two-sixty-one for Robinson."

Cheers could be heard throughout the hotel. Grant and Wagner took turns shaking the hand of the President-Elect.

"I've got to wake Ellen, "Atkinsen said, "Steve, please call Styles in Albany and thank him for me. And once I get a call from Robinson, I want to see you privately."

"Ellen, are you awake? How do you feel?"

"I've been awake, Herbert," Ellen said, rubbing her eyes. "I know you've won."

"How the heck did you know? It was so close." He grinned like a child and lifted her by the shoulders off the pillow to sit up. They embraced for several moments.

"I just had a feeling and I prayed you would get what you wanted," she said, as her eyes glistened. "You deserve to be proud."

"It couldn't have happened without your support … and your love." He almost lost it as he bit his lower lip.

"Thank you. But you were the one accepted by the voters."

"How about you freshen up and come outside. Harry Grant wants to make a toast." He stared deep in her eyes and kissed her cheek.

"I'll be there in a minute," sounding indifferent as she sauntered to the bathroom. "Guess we'll have to leave our home in Atlanta for awhile."

Atkinsen stood at the bedroom door for a moment. At this grandiose time in his life, he had overlooked the impact on his wife. He had witnessed her melancholy moods all too often. *I hope she can be happy and secure in Washington.* He felt a knot in his stomach realizing she will miss the contentment of their Atlanta home.

Senator Robinson called from Frankfort to offer his opponent congratulations and officially conceded, of questionable sincerity, at 1:15 a.m. The Atkinsen legacy began at that moment, manifested by the contingent of Secret Service agents on the scene. His first official act was a meeting with Wagner.

"Steve, the way you managed the itinerary, avoided *faux pas'* and kept the press at bay were all critical factors in my election. We had our disagreements but that's over with."

"Thank you, sir. However, I must apologize for being so direct at times."

"I have to admit you upset me once or twice," Atkinsen said, as a wily grin crossed his face. "But I respect your no nonsense approach during the pressures we faced in a fast-moving campaign." He clasped Wagner's hand and said, "You're the man I want as Chief of Staff in my administration."

"Mr. President, it's an honor to be chosen as your Chief of Staff and I accept. I'm thrilled to serve at your pleasure." A boyish smile temporarily erased Wagner's tough appearance.

With Ellen at his side Atkinsen accepted congratulatory toasts from his closest political friend and advisor, Harry Grant, and Steve Wagner. Grant warned, "We haven't heard the last from Robinson, Mr. President." He shook his head; his furrowed brow was a trademark for the cartoonist pen. "He'll be a thorn in your side for the full term of your presidency."

The President-elect nodded and said, "You may be right, Harry, but at least let me enjoy this moment. *Prosit!*"

They raised their glasses of California sparkling champagne to celebrate the occasion and the singular honor.

"Only in America could something so unexpected happen," Ellen said. Her tears of joy were for the man she loved.

Newspaper editorials likened the Atkinsen/Styles slim upset victory to Truman's defeat of Tom Dewey in 1948.

Chapter Four

"Come on in, Harry," said the President, greeting his friend at the door to the Oval Office. "How were your holidays?"

"Same as always, Herb. How were yours?"

"Oh, I had a few up and down moments," he replied, an ungainly smile on his face. "Too much free time spent reminiscing."

"Have you lost weight?" Grant asked.

"It's that obvious?" the President gave a shrill response. "I guess ten pounds or so."

"Really!" Grant responded, solicitous of a friend who happened to be President. "So, let me see, I've missed the scuttlebutt inside the Beltway but—"

Atkinsen interrupted, "Hey, I'm the last one to hear anything if you or Wagner don't tell me." He snickered, as he removed his suit jacket.

Informality was the modus operandi of the two men ever since their first meeting at Georgetown University. Grant never took for granted that the President accepted his information as the straight scoop and his advice as an unpretentious confidant.

Grant often joked, "Don't forget I'm almost twenty years older than you," to take leeway in their private, candid interactions.

"So you're not talking to your cabinet these days," Grant said. "What's going to happen to national security?" he added.

"Very funny, but not to the Department of Defense. The Generals are banging heads with Homeland Security again about border guards and the National Guard troops on the Mexican border."

"Herb, I suggest you stay on top of that one. The government in Mexico City has its problems, so they'll eventually throw blame at us. Before you know it, chaos could spill over the border. Someday there may be a mass exodus from south of the border."

Atkinsen looked askance at Grant, as if his speculation was absurd and not worthy of comment. "Wagner didn't like it, but I tabled the Jordan Brown matter until after the State of the Union. I must say, however, I think Steve may have a point about Brown's performance."

"Good. Let the dust settle for a while and see what Frank Simon has to say," Grant said, with a nod of approval.

"Here's the subject that needs attention," the President said, changing to a more serious tone. "Jackman of the National Committee wants me to announce my candidacy sooner rather than later. I have a meeting with him next week."

"I wondered when we'd finally face up to this subject. Or, should I say, when you were ready to make a commitment." He crossed his legs, left arm resting on his lap, and held his chin with his right hand, assuming the position for politicking similar to an athlete's stance or posture to compete.

Grant had detected the subtle changes in the President's interactions with others, and moodiness after his wife's death. He had been aware of Ellen's health problem ever since he was taking into Atkinsen's confidence. As the President's advisor, he would bide time to offer his counsel.

"All these months after her death have not eased my loss or helped me forget," Atkinsen said, tapping the desk with his reading glasses. "It should be obvious to you of all people that my drive is not what it used to be."

"Yes, I know," Grant said. The time was right not only to support his friend but also to encourage further dialogue.

"So, what do you think, Harry?"

"Okay Herb, let's take it one step at a time. First, what about Vice-President Styles?"

Atkinsen appeared surprised at the question or the relevance. "What do you mean?"

"I mean, are you satisfied he's the right guy as VP? Has he met your expectations?"

"Our expectations. Remember you and I selected him after the party convention four years ago. Hell, I hardly knew anything about him."

"Sir, let's not rehash that subject again," Grant said, a note of frustration in his voice. "You needed someone from the Northeast, preferably New York, and it worked, didn't it?"

"Okay, okay."

"So has Styles been the right guy?"

Atkinsen stood and paced around the office, collecting his thoughts. "Clark Styles is an honest guy. Remember, he played devil's advocate face to face with President Washburn on military appropriations a few years ago."

"We already knew that."

"Styles' has a fine image. Very pragmatic. He's well liked and does a good job representing me and the administration." He paused and shook his head. "Frankly though, he's not a decision-maker, and he gets bogged down in legislative details that reduce his effectiveness."

"Have you told him that?" Grant probed, sensing the President was refocused on what was at stake.

"Sure, we had candid discussions until my wife died. For example, I told him he didn't delegate enough." Atkinsen paused, thinking he was too critical. "But I still respect the man. He tries to do the right thing and was an effective senator. He's not egotistical at all—a unique politician."

"Herb, I believe you just pinpointed a basic issue for next term. The party and its presidential candidate need a stronger running mate, probably from the West Coast this time given the population shift."

Grant scrutinized Atkinsen's body language as his point became clear-cut to the President. He intuitively felt that the business of politics reenergized Atkinsen.

"Maybe you're right, Harry. But I'm not about to cast him aside at this point. It smacks of inefficiency on his part and disloyalty on mine." He hesitated and added, "Jesus, he's the only one at the beginning who helped me as an outsider get through the legislative pitfalls working with the congress."

"Just think about this. Can the party afford to discard both leaders?" Grant knew he had the winning poker hand. "You're at the top of your popularity. Take another day or two to consider the alternatives—and the possibility of a President Robinson."

Atkinsen grimaced at the thought. "That would be a bitch," he said, throwing his hands in the air.

"Unlike your first term, you have Wagner and the Cabinet on board from day one. You're in synch with Josh Cohen on your speeches. And there's a wonderful opportunity to pick a Vice-President who could lead the party four years from now. The entire team is ready to support you. Just give them the word." Grant realized he may have sounded too pushy. "Of course, you still have me."

"Yeah, and I still have gridlock to deal with here in DC." His right hand covered his face. "Let me sleep on it, Harry. I'll call you in the morning."

"Good day, Mister President," Grant said, enunciating each word.

He smiled and exited the office, leaving Atkinsen in deep meditation.

Chapter Five

"Harry's wrong on one aspect of the team," Atkinsen sighed, after his advisor left the Oval Office. *He's forgotten there's one person missing.* The President toyed with his wedding ring.

Only eight months after his Inauguration in the first term, Ellen Atkinsen died. The cancer metastasized and, seemingly overnight, except for her mental faculties, she deteriorated in strength and body weight.

"Mr. President, your wife asked for you," the doctor had told him, following a final examination. He placed his hand on Atkinsen's shoulder. Words were unnecessary as the doctor avoided eye contact with the President.

Atkinsen had prepared for the worst. He didn't expect Ellen would be smiling at him as he approached her hospital bed. She moved her fingers to signal to him to hold her hand. He tried not to tremble. Her grip was firm, like the first time they held hands and he kissed her, but there was no color in her face.

"Come closer."

He knelt at her bedside in order to hear her speak. Her voice was weak but clear. He smiled at her with downcast eyes; it would make a dreadful photograph.

"Herbert, you often said you were proud of me for coping with misfortune. You're a good man, an honest man with a good heart. I know you love me as I love you. I want ..." she gagged. "I want you just to be yourself as President, for me and the country. Make me proud of you! God bless you."

He lingered at her bedside as she slept, at times fidgeting with her blanket or touching her forehead. She appeared to be at peace and without pain, which gave hope to his aching heart.

The hours wait seemed like days. He felt guilty when he smiled recalling an incident on their honeymoon in Bermuda. As they strolled around the lavish pool setting, a frisky Ellen lost her balance and fell into the pool with her clothes on. As he reached down to help her out, she pulled him in.

Atkinsen forced a cough to hide a juvenile laugh at the sight of them splashing around in the pool, blind to the stares of hotel guests.

The time came.

She opened her eyes and moaned, "I'm glad you stayed with me, Herbert. Hold my hand again."

Before he could utter a word, her eyes closed for the last time.

"Ellen. Ellen," he repeated, raising his voice to no avail.

He sat alone in the funeral home in Savannah late the first night, eyes swollen from grief. He understood her words had forgiven him, once again, and emboldened him to be himself; to trust his instincts. He slouched around the morbid parlor. Each time he passed the urn containing her ashes, he kneeled for a moment. At one point he placed his hands above the vessel as if he expected, like a magician, there would be a puff of smoke and a figure would appear.

There's so much I wanted to do to make up for the past and show her I love her.

Secret Service agents kept a remote vigil with the President.

Atkinsen remembered a disagreement just two months into his presidency. Her negative reaction to a controversial decision coincided with a sharp drop in his ratings, an exception for a new president.

"I don't know why you would break your campaign promise," she had said, seldom so upset as she gestured and pointed a finger at him.

"Please understand, Ellen. It was a political favor I had to make. I weighed the consequences and did what was necessary."

"Well, you've let down your Israeli friends. They expected you to support additional funding. I certainly hope this is not a forerunner of compromises and reneging on your principles."

To soften her critique, he admitted that, "Rather than approve a similar funding to certain Arab states to maintain parity, I changed my position in order to take no part in further escalation of arms year after year."

His heart beat faster as an unwelcome thought of their one serious marital conflict in twenty-nine years crept into his mind. A piercing pain erupted in his brain and was gone as quickly as a lightning bolt.

* * *

"I can't wait for him to get home so we can celebrate his victory together," Ellen Atkinsen said to herself, as she put on lipstick.

The brass candlesticks on the dining room table were lit and a vase of fresh-cut flowers brightened the room. She had prepared lasagna, his favorite Italian dish, and bought their preferred Chianti.

When he hadn't arrived by nine-thirty, she put the meal in the refrigerator and tossed the flowers in the garbage. She was angry he had not called. "What's wrong with him?" she muttered, as she changed into bed clothes.

Ellen hopped off the living room couch when she heard the front door open. It was after midnight.

"Herbert, I'm so glad you're finally here!" she exclaimed, momentarily forgetting her displeasure at him.

"Ellen, you scared me," he said as his head jerked back. "I didn't think you'd still be up."

She gave him a hug, and then bolted away. The scent of perfume—not her own—was too distinctive.

"Where were you?"

"We all celebrated the trial verdict," he replied. "The District Attorney was real happy with how I handled my first important case. I just got carried away and forgot to call. Real sorry, hon."

She thought his response was too automatic and condescending. "Where were you, and who were you with?" Seeing his blank stare, she stated in a deliberate tone, as her jaw quivered, "You were with another woman?"

"Well, yeah. My associate, you know, Mary Stevens and I had a drink and … and …." He just shrugged and started to turn away, as if there were nothing more to say.

"So what went on all this time?" she ordered. "Tell me the truth!" Her sad eyes anticipated the worst.

"Ellen, I'm sorry. I just couldn't call you."

"The heck with the phone call. I wanna know what you were doing."

"Nothing," he said emphatically.

She felt weak from the pang in her stomach.

"Well I'm calling her right now."

With her husband close behind, she stomped into the kitchen and snatched the phone.

"Ellen, don't!"

He watched her punch in the number.

"Please don't, it's late," he said with wide-eyed anxiety. He raised his clasped hands to his face as if to pray. "Something happened on the spur of the moment. She … we just …" He stuttered and reached out to hold her hand, as she dropped the phone.

Fists clenched, she pounded his chest once before he grabbed both her wrists.

She pulled away. Her rage held back tears as she cried out, "I don't believe this. You deceitful bastard!"

"Ellen, please—"

She cut him short, shouting, "This is how you value my love—how you feel about our relationship. How could you?"

"It meant nothing. I promise it will never happen again," he sobbed. The pained look on his face was as if a molar were extracted without Novocain.

"You're damn right it won't happen again," she announced, weeping. As tears finally flowed, Ellen marched off to her bedroom. She held her hand over her mouth and rushed into the bathroom expecting to vomit.

The aroma of coffee attracted her to the kitchen in the early morning. With no make-up and little sleep, Ellen looked haggard.

Her anger was downgraded to extreme disappointment and apprehension.

"Can I pour you a cup?" he asked.

"I'll get it myself," she said. After taking a couple of sips, she turned to him and said calmly, "Let's talk!" She looked him straight in the eye, with an anguished feeling of pending loneliness. "Do you want a divorce?"

"Omigod, no. Absolutely not."

"Then here's the way it is. I can't live my life under this cloud." She wiped a tear from her eye. "I'm not going to ask you for a divorce so there has to be a change. It's up to you." She paced around the kitchen table, clutching her damp handkerchief.

"Yes, I know, and I will," he said, subdued like a guilty child.

"I want to put this behind us. My anguish will not go away, but I will try to forgive what happened last night. I don't condone it and if anything like that happens again, it's over between us."

She stopped to catch her breath.

"Herbert, you broke my heart. How you do your penance and make it up to me is up to you. In the meantime I'm staying with my sister for a few days."

* * *

The President finally had some privacy during the mourning period. The good and sad memories of married life with Ellen continued to haunt every waking moment. He slept in a guest room in the White House so as not to disturb her space in their bedroom.

Vice-President Styles had carried on routine duties and protected the President from the more mundane matters in the Oval Office. One opposition newspaper gave a cynical analysis of the President's ten-point rise in his popularity rating, purely on the basis of sympathy. "A heck of a way for the President to reverse his earlier decline," wrote the biased reporter.

One of the many letters of condolence from all over the world came from a noted historian who pointed out to Atkinsen that, "Woodrow Wilson is the only other President whose spouse passed away during his time in office."

Atkinsen wondered how Wilson dealt with the loss. *Did he miss his wife as much as I miss Ellen?*

Chapter Six

Steve Wagner made an impromptu visit to the President's speech writer to check on progress with the State of the Union address. He walked into the office on the lower level of the West Wing thinking, *Atkinsen seems too nonchalant about this important address.*

Josh Cohen was the epitome of the perfect wordsmith. He had the absolute confidence of the President and reciprocated with prose that reflected his boss' views and manner of delivery. Cohen was a magna cum laude graduate of Notre Dame—and journalism was his true passion. His article on Foreign Policy Consistency had appealed to the new President, which led to Cohen joining the Atkinsen administration, despite lucrative job offers.

"Josh, the President wants to low key his message this time," Wagner said. "Stress a bipartisan spirit on domestic issues."

"I know," said Cohen, "but he seemed more distracted about this State of the Union than previously and—"

"The President wishes to present a broader perspective and tone, given we're in a period of delicate peace," Wagner said, unwilling to divulge any information about the President's state of mind. "Don't specifically mention the Israeli-Palestinian situation. It's an occasion to look back at our history—something different, you know. And don't make it as drawn out as Clinton's."

"Has the President decided to run again?"

"I'll let you know in due course."

"I sure hope so," Cohen said, wringing his hands together. "After working at this job, I'll hate to go back to dullsville."

"How about we get the next draft by this Friday? The President plans to spend the weekend at Camp David, so he can give it a good read." Wagner wondered if Cohen ever fell over backwards in that old chair.

"Will do," Cohen replied, thrilled at the challenge. "I have all the notes from my meetings with him. They're indexed and organized. Unfortunately, Senator Robinson has put the kibosh on several pieces of domestic legislation."

Wagner started to leave and then hesitated. He turned to look at the baby face writer and said, "You really want the President to be reelected, right?"

"Yes, sir. Of course."

"Well you better do your best work on this speech. It's the most meaningful of his presidency, and his future depends on a strong, substantive message, not just in the view of the general public, but from his own perspective."

Immediately after Wagner left, Cohen plunged into the task. He pushed some reading material aside on the desk in his small office, with books on the floor as well as on shelves.

"Let me check some history on speeches."

He typed without pause: *the most influential, the Monroe Doctrine; Reagan and the second Bush identified evil empires; the most candid in modern time has to be Gerald Ford's address in 1975: "I must say to you that the state of the Union is not good."*

"Enough of the past. They're okay as trivia questions."

Cohen leaned back and closed his eyes. He realized the President wanted to appeal directly to the psyche of Americans and stress that 'Technology and other advances haven't—no shouldn't—change the fundamental character of a nation or its people.'"

He reviewed his notes for other quotes of Atkinsen, "Elementary school curriculum should stress American History and Civics to encourage patriotism."

He stood to stretch and relieve a cramp in his hamstring.

"Let me get down to business," he whispered, hands on his hips. "The President is depending on me. I better call my wife and tell her not to hold dinner."

Chapter Seven

"Good morning, Mr. President. I trust you had a good sleep." Harry Grant had been waiting by the phone for the President's call. He knew the earlier the call, the better the news.

"I'm feeling fine, Harry. Hope you're staying warm. The temperature is expected to go below freezing."

Grant put down his coffee cup and reached for a writing pad in the lower drawer of his desk. "No problem for me. I'm preparing a lecture on the Supreme Court so I'm staying home all day."

"I've already had the briefing from Homeland Security ...more of the same," the President said. "It just seems as if countries are throwing arrows at us at every turn, like we started all the conflicts."

"I know what you mean. We're the eight-hundred-pound-gorilla," Grant interjected, sensing Atkinsen's downcast mood.

"Ambassador Kirkwood will give me the report I requested on UN programs next week," Atkinsen said, sounding frustrated. "I'm not at all happy with Secretary-General Rickman and his self-serving opinions. He actually believes the procedural reforms he has enacted are adequate."

Grant had to change the subject. "So, have you thought about our discussion yesterday?"

"You know I have." There was a pause, followed by the sound of a forced cough. "I'm not convinced that Styles should be removed from the ticket. After all, how often in history have men risen to the occasion as president? Truman's the most obvious one who comes to mind. I think Lincoln is the best example."

Another pause suggested to Grant that the President remained undecided. "If you don't mind me saying, sir, Styles is no Lincoln."

"Good line," Atkinsen said chuckling. "Styles is strongly patriotic and never plays politics on the major issues," the President said, as a definite statement that could not be challenged. "I just don't want to have the press report I dumped him, you know what I mean."

"Of course, if that's how you feel," Grant said, evading a squabble. "Since you're considering a replacement for Brown at Interior, it might appear as the beginning of a major shake-up in your administration."

Grant thought for a second and continued, "As long as you indicate your own intention about running, there's no need to make any announcement about Styles or the VP position on the ticket until the convention in August. What do you think?" He knew he pinned Atkinsen down with that question.

"You're an SOB, Harry," the President said. "When I meet with Oscar Jackman next week, I'll tell him I'm committed, although a new ticket never entered my mind. Every time you mention the likelihood of a president Robinson, my stomach churns."

"Great news, Mr. President. I'm delighted for the party, but, more importantly, for the country." Grant put the phone down and raised his right arm, fist clenched, in a victory sign.

"Are you there, Harry?"

"Yep, I'm here, Mr. President."

"I'll hold off any discussion about a running mate for now and focus on the State of the Union." Without waiting for a reaction, he ended the call.

Grant was satisfied the decision had been made. Nevertheless, his concern for his friend's physical and mental stamina to cope with a vigorous election campaign against Senator Robinson persisted. He entered a note in his diary—*not as engaging as before and seems insecure at times.*

* * *

Harry Grant was brilliant, intellectually and as a political strategist. He was also called "an enigma." The press referred to him as "the President's kitchen cabinet of one." He seldom granted interviews, unless his motive was to advance an issue or individual. Unflappable even in the face of heated arguments, Grant's insightful views were highly regarded and he earned the reputation as a constitutional scholar.

After graduating from Yale near the top of his class, he earned his Ph.D with a thesis on *THE SEVENTEENTH AMENDMENT— THE CASE FOR REPEAL*. Grant made a well-grounded constitutional case that US Senators should not be elected by the people, but be appointed by their state legislature. While he could see both sides of the issue, he opted to go with the views of the Founding Fathers, who judged the lesser number of senators should not be elected by an uniformed state-wide electorate. He concluded:

"The Seventeenth Amendment was passed in 1913. The fact is the main proponent, William Jennings Bryan, the Nebraska statesman who ran for president three times, protested against local legislators in retribution for their opposition to his presidential ambition."

Grant met Herb Atkinsen for the first time at a Georgetown University Debating Society tournament—the oldest educational debating society in the country. Grant had taken a professorship of Political Science at Georgetown. Atkinsen, the Georgia cracker, impressed Grant with his command of the subject—Church vs. State in a Democracy—and his forceful presence in front of the audience. The clarity of Atkinsen's argument accentuated his sincerity in Grant's eyes. The young man's opening had disarmed the other side.

"The Preambles of all fifty states invoke gratitude to an Almighty God, to a Creator. Can anyone among us disavow these introductions to the lawful existence of God in our society? Furthermore, there are phrases, in Hebrew, of the Ten Commandments in the Supreme Court Building of all places."

"You were very good and convincing," Grant said to Atkinsen when they were introduced after the debate. Once the tournament ended, Grant asked him, "Do you have plans for dinner?"

"No, I don't, Professor. I'd be delighted to join you."

The two hit it off immediately. Their interest in political matters put them at ease, like golfers relating to handicaps and their favorite golf courses.

"My inkling is you should consider political office at some point in your career," Grant said as he drank the last drop of his coffee.

Grant had reconciled himself to the fact that his public speaking style, with a noticeable stammer, and his homely appearance precluded him from running for public office. From a stroke suffered years ago, his left harm hung awkwardly down at his side.

"I enjoyed having dinner with you, Mr. Grant, and our discussion," Atkinsen said smiling. "I'll keep in mind your suggestion about politics. My girlfriend, Ellen, says the same thing. I would like to stay in touch with you."

"Sure thing and you can call me Harry. You know I thought your closing was great."

Atkinsen laughed, "Oh, you mean, 'Give to Caesar the things that are Caesar's; give to God the things that are God's.'"

"Perfect for a Jesuit school," Grant added, making a mental note to obtain the address and phone number of his new acquaintance.

As Atkinsen turned to leave, Grant said, "Remember, DC is where the action is."

They shook hands like old friends outside the restaurant.

Grant watched the young man walk away.

"That fella could go a long way in politics," he asserted.

Chapter Eight

"Will there be much of a delay before I meet with the President?" asked Morgan. After waiting around for ten minutes past the scheduled nine a.m. meeting he had requested, FBI Director James Morgan was downright alarmed, pacing back and forth in front of the secretary's desk. The national security report he was about to give the President would be shocking and a political bombshell. He had agonized about communicating directly with the President an issue that went beyond the non-political role of the FBI.

"The President is running a few minutes late with the UN Ambassador Kirkwood," the appointment secretary answered.

The previous evening Morgan had met and reviewed every detail of the findings presented by the Deputy Assistant Director (DAD) and the Unit Chiefs in Charge of Public Corruption and Organized Crime. The facts were swirling in his mind as he sat in the outer office and waited.

"Are you prepared to back this information up without reservation?" Morgan had asked, pointing at the three men. His tone was harsh and incredulous.

"Sir, at this point we have conclusive evidence of a connection to the mob and a possible crime," the DAD answered. The intensity in his voice was obvious to Morgan.

"There are two sides to the story," Morgan interjected, dismissing the certainty of their opinions.

"Director Morgan," the senior Unit Chief added, "only recently did we coordinate two separate investigations at our levels, and all the facts tied together."

"What have you got?" Morgan had always valued the recommendations of the experienced Organized Crime head, who had been instrumental in numerous convictions.

The Unit Chief continued, "Our undercover team has been tracking *La Cosa Nostra* in Chicago for some time and recently picked up this wire tap conversation." He pressed the play button on the tape recorder and everyone fell silent.

Static

"What's happening with that fucking office building contract on Michigan Avenue?"

"We're still working on it."

"You guys better get off your ass. Nobody else should end up with it or else."

"Finabala, we've already made offers to a couple of big shot executives from Jersey in charge of their real estate in the Midwest."

"Well, don't leave no stone unturned on this!"

"Yeah, right. I have an idea but I dunno how we can work it out."

"Yeah, what is it?"

"We can lean on the veep."

Four seconds of silence.

"You mean Styles?"

"Right. Our operation in Utica let him off the hook for his gambling debt years ago when he was a State Senator."

"Really. Hey, that's good shit. Half the space in the building will be occupied by federal government agencies. He better have a long memory and help us out. Lemme follow-up on him."

"I'll wait to hear from ya'."

Static

Morgan stared at his associates. "First, did you get the court order for the wire tap?"

"Yes, sir."

"What do we know about his gambling problem?"

"You may go in now, Director Morgan ... Director Morgan," the secretary repeated in a more pleasant tone than earlier.

"Yes, ma'am."

"I've rescheduled Mr. Cohen to meet with the President on his State of the Union speech," she said, a subtle hint to keep the meeting short.

"Thank you," Morgan said, replacing his thoughts of yesterday and bracing for the meeting with the President. He passed UN Ambassador Kirkwood exiting the Oval Office looking displeased.

James Morgan had a distinguished career in law enforcement. After graduating from the University of Georgia, where he played third base on the college team alongside shortstop Herb Atkinsen, he joined the FBI as Special Agent in Atlanta. Before his appointment as FBI director, he had been the Special Agent in Charge of the New York office during 9/11 and distinguished himself with valor in the investigation of the World Trade Center site.

* * *

"Good morning, Jim," President Atkinsen said, smiling at his friend from college days. "How were the holidays with your family?"

"Very nice, Mr. President," he replied; it was an automatic response.

"I'm about to have my second cup. Would you—"

"No thank you, sir," Morgan said softly, uncharacteristically cutting short the President.

"What have you got for me, Jim, it sounded urgent?"

"Yes sir, it is. Frankly, it's a matter of national security."

"Well, you know I've already met with Homeland Security early this morning so—"

"I'm sorry to interrupt, but this matter concerns an investigation of someone in your administration." Morgan was fiddling with the two sheets of paper in his hand. A cough was forced, as if to apologize for being blunt.

"You seem uptight." Atkinsen said, as he walked around his desk, with his coffee, motioning to a couch in the sitting area of the Oval Office. "Have a seat."

"Mr. President, I have to advise you that our report refers to Vice-President Styles."

Atkinsen held his cup in mid-air for a moment, as his easy smile disappeared. He sat upright and said, "Go on."

"Before Styles was elected US Senator, and as a New York State Senator, he played a role in the awarding of a hotel construction contract in Utica for a company controlled by *La Cosa Nostra*."

"Hmm. That's upsetting," the President said, taken aback by this revelation. "Unless there was a quid pro quo or some impropriety though, there's no basis to make a big deal over it. That kind of thing is a common city government transaction." Atkinsen's mild manner was noticeably strained, anxious about what he might hear next.

"Yes sir, it normally is routine. But, first of all, he injected himself in the approval process for the project, which raised eyebrows among leaders in the community. But it's the reason he did it that's the problem."

"Which is?"

"For his perceived part in getting the transaction approved," Morgan paused, running his free hand through his hair several times, "a significant gambling debt was forgiven."

"I don't believe it," Atkinsen said, looking like he heard a bad joke. "How much … You have proof of this?" Atkinsen sounded defensive at the outlandish charge.

"Yes, at least enough to have him questioned under oath. We—"

"How come the FBI didn't discover this problem a long time ago, dammit?" The President stood, agitation distorting his face, and stomped back to his desk.

"Our Public Corruption Unit did investigate rumors of a gambling habit while he was a State Senator, but concluded the allegations were unfounded. I regret it wasn't pursued further." Morgan's eyes searched the floor to avoid the President's glare. His body was as rigid as a mannequin; a forlorn look whitewashed his face.

"Why does this situation involve national security?" the President asked, gesturing with his arms. He was apprehensive of the Director's answer and closed his eyes.

"We believe he has compromised his position by a relationship with the mob. While we have no credible evidence there has been direct contact with the Vice-President, the possibility exists they may put the pressure on, perhaps on international issues, to blackmail him."

Morgan stood and slowly walked to the front of the President's desk and said, "Sir, allow me to say this. If the press or opposition party gets hold of this information, I'm not sure you could survive the scandal."

"All right, stop right there!" Atkinsen exclaimed, annoyed at Morgan's inference. "I interpret what you're saying, but you're out of bounds. Don't go beyond your expertise or authority!" He thought for a moment and asked, "Who's aware of all this?"

"Just a couple of us at the Bureau and one or two at Justice. The reason we didn't bring it to Homeland Security is because Styles has become too friendly with their people." He stuttered, which caused an awkward silence. "May I leave our report with you?"

"Yeah, sure. I'll talk to the Attorney General—no names mentioned—to figure out how to approach this as a generic issue." Atkinsen glanced at the two sheets of paper. "Hold off any further activity until you hear from me."

The President was flustered about the next step and the implications of this information. He paused for a few seconds and said sarcastically, "Why didn't you just hit me with this when I was about to give the State of the Union two days from now, for Christ sake! The FBI sure blew this one." He turned his back on Morgan and ordered, "Please leave."

The red-faced Director turned to leave the Oval Office and meekly said, "Thank you, Mr. President."

As he perused the report, Atkinsen buzzed his secretary and ordered, "Have Mr. Grant come and see me right away."

Jesus, how did Styles let something like this happen?

He read the transcript of the two mobsters' phone conversation. His legal mind concluded that Clark Styles had some intense explaining to do. *Hopefully, he'll be able to account for the damaging wire tap. Or else.*

Chapter Nine

Professor Grant had finished his lecture on the American Judicial System and introduced, in his unique style, a trivia contest to advance class participation. He felt this approach to teaching the workings of government grabbed the attention of freshmen students the best.

"How about this one? I've told you before that one of my favorite books is *Catch 22*. The federal system and government policies are full of bureaucratic situations that make you scratch your head. They can defy logic and contradict other policies. Can you give me an example?"

A student spoke up. "In order to counter the growth of the Iraqi Communist Party, we helped Saddam Hussein's rise to power."

"No, no. Your facts are right, but that case illustrates the lesser of two evils principle—a common pragmatic choice. Since you brought that up, there's also the choice between two undesirable options— damned if you do and damned if you don't. It's referred to as *Hobson's Choice.*"

Several other responses missed the point.

"Professor, can you give us an example of catch twenty-two," a student piped up.

"Here's one, but I expect you to think about it as part of your homework assignment for our next class. Secret Service agents are dedicated to protecting the life of presidents. If an agent comes on too strong in dictating and controlling the activities of the president, he risks being removed from the protection detail. So he's prevented from performing the best job he's expected to do."

Grant checked his notes to move to a different question. "The other day we covered the Reagan years, and I mentioned his kitchen cabinet, that is, friendly advisors who are not part of the administration or on the payroll. What's the origin of that term?"

"Professor, your name has been quoted in the press as a special advisor to President Atkinsen. Are you—?"

There was a knock on the door and a secretary entered with a note for Grant. He turned his back on the class and read it.

The President wishes to see you right away. Two men are waiting outside to drive you to the White House.

"Class is over. Oh, the answer goes back to Andrew Jackson's presidency." He shoved several magazines into his briefcase and hurried out of the room.

* * *

Grant knew something was amiss as soon as he entered the Oval Office. The President was pacing the floor, a dour look on his face. Grant wondered if there was trouble with the State of the Union address. He waited to be recognized; this was not a time for jovial banter.

"Have a seat on the couch, Harry," Atkinsen said, as he gathered papers from his desk. He sat opposite his long-time advisor and said, "I've got a problem."

Grant was accustomed to meetings starting out this way. He would often say, "What's an advisor for but to discuss issues, identify options and recommend courses of action." This had been his forte, which enhanced a professional relationship into a close personal friendship. But the President's manner seemed icy this day.

He feared this urgent call related to his disturbing meeting with the President one week earlier regarding the announcement he was a candidate for reelection. When Atkinsen confirmed his intention to the National Committee, Jackman had urged that the decision be made public before the State of the Union address. He indicated, "George Granger's entry to oppose Robinson in their primaries is capturing all the headlines. Robinson has stepped up charging you with a do-nothing administration. We need a quick announcement that you will run for a second term."

Shortly thereafter, a press release read, *President Herbert Quinton Atkinsen announced he will seek reelection to serve a second term. The President wishes to build on the achievements of his first term.*

Grant had recoiled at the premature release and informed the President, "That simple message failed to show your dedication to the hard work ahead. The public wants to know you're still committed and aggressive following the death of your wife." He flipped the one page statement on the coffee table between them.

"Take it easy, Harry! I'll have other opportunities to show I'm in the race to win."

"I'm not mad at you, sir. I'm upset with Jackman and Wagner." Grant calmed down and said, "I'm sorry."

But that incident was a week ago, and a week inside the Beltway can bring a world of new problems.

"What's it about, Mr. President," Grant asked, anxious about what sort of problem he would hear.

"Morgan came to see me this morning," the President stated. Since his head faced down, the words came out like a murmur to Grant.

"Uh, huh." So it's a law enforcement issue, Grant surmised.

"The FBI has linked Clark Styles to gambling and a possible link to La Cosa Nostra."

Grant leaned forward on the couch, careful not to appear shocked. "Does the FBI have evidence he's done anything illegal as Vice-President?"

"Morgan told me the gambling occurred when he was a New York State Senator. He suspects the *LCN* believe they have Styles in a blackmail situation. He—"

"But nothing illegal as the Vice-President," Grant interrupted.

"Right."

"Herb, are you aware of or recall any hint of favoritism shown by Styles that might advance their interests?"

Atkinsen was silent for several seconds. "No, I can't think of anything resembling impropriety. It's simply out of the question. As I said the other day, I respect him. He's been loyal and honest during the time I've known him. What's your point?"

Grant stood and walked to the back of the couch, folding his arms across his chest. "I want to differentiate between a crime and a personal scandal if it all came out."

"Of course, it will come out," the President said, abruptly sitting up straight on the couch to signal his irritation. "That's why I can't sit on this information."

"Yes, of course. I meant how it comes out. About his gambling, it's a smear on his character, but they're not treating it as a crime, are they?"

"Styles was involved with a gambling ring to begin with. I decided not to discuss this with the Attorney General yet, since I don't think he'd be prosecuted for that. The bigger problem is his debt was forgiven for possible influence in awarding a construction contract."

"That's something we have to verify. So far none of this taints his position in your administration." Grant scratched his head and moved his hand to the back of his neck. "Is Styles or anyone outside the FBI aware of the investigation?"

"Not to my knowledge. Wagner may not like it, but I don't intend to get him in the loop yet either."

"Obviously, you have to get Styles to admit to this and to tell if he's been contacted by the mob since becoming Vice-President," Grant added, as a clearer picture of the problem took shape in his mind. "If he can conclusively say his gambling habit ended years ago and he has not been approached by these shady characters, then we're left with just a potential scandal—not a legal problem."

"Right, and probably end my chance for reelection."

"Wrong! You were not committed at first to Styles in the last election and you're somewhat ambiguous about him as your running mate this time," Grant explained, continuing his thought process. "So, one way or another, he's got to go as VP."

"I can let him resign, period, as long as he hasn't committed a crime. But it will reflect on my record. The only other VP to resign was Spiro Agnew, which he did under duress for his crime." Atkinsen stared down at the floor shaking his head back and forth. "That may be the price I have to pay."

"Agnew was a classic Greek tragedy, no pun intended," Grant stated. "But his corruption as Vice-President has no relevance to this situation. And Jefferson's reputation wasn't stained by his infamous

VP, Aaron Burr."

Grant suddenly advanced toward the President and spoke just above a whisper, "Suppose you give Styles a reason to resign."

Atkinsen looked startled. "What the hell are you talking about? Either way the effect is the same."

"Let's say you do something totally out of character. It gives Styles an out to resign on the basis he can't function with you any longer."

"Jesus, Harry, what would I do to cause that reaction, and how do I survive the campaign? It puts the onus of blame and doubt on my presidency."

"Herb, the good news is I sensed at our last meeting you'd put friendship aside and drop him anyway, in which case we might not have to deal with a scandal. So you—"

"Wait a second, Harry. You're assuming he hasn't committed a crime. I still don't see how I can get out of it unscathed." Atkinsen jumped up, releasing nervous energy and walked to the French doors.

"Okay, we've already agreed that a crime changes the scenario," Grant said. "For now I'd like you to focus on what you could say that would piss off Styles."

Grant watched Atkinsen pace around for a few minutes. *He doesn't need this quandary,* Grant thought, feeling sympathy for his friend.

What a bizarre discussion! Grant had not considered how Clark Styles would react, even if a resignation for a trumped-up reason was to help rather than hurt him.

Atkinsen returned to his desk. He reached for stationery to take notes as he spoke. "Let me go over how this scenario, as you call it, plays out. First, I meet with Styles to lay out the charges against him. It will be clear that his resignation is expected. Then, I'll make a statement or decision that gives him a reasonable reason to resign. Oh, and I need to think about his replacement a lot sooner than planned."

"Okay, the explanation might be a policy disagreement. You've let him off without damaging his reputation, which obviously is important to you." Grant was riveted to their dialogue, testing the logic of the plan in his mind.

"So, I create a rift between us that does not impair my reelection. That will be tougher on me in the convention then in the general election. Styles is considered next in line within the party. After all, there are influential Senators who would support him."

"Of course," Grant jumped in, sensing he had the upper hand, "but he has to decline any back-room maneuver to be the party's nominee or he's exposing himself to disclosure. You can make that fact abundantly clear to him during your meeting."

"In other words, I'll hold the real problem over his head."

"Correct."

"Frankly, not the way I do business, as you know." He resumed pacing the floor, as he tore his notes into shreds. "For God's sake, I wouldn't be President if it weren't for his leverage in New York. Let's not forget that!"

Grant studied his friend's bearing. This is an instance where good character stands in the way of smart politics, he thought.

"Remember, Herb, you still have much to accomplish as President. Unfortunately, there's no one else on our side who can beat Robinson."

"So now I must confront Styles and then come up with a cover-up scheme," Atkinsen repeated. A chagrined look clouded his face. Like a soldier on guard duty, he walked back and forth. *And can I be comfortable with a new running mate in the election*?

He buzzed his secretary and directed, "Please ask the Vice-President to join me for a cocktail at the White House tonight."

"Too bad all this came out now," Grant said. "Couldn't be at a worse time."

"Accept the good and cope with the bad," Atkinsen said, smiling for the first time in the meeting. "I recall a pretty savvy guy counseling me when I was a smart-ass college kid."

Grant beamed at the compliment and said, "I hope it goes well with Styles."

* * *

After Grant left, the President read several reports Wagner had prepared, but concentration was out of the question with the omnipresent Israeli-Palestinian hostility crowding his mind.

He wondered how often personnel information fall between the cracks, like the Styles slip-up. *I'll ask Wagner to speak to Morgan and review the procedures for background checks.*

Since he had three hours before his meeting with the Vice-President, he selected bourbon from the liquor cabinet and poured a short drink. *Maybe the alcohol will ease my distress for a friend.*

"Ellen, is all this worth it?" he sighed. He picked up her photo on his desk and placed it face down.

Chapter Ten

President Atkinsen lingered at his desk in the Oval Office longer than usual, despite the fact the Vice-President had already arrived in the upstairs residence for the appointment. He inserted several notations on the margins of the last draft of his State of the Union speech.

Josh Cohen had said to him, "I think this reflects your views and strikes the right message to the American people. It may be your best."

Atkinsen's mind wandered to his earliest encounters with Clark Styles. The party bosses and Harry Grant felt a northeasterner was vital as a running mate—someone non-controversial with an acceptable public record and a presence on the national scene. Styles, as a highly respected senior New York Senator, filled the criteria to perfection. His Keynote address seven years ago at the convention in Los Angeles endorsed Craig Washburn as President which enhanced his reputation among the party faithful.

The Atkinsen and Styles staffs coordinated the schedules and talking points like "a well-oiled machine", as one reporter described their campaign, with much credit attributed to Steve Wagner. The candidates complemented each other well in political acumen, and, as time went on, their political relationship grew to friendship. Nevertheless, Styles understood and accepted their business-like rapport and who was calling the shots.

Both before and after becoming President, Atkinsen took delight with how Ellen and Joyce Styles nurtured their relationship. "Joyce is a wonderful, down-to-earth woman, a dear friend," Ellen had said to her husband on more than one occasion.

He gazed at the picture on the mantel of his wife in her inauguration gown. *She looked so beautiful that evening, and her brief remarks charmed everyone, reminiscent of Jackie Kennedy.*

The President placed the speech in his center drawer, locked it, and left to meet the Vice-President.

As Secret Service Agent Ashton Williams walked just ahead of POTUS, he advised the agents in the area that, "*Shortstop* is on his way up to his living quarters." When they reached the elevator, another agent stood at attention. Williams said, "Mr. President, I'd like you to meet the newest member of the detail. This is Russell Barrett."

"Hello, Russell Barrett, nice to meet you."

As they shook hands, almost on the run, Barrett said, "My pleasure, sir. It's an honor."

"Good luck, Barrett," the President said, as the elevator door closed.

* * *

"Good evening, Mr. President," Styles said in his usual upbeat manner.

"Hello, Clark. Sorry I was delayed. Where are you off to? I forget."

"A fund raiser at the Kennedy Center. I'm supposed to meet Joyce there at eight."

Cocktails were brought in—bourbon and water for the President and scotch on the rocks for Styles, who sat back with his legs crossed, looking relaxed.

"I've read the most recent draft of your address," Styles said, while Atkinsen sipped his drink. "I think it's a forthright commentary on conditions today and programs for the future."

"I agree … it's a good start." The President leaned forward in his chair. "Clark, something serious has come up I have to talk to you about." His informality had turned serious.

"Yes, sir," the Vice-President said, uncrossing his legs.

"This concerns your time as a state senator. Your connection in Utica to—"

Styles interrupted in a flash. "Sir, there's nothing to that construction contract thing. I didn't do anything wrong and was never accused of impropriety. It's really old news."

"Let me finish, Clark! I'm not going to dwell on that issue specifically. Director Morgan has presented me with new information regarding your personal finances."

The calm, innocent look disappeared from Styles' face. He squirmed in the chair. "What is he saying?"

"The FBI has evidence of your gambling habit."

"God, that was a long time ago. I haven't been involved in any gambling since. Believe me."

"Clark, there's more to it. You weren't able to cover your gambling debts, were you?"

Styles wiped non-existent lint off the lapel of his tuxedo. He now appeared dazed as his eyes scanned the entire office. He opened his mouth, but no words came out.

"Clark, we've always been open and honest with one another. Let's not make this any harder than it is," Atkinsen lectured.

"I had a problem then. It really didn't amount to much. So I ..." He started to tremble, holding his hands over his face. Taking short breaths, he stuttered, "You've got to believe me, sir. I didn't do anything to get out of what I owed. The operators wanted me to support gambling casinos in upstate New York to compete with the gambling on Indian reservations. There was no way that could happen, either with my help or anyone else." He stopped to blow his nose into his handkerchief.

"What about the construction contract in Utica?"

"Sir, that was a bogus issue. The operators never had any interest in that project at all, to the best of my knowledge."

The President stared at his Vice-President. He had been studying Styles' gestures and voice intonations. *His emotions and explanations come across as sincere and make sense.* He wondered if Styles had told Joyce about the problem.

"Mr. President, I'm truly sorry this came out at this time. I've let you down. It all happened so long ago. Even my wife doesn't know about it."

The phone rang. Atkinsen picked it up and stood with his back to Styles.

* * *

Nervous perspiration had soaked Styles' shirt. He gulped down the last of his drink, wishing he had another. While he waited, he reflected on a meeting at a labor union convention in Las Vegas two years earlier at the end of his first year as Vice-President. He had been invited to the suite of the union president and was introduced to a Joseph Vitale. Their conversation was brief, but he remembered Vitale's not-so-subtle message.

"I hope the administration resumes normal relations with Cuba. You know, like it was before Castro. I'd like to count on your support."

Months later, Styles ascertained that Joseph Vitale was head of a Florida *La Cosa Nostra* family. *How did I let myself get into that position?*

He wondered what would happen next, as he grimaced at his stupidity. *To think I expected that he would ask me to be his running mate again.*

* * *

Atkinsen resumed his position opposite Styles. He placed his hands together as if to pray.

"Clark, this presidential race will be tough. Robinson is mad as hell for losing last time. Right now, you represent baggage to my reelection."

"But no one knows—"

Atkinsen interrupted him, "Stop right there! You know how these situations get out in Washington. The scandal will crush my chances for a second term." He stood in front of Styles, arms folded across his chest. "The fact is you cannot be on the ticket."

Styles lowered his head, eyes closed tight.

"Even if you avoid prosecution, which I now believe you can, you've been compromised."

"Herb, I can't believe you'll throw me out. After all I've meant and done for you since your wife died."

Here comes the denial and anger, Atkinsen thought, regretting it would end up this way.

"Is there anything I can do?" Styles pleaded. "I've been loyal and trustworthy as your vice-president. Without a blemish on my record."

"Clark, you have to realize your political career is over,"

Atkinsen said in an unequivocal tone. He felt compassion for his friend as he declared this terminal judgment. "There are choices about how we proceed from here."

Styles stared at the President. The sadness in his eyes communicated his shame.

"You could stay on until the convention in August and then a new VP nominee would be announced. However, it would look like I dumped you and the onus would be on me. Besides, I'm obliged to deal with this problem long before then."

Styles continued to stare in space, as if he were hearing a foreign language. He brushed a lock of hair off his forehead.

"I could insist you resign after the State of the Union. The suspicions regarding your reason and why I accepted your pulling out at this time would lack substance, so the press and Robinson would dredge up something that might hurt us both."

Atkinsen hesitated to allow the alternatives to sink in to his downcast VP. "We might try another approach."

Styles had the look of a penitent sinner, head down. "What would that be, Mr. President?"

"Suppose I gave you a reason to resign—a policy difference, let's say. I'll still expect your letter of resignation, and you can be as specific as you want to state your disagreement with me. But, no character assassination and speak the truth! Okay?"

"Sir, I've supported your decisions so it's impossible—"

"Just think about it for the next couple of days," Atkinsen cut in, patting Styles' shoulder. "Look at me," he said, as Styles raised his head. "It will work out for the best."

They stood facing each other. The President motioned to the door.

"Good night, Mr. President. I'm truly sorry about all this."

The President reached out and held Styles right hand in both his hands. "Good night."

"Harry, did I wake you?"

"No, sir," Grant replied. "I was reading the draft of your State of the Union address. It sounds presidential."

"My meeting with the Vice-President went as we discussed. It's a shame … and I know he's disappointed with me. Now the ball is in my court."

"I know how tough this is for you," Grant said. There was an awkward silence. "If I may, allow me to suggest one more thing."

"Go ahead."

"Let's wait 'til after the State of the Union address and see how it's received around the world. Then, meet with him again to identify a domestic or foreign policy he can take issue with. He's got to come to grips with his situation. Provoke him if need be!"

"Hold it!" the President shot back. "You want me to deal with this in the next few days. Why so fast? And what about his replacement?"

"First, the chances are better than even money that the story will leak out," Grant replied. "Then we're back to the scandal we wish to avoid."

"I guess you're right, but I have to think this through. What about—"

"Filling the vacancy is more of a problem. You have a short list you're considering for your next Vice-President, I know."

"Yes, but no one stands out as highly qualified except Allcott and I want more time to evaluate other candidates." Atkinsen stood and paced around the Oval Office like a caged lion.

"Mr. President, we may be able to keep the position vacant until August."

"You're kidding," he said. "I thought the Twenty-Fifth Amendment covered this situation."

"It does, sir, but there are no specific time requirements for you to nominate a Vice-President to obtain congressional approval. If memory serves me right, Nelson Rockefeller wasn't sworn in as Vice-President until five months after Ford replaced President Nixon. That was a long time for the position to be vacant."

"I think you're right about that, Harry, but you can bet that Robinson and the opposition will scream bloody murder if we wait until August. It places Speaker Allcott, who is on my short list anyway, next in line of succession to the presidency for seven months. Besides, Robinson dislikes Allcott, and he doesn't hide his opinion."

"That makes my point," Grant squealed into the phone. "If you nominated Allcott now to fill the vacancy, he'd get House approval but not the Senate's even though we have a slight majority. Robinson would use his influence to persuade the senate that a margin of 51-49 to pick a VP position would be too divisive. The rejection of your nominee would give Robinson a major victory right at the start of campaigning."

"Christ, you have my head spinning. Let me sleep on it."

"Thank you, Mr. President. Good night."

After ending the call, Atkinsen was more confounded than ever. There were pitfalls no matter which way he went. *Who's going to be on my ticket?*

"This was a hell of a day," he said to himself, as he fell into bed.

Chapter Eleven

The Speaker of the House, Bob Allcott, pounded the gavel three times and announced, "Members of Congress, I have the distinct honor and high privilege to introduce the President of the United States."

Once again applause erupted, somewhat muted on the Minority side of the aisle, and lasted about a minute. Although not as long, the response was more fervent than the cheers when the President had first entered the House chamber only moments before to be escorted to the dais. This annual event in the last week of January had become a command performance, to the delight of all politicians, especially the party in power.

As Atkinsen strolled down the middle aisle, shaking hands and beaming, he felt humbled at the memory that Dwight Eisenhower, his father's hero and golf partner, once shared the same stage.

As the applause went on, Atkinsen's gaze ranged from left to right, and to the respected Joint Chiefs and Supreme Court members in the front row. He made eye contact with the Justice who cast the deciding vote on a clear definition of pornography that disposed of the "I know it when I see it" concept.

Next he caught Senator Robinson's smug look, like a tiger ready to pounce on its prey. *How does that charlatan garner such broad support?*

The President made the usual opening comments and acknowledgments. He proclaimed in a vigorous voice, "The state of the Nation is strong," prompting a standing ovation.

He glanced up to his left, to the packed gallery—and the empty seat in the first row.

Oh, how Ellen loved the enchantment of this evening. "Why not play *Pomp and Circumstance* when the president enters wearing a cap and gown?" she had joked. *Or was it to suppress conceit on my part?*

As quickly as a wave of sadness swept over him, the mental curtain of necessity dropped, shutting off the memories. For the next thirty-five minutes Atkinsen spoke in specific terms of the economy and domestic policy achievements. He outlined the challenges confronting the world and the United States role in promoting peace. He received spirited applause for stating, "The education of our youth must be improved."

Sounding Lincolnesque, he spoke with emotion, "In terms of America as a civilization, we here in this chamber tonight are neither indispensable nor permanent. The demographics of the American people may change, but the core values and ideals upon which this institution was founded are essential for and inseparable from our very survival."

Mixed applause delayed his speech eighteen times. This was his element, his comfort zone. Atkinsen held back a grin at Josh Cohen's line regarding the camaraderie in the chamber, which he decided to skip given the animosity that exists.

The President appeared calm, his delivery smooth with aplomb. There was no trace of nervousness, except for occasionally wetting his lips. His alternating smile and serious appearance was genuine.

He had just concluded remarks related to alternative energy sources when a sudden change in his behavior was apparent. His eyes narrowed and he fixed his gaze directly at the television camera. As he reached for a glass of water, he turned toward the Vice-President for only a second and then, as a conscious decision, removed the typed speech from the rostrum.

Clark Styles had been sitting behind the President next to the Speaker of the House in accordance with protocol. The TV camera highlighted his stone-faced look. When the President stared back at him, a twitch below his left eye appeared on the TV screen like a hairline crack in the face of a statue.

The President hesitated for several, tense moments as he observed the anxious faces of friends and foes alike. *I don't need the teleprompter any more either.*

"There's no point of my asking for bipartisan support on my energy proposal, so I won't," he said, glaring at the startled audience. He noted Congressmen check the advance copy of the speech for this line; then stare at him with a quizzical look.

"Therefore, I am initiating actions to resolve long-standing thorns in the sides of our citizens. First, there has been enough unjust criticism incessantly directed at our great country. I'm putting the United Nations, a dysfunctional organization, on notice right now that all funding and dues will stop immediately. The Oil for Food scandal is but one symbol of their ineptness and corruption."

An uncomfortable stirring filled the chamber, like a bee hive was loose. Close advisors to the President looked at each other, clearly baffled by the departure from script. The junior Senator from North Carolina, a Jesse Helms protégé, stood alone and applauded, but quickly sat down.

"Furthermore, I refuse to sign the Clean Air Treaty." Pointing at the opposition side, he charged, "Put politics aside and let's do what's right for the country."

Hissing and shouts from the minority became shrill. Political moderates seemed stunned, sitting speechless.

For the moment Atkinsen could not mask the anger in his delivery, needlessly vengeful. "And I expect the Mexican government and US companies to do more to stem the tide of illegal aliens."

The uproar from the Minority party eclipsed the embarrassed rumbling of the President's own party.

"Lastly, I propose we reintroduce the draft to strengthen our military."

The President paused, his emotion under control once again, and pictured Harry Grant sitting at home in front of the TV pulling his hair out.

The jeering was widespread.

"From now on we must face facts and eliminate the political-correctness that has been forced down the throats of our citizens. This is how—"

The clamoring of disapproval drowned out the President's words. The Speaker pounded the gavel calling for order.

Atkinsen looked determined as he concluded in a loud voice, "I believe these steps are in the best interests of the country. God bless America."

The Sergeant-at-Arms waited for the Secret Service to take charge of the President and lead him out the chamber, without the usual cadre of congressional leaders. As they walked at a fast pace up the center aisle, angry faces shouted at the President. Less than an hour ago, these same lawmakers were applauding him and begging to shake his hand. Keeping his head down, Atkinsen was soon in the limo heading back to the White House, leaving behind a chaotic scene.

"What the hell did you do?" shouted Steve Wagner, disregarding the proper courtesy. Not waiting for an answer, he pleaded, "Why? Tell me why?" His face was bright red, like the worst sunburn imaginable.

"Shut up, Steve! I want to get back to the White House, have a double bourbon, and go to bed. I'll explain it all to you in the morning ... at seven as usual."

"But what do I do?" asked an exasperated Wagner. "Everyone will want an answer now—the press and Foreign Ministers, not to mention congressmen from our own party. Before the nights out, I'll hear from the Cabinet and the UN head. This is crazy." He buried his shaking head in his hands. The world was collapsing around him, like a seven-point-five earthquake.

President Atkinsen leaned back on the headrest and stared straight ahead, oblivious to his Chief of Staff's predicament ... and his own.

Chapter Twelve

"It's unbelievable," Granger said. "In all my years in politics, I've never witnessed a breakdown like that. I almost feel sorry for him." He leaned his head to the side resting on the palm of his hand.

Granger's associate, Stan Flanagan, nodded in agreement. "The damage President Atkinsen did to his party tonight is staggering," he said, unsuccessfully holding back a smile. "As you ordered, the prepared response from our side was cancelled for good reason."

"Funny thing is if he had only indicated his disillusionment with the UN, I could have met him halfway. He had balls to say what he did." After drinking a sip of water, he continued to shake his head in disbelief.

George Granger sat in the large leather chair in his office in the Sam Rayburn Building, still in wonderment over what had happened just an hour ago. Although he was the House Minority Leader, he didn't want to be out in front with a statement about the President's tirade.

"Let him stew in his own broth," he advised his aide. "Journalists and TV talk shows will have a field day with this for months and years to come."

Granger had learned the hard way the good and bad of his profession from political in-fighting in the Louisiana Parishes. College life and a political science major had not prepared him for his state's brand of politics—a holdover from the Huey Long days.

During one bitter debate, Granger was called a bigot. His retort prevailed with the voters. "While I am a Roman Catholic, my wife is Baptist and I attend services with her periodically."

His legislative credits in congress were modest but of real substance. The Granger/Waddley bill protected children from child predators on the internet. Cloak-room arm twisting and compromises were his forte, for which he was compared to Lyndon Johnson, with an added high mark for honesty. Based on his proven ability to get things done, his colleagues in the House had unanimously chosen him as Minority Leader.

Granger's claim to fame came in years past due to an act of God, namely Hurricane Katrina. From what had been the front lawn of a tottering home in New Orleans, he had shouted to TV reporters, "This is a disgrace. I intend to raise the roof back in Washington with the administration and with FEMA. We need change and we need action. Furthermore, the big Insurance companies must own up to their obligation."

Although the situation had not improved in the Ninth Ward of New Orleans, his reputation as a fighter remained intact. He received significant support from the large Cajun population. There was little doubt that Cajun blood was in the Granger genealogy.

Granger's gangling appearance and bushy black hair made him a focal point at gatherings. Political insiders respected his astute judgment on complex issues. At age fifty-two he had become an articulate spokesman of moderation for his party, which had been in the minority for seven years. Even Majority party congressmen admired his political intuition.

A combination of his reputation and words of encouragement from family and friends had induced him to form an exploratory committee to be the nominee of his party for president. "I've been behind the scenes too long," he acknowledged.

"I think the President's outburst tonight is going to help your chances in the primaries much more than Robinson's," Flanagan proclaimed.

"I'm not sure of that, Stan," Granger replied. His head tilted to one side and his eyes squinted as if he were reading fine print. "The Senator's team has been together a long time. He's still seething at losing the last general election to Atkinsen. Hell, he's already taking pot-shots at my record."

* * *

When Granger had turned down the overture to be Robinson's presumed running mate one month earlier, his loftier ambitions were no longer a secret.

"George, you've done a great job in the leadership position," Senator Robinson had said, in his unique lusty style. "After all, you have a better sense of what the voters want than most of us on the Hill. You deserve to be considered on my short list for Vice-President."

Granger recognized that the opinions of Robinson, as titular head of the party, carried a lot of weight. He hesitated before he responded, uncertain if this was the proper time to spread the news of his personal intentions. At one time he had great respect for the aging, back-slapping senator with flowing silver-grey hair. The better he knew Robinson, the more he discerned the nuances in their views.

Granger knew they'd be competitors from here on out.

"John, I appreciate your confidence and support," he began, making focused eye contact with his new adversary, "Frankly, I think it's time for me to look ahead to a broader role in our party and influence our national direction. So—"

"What are you saying, George?" Robinson interrupted, seemingly taken aback by the firmness and implication of the response.

"Just what it sounds like, John. I believe I have the credentials and the financial backing to seek higher office."

Robinson reached back his left hand to scratch his neck. Then he folded his arms across his chest and smiled. "You know what you're getting yourself into?" he asked. His tone had changed to an exaggerated drawl.

"Yes, I do."

"I'm not sure you do. We're shooting at the same target—head to head, you get the picture? Why don't you reconsider and we'll keep this discussion to ourselves?" He put his hand on Granger's shoulder and said, "Let me make it quite clear. You're at the top of my list for Vice-President." Robinson offered this incentive with a smug look on his face.

Who's he kidding? There's no way our party's ticket would include two men from the South.

Granger knew that as a political opponent of Robinson, he would face the dirty tricks of the senator's team. He recalled the gossip from Robinson's last Senate race. The senator had doled out favors, and female companions, for special guests to the three-day Kentucky Derby extravaganza. His "winnings" were tallied not at the pari-mutuel window, but in the voting booth and his campaign coffers.

"My mind's made up, Senator," Granger said, ignoring Robinson's condescending tone. His jaw locked in an outward position.

The senator stared at his newest opponent. Turning, he left the room abruptly without shaking Granger's outstretched hand.

"I guess he's used to getting his way all the time," Granger told his wife, Mary Jo, that evening.

"I can't believe it," she said. "He seems so nice."

"I'm not looking forward to the next time his friendly facade fades away."

Christ, is this what the national campaign will be like?

* * *

"George, the producer of *Meet the Press* called," Flanagan announced with bated breath. "They want you on this Sunday for your reaction to the President's address."

"Perfect timing," Granger bellowed, as he put his feet on the coffee table and leaned back in the armchair. "Stan, let them know I'll be there." He realized he had to seize the opportunity to outwit the opponents from both parties. He jumped up from the chair feeling the rush of excitement of a presidential campaign.

"The grapevine has it that Robinson is pissed that *NBC* didn't invite him," Flanagan said.

"Jesus, what an incorrigible old cuss," was Granger's reaction. "He's been on that program a half dozen times already."

Granger's adrenaline rose at the thought of his first appearance. He closed his eyes to visualize the setting and the questions from Tim Russert.

"Congressman Granger, how do you expect to gain the nomination against the titular head of your party and why do you think people should vote for you?" *That's probably his first questions.*

"I'll be prepared for him," he told Flanagan. "Meanwhile, I don't get it. Why did Atkinsen lose control like that?"

He tossed a magazine across the table sending it and the *Washington Times* to the floor.

Chapter Thirteen

The annual meeting of the John Wilkes Booth Fraternity was always held on the night of the State of the Union address. In point of fact, this was their only group gathering each year for the past two decades, except during the Waco, Texas incident and the months following 9/11. Ever since John Hinckley botched their stalking of Ronald Reagan, the group had split up and kept a low profile.

The five middle-aged men used the occasion to vent their long-held grudges against authority and their frustration with the Federal government. To them, the presidents, regardless of party affiliation, were the culprits—the authority figures.

"I'll lose my good-paying job at the UN," Pete Tomlinn cried out at the television. After sixteen years in Food Operations, he had been promoted to Assistant Manager, Dining Facilities at UN Headquarters two years earlier.

"The guy's off his freaking rocker," Justin Morse exclaimed, reacting spontaneously to President Atkinsen's tirade. His home in the Riverdale section of the Bronx had been their meeting place ever since he formed the JWB Fraternity.

"We can't sit by twiddling our thumbs with the country run by ass-hole, arrogant people. What do you guys think?" Morse stood and walked around the living room, pounding his fist into his open palm. Following his military experience, his antagonism toward the federal government induced a paranoiac mindset.

"I dunno," said Shorty, "This guy's got some good ideas."

"Are you kidding?" Morse asked. "He's trampling on peoples' rights. Our rights."

"So what are we supposed to do?"

Morse advanced to Shorty and lowered his head until they were nose to nose. "I'll tell ya. His actions are destructive to the country so we can terminate his presidency. It says so in the Declaration of Independence." Morse checked the faces of his companions. A superior air reflected his attitude and dominance.

"Yeah, I agree with you, Justin," said Pete's brother, Butch. "This guy better not get reelected in November. Shit, he'll increase our taxes to pay for the draft. And what's gonna happen to our eighteen year old nephew, Pete?"

Shorty Polski said, "Don't worry 'bout it. After tonight, he'll never get reelected. The stupid jerk."

Pete seemed in a trance, bewildered by the President's attack on the United Nations. "What the frig am I going to do now?"

Horny Jess Brocce drank his beer down in one slug, laconic as always.

The President had sounded unbalanced to all five men, and they were pumped up for action, with Morse as instigator.

"Who's to blame for your low paying jobs and bachelor existence?" Morse took delight in goading them out of their self-pity and personal plight.

"What can we do about it?" Butch complained. "And who the hell are you to talk anyway? The sub-prime mortgage problem has messed up your business and the government's not doing a fucking thing about it."

"Yeah," Pete blurted out, "I'm doing a lot better than you are right now."

Morse glared at the brothers. "Shit, you guys. Don't you see! All the more reason it's time we develop a plan like years ago. It woulda worked then."

Morse was their uncontested leader, supported by Butch, for his outspoken accusations about federal regulations and injustices that disadvantaged the average working man. The pulpit was like a weapon for him to incite his followers.

"The government's to blame for closing our veteran's hospital and taking away our benefits, for illegal immigrants, high taxes, you name it. Politicians haven't done shit about gas prices. We've been crapped on long enough." Arms folded across his chest, he scowled, "Okay, are you with me or not?"

"Hey, don't forget security is much tighter after nine-eleven," Butch said, dashing their exuberance.

"Sure, but it's not impossible if we have a fool-proof plan," Morse responded.

"Man, you guys have been nothing but talk for years," Brocce said, exuding sarcasm and waving his arms at his buddies. "Remember, I wanted to get that bastard Clinton after the massacre of David Koresh and those innocent people in the compound in Waco and you guys—"

"Bullshit. You chickened-out when I had a plan to get him at one of those inauguration parties in 2000."

"That would never have worked and you know it, Morse."

"Go to hell!" Morse shot back, edged on by Brocce's doubting Thomas attitude.

"Okay, okay, this time let's do it," Butch declared. "Come on, Brocce! What the hell do we have to lose?"

It was unanimous. They shook hands, feeling the excitement of a daring intrigue ahead.

"This is like old times, guys," Morse said. "Atkinsen deserves it and we'll be doing the country a favor."

* * *

The five men had been Army buddies. At one time or another each had served time in the stockade in Fort Campbell, Kentucky, and each received a dishonorable discharge. Morse, the worst offender, had Ranger training at Fort Benning, Georgia and excelled at the physical demands, including parachute jumps. His Commanding Officer wrote, "He's a prime candidate to lead a covert action."

Morse was scheduled to go on a secret mission to Iran until he went AWOL and had a fistfight with a Second Lieutenant, breaking the officer's nose. As he was led to the brig by MPs, Morse mumbled, "Sonofabitch gave me too many shitty orders."

After a night of heavy drinking following their discharge, the malcontents discovered their affinity—a strong dislike of the sitting president, Jimmy Carter, and political leaders in Washington.

"Those high interest rates and inflation are killin' my parents," Butch lamented.

"What about those poor Marines and civilians held captive in Iran?" Pete bitched. "The country's going to hell."

"I remember how a couple of broads almost killed President Ford in the same month a few years ago," Morse said. "It's not that hard if you have a good plan. Would you believe those Secret Service guys were partying the night before Kennedy was shot?" He held his head high showing off his knowledge, imitating a Mussolini pose. "What did Oswald accomplish by killing Kennedy? We've got better reasons."

Morse started the JWB Fraternity gang during the 1980 presidential campaign between President Jimmy Carter and former California Governor Ronald Reagan. They were committed to assassination as a means of ending US involvement in the Middle East and isolating America from the Israeli-Palestinian problem. "We have to end our dependence on foreign oil," he would preach to co-workers and in Letters to the Editor—not a radical position to have, unless it was backed up with violent intent.

Morse, an exercise freak, had one year of Community College, which exceeded the educational level of his followers. He had made a decent living selling real estate in Yonkers until the extended buyers' market cut his income in half. Renting apartments to students attending Manhattan College provided steady, but modest, cash flow.

Morse took every opportunity to attend lectures on American history. A self-proclaimed history buff, he read everything about the Civil War, including his preferred works by Carl Sandburg and Bruce Catton. The life of John Wilkes Booth fascinated Morse. He was fixated with Booth's conspiracy plan to assassinate both the President and Secretary of State Stanton at the same time.

"Booth even rehearsed his plan a day earlier," Morse described to his followers, as if Booth were an old friend. "He got a big break when General Grant cancelled plans to attend the play with Lincoln. So there was less of a military presence at the theater."

He never missed a chance to tell whoever would listen, "The deed only took sixty seconds. If Booth had not broken his leg jumping onto the stage of the Ford's Theater, he could have escaped to the South as a hero."

The fact that the assassination was successful on a Good Friday was a meaningful, indelible sign to Morse that fueled a lifelong obsession.

By the time a plausible plan to assassinate Carter had been developed, Ronald Reagan was in office. Morse was determined to move ahead with the plot.

"I don't care that he got the hostages back from Iran," he said, as the group argued about the proposed plan with the uncertain movements of a new president. "We have plenty of time to test the plan before Good Friday."

"We'll have to get his itinerary pretty soon or else call it off," Shorty said, expressing the concern of the others.

"Come on!" Morse answered, his lips curled in defiance. "We can't back down now. From my inheritance I'll pick up the cost of whatever travel is necessary. Let me worry about his daily schedule. We'll all meet at a Holiday Inn in DC next week."

Shorty was assigned the job of tracking the President to pre-announced locations. He would observe the Secret Service protection and the closeness of the public to the Commander-in-Chief. "How the hell do we get away even if we get a shot at him?" he said to himself.

Plans were drawn on paper, like a football coach draws X's and O's. By Monday morning, March 30, 1981 things had fallen in place—Pete Tomlinn had stolen a car and license plates; Morse, under the guise of a former journalist, had mingled with reporters who often knew the President's schedule in advance; and Butch Tomlinn had acquired several weapons.

After a late breakfast with the group, Shorty took off to the Washington Hilton Hotel where Reagan was to speak to the Building and Construction Trade Union. Morse had told him, "It's your turn again to stalk him. Pay attention to how those Secret Service guys operate. Then, get back here as soon as you can."

Just nineteen days until Good Friday, Morse thought.

"What's going on?" Shorty asked a bystander.

"The President is due here in ten minutes," the man replied, straining to get a better look. "Those well-dressed guys over there are Secret Service."

Reporters and photographers pushed Shorty out of the way. He noted their credentials permitted closer proximity to the President's entourage when they exit the hotel.

Because his hands were buried in his leather jacket on this blustery day, a police officer asked Shorty to show his hands and patted his jacket pockets for a concealed weapon. *They're not checking all those reporters gathered near the exit. I even see one guy without any credentials. Why pick on me?*

He decided to pull back to higher ground to watch the President emerge and wave to the crowd. *Wow! He's out in the open.*

Suddenly, gunshots rang out and there was pandemonium as spectators scrambled away or fell to the ground. Shorty was too stunned to move, but he could see Secret Service men with raised weapons knock someone to the ground. He believed Reagan was shoved into his limo, unharmed. He walked away from the scene quickly, hiding his face, as photographers snapped pictures at random.

Within days the fraternity members heard that the would-be assassin was a suicidal loner, who was infatuated with an actress. Somehow, John Hinckley was able to get within twenty feet of the President.

"I don't believe it," said Morse, as the group scrapped their plan and disbanded because of a deranged kid. "Don't worry," he told them, "our turn will come."

The gang vowed complete silence on the plot. It would never be revealed that President Reagan had been twice a target.

* * *

After his buddies had left after midnight, Morse couldn't sleep. He hoped it wasn't the liquor that influenced their commitment to carry out an awesome and dangerous act. He rambled on in his mind about all the things that had to be done in a secretive plot. Regretfully, too many years of inaction by the group had gone by— just bitching and loose talk. This was the opening he was waiting for. This President had given him and his followers a gift with his diatribe in the State of the Union address.

He got out of bed and lit up a cigarette.

This is the opportunity I've wanted. A snide smile crossed his face.

Crushing out the half-smoked Marlboro, he climbed back in bed and turned on his stomach to sleep.

"We have only three months before Good Friday." He mumbled into his pillow.

Chapter Fourteen

J.J. Rickman, UN Secretary-General awoke earlier than usual. Notwithstanding a restless sleep, he was keyed up to start a challenging day. The President's words still rang in his head as he showered and dressed. An early morning meeting with his Deputy had been scheduled immediately after he heard the President's address.

"There's sure to be TV cameras and reporters expecting my reaction." The limelight was his narcotic.

He selected a blue stripe suit, a light blue shirt, and a matching Bill Blass tie. He slipped on expensive cuff links and Gucci shoes to complete the ensemble. His debonair image—impeccably dressed, a slender six foot frame and well-groomed mustache— would outdo any actor auditioning for the part.

The official residence of the Secretary-General was at Sutton Place, one of the most exclusive sections of Manhattan. The City of New York donated the elegant twenty room, four story townhouse for the UN Secretary-General. This tax free real estate more than matched the Waldorf Astoria Hotel Towers apartment occupied by the US Ambassador to the United Nations.

Rickman's daily routine started with breakfast prepared by the residence's staff. Not today. His singular focus was to get to his 38th floor office as quickly as possible.

A cup of strong black coffee did little to disquiet his anguish at what was ahead. The tense feeling in his stomach reminded him of his turbulent days as Commissioner-General of the United Nations Relief and Works Agency for Palestinian Refugees—and his rise to that position.

* * *

Without family connections to depend on, Rickman had progressed rapidly as Assistant Minister of Finance in the Executive Branch of the Austrian Government. His intellect and work ethic were praised, but his cleverness in writing reports to promote his reputation went undetected. "I discovered the misappropriation of funds in our Swedish Embassy," he reported to the Vice-Chancellor, taking credit for the findings of a clerk.

Rickman was driven to achieve at the highest level. At the Vienna University of Economics and Business Administration, one of the top business schools in Europe, he graduated at the top of the class. His enviable advancement in government service and ambition resulted in a unique opportunity.

"Herr Rickman," the Vice-Chancellor of the Ministry of Finance said, "the President and I have discussed your future and believe you can best serve Austria under the tutelage of our Ambassador to the United Nations in New York."

Rickman was taken aback, as he had hoped for a ministerial post. Nevertheless, he accepted the assignment. *I'll make the most of this experience.* A year later, he learned that a report he had drafted led to the sudden resignation of the Vice-Chancellor.

"I knew it," Rickman said. "He was guilty of tax evasion, which explains why they transferred me. It's the last time I don't use leverage to my advantage."

Rickman adjusted quickly to living in Manhattan.

Half the people here just go through the motions of pushing paper and only look forward to their evening parties.

His performance, political acumen and social graces were noticed within the Secretariat at UN headquarters and by several Ambassadors, who influenced his promotion to a prominent international position administering the complicated Palestinian problem.

Rickman knew he had to be a fast learner. The General Assembly established the United Nations Relief and Works Agency in 1949 to carry out relief work for refugees. This followed United Nations Resolution 181, which partitioned Palestine and led to the first Arab-Israeli conflict. The resulting 700,000 refugees had grown over the years to some four million men, women and children.

Rickman was appalled by the sights on his first visits to the Palestinian camps. Constant strife among Arabs or with Israeli forces made it almost impossible to maintain schools and the infrastructure. Teenagers had nothing to look forward to other than demonstrations or assaults against the Jews. He kept a diary of his observations as he shuttled between his headquarters in Gaza City and Amman, Jordan.

Yassar Arafat had been named President of the Palestinian Authority. Rickman held several meetings with Arafat, but it was the first and last contacts that were most memorable.

"Mr. President, I've read the reports of my predecessor," Rickman stated, attempting to put Arafat on the defensive. "I have not seen any improvements in the infrastructure despite vast sums of contributions to your cause."

Waving his hands in surrender, Arafat responded, "You have to appreciate my people have many needs. The Israelis continually undermine my efforts."

"Do you speak for all of the people?"

"Of course, you can see for yourself the support I receive here. And in Europe too, I might add." His smile couldn't hide a battle-worn face. "But we must respond to Israeli intrusions into our camps."

"I've been informed that Saddam Hussein compensates the families of suicide bombers. Where does—?"

Arafat interrupted, "There are small amounts of humanitarian donations to families in distress. We must share to help all our people until we regain our occupied land."

"I recognize the hardship," Rickman sympathized.

"And we appreciate the United Nations sustenance and commitment," Arafat affirmed. "As you know, we'll continue the two percent administrative fee."

Rickman nodded as if he understood the point. *Is this what my predecessor meant about the benefits of acceptable practices?* Later he was surprised that funds were deposited in an account only he controlled.

Rickman's diary recorded his last private meeting with President Arafat.

The man is a wonderment—with nine lives. Even during a period of relative quiet, his popularity is strong while decay best describes living conditions in the camps. Yet, there are more and more babies. At least Palestinian statehood appears more likely. Arafat speaks out of both sides of his mouth. He declares with strong emotion peace will only come when his people have uninhibited access to the old city of Jerusalem.

Sometimes it seems the leadership want the status-quo, which has plagued generations of innocent Palestinians. What would happen if there were no longer any refugees?

After four years, Rickman was called back to UN headquarters by the outgoing Secretary-General. The Austrian President supported the transfer. Privately, Rickman had lobbied for the open post and urged Vienna to actively promote his name. *It's payback time.*

Based on the recommendation of the Security Council, the General Assembly elected him to the position of Secretary-General. Only Israel opposed his appointment.

The issues in his first five years were handled with skill, which helped him solidify his position and stature in the international community. Employing the "good graces" of his office with dynamic public relations, Rickman was easily reelected to a second five-year term. The bureaucrats were overjoyed with the status-quo.

* * *

The black, tinted-windowed Cadillac drove the short distance from Sutton Place to the UN building. Rickman had time to read the editorial in the *New York Times* under the headline:

PRESIDENTIAL MISCALCULATION AND/OR MISCONDUCT

Each President must cope with pressure, at times intense and nerve-racking. Each President learns to deal with the stress of the job in his own way. Sadly, President Atkinsen has allowed the burden to affect his judgment. His State of the Union address displayed a flagrant abuse of his responsibilities as President, and irresponsible behavior.

Rather than speculate on his rationale or conduct, we leave it to the President to explain the unprecedented drama last evening.

"Good Morning, sir," Deputy S-G Kato Hitoshi said. "Coffee will be here shortly." The wall clock read 7:15.

After greeting his assistant, Rickman dropped his newspaper and briefcase on his desk and sat at a round mahogany table. He read the faxes and notes left for him in a manila folder, as customary. The unusual number did not surprise him—from Embassies, Ambassadors, Under-Secretaries, and major television networks. After an aide had served the coffee, he said, "Shall we get down to business, Mr. Hitoshi."

"Sir, the President's comments were totally unexpected and unwarranted," the Deputy said, expressing his rehearsed reaction. "He has ignored all protocol and," he stopped to catch his breath, "and blasphemed the members, who are dedicated to world peace. I am—"

"Was there any advance warning of his intention?"

"Absolutely not, sir. I had been informed by Ambassador Kirkwood that the President had shown greater interest in UN matters recently, but no indication to discontinue funding. A callous decision and typical American arrogance!"

Rickman was taking notes, almost disregarding Hiroshi's remarks and the unusual behavior of the normally unobtrusive diplomat. He offered the thought that, "The press has suggested it was a political stunt to jump-start his reelection effort."

"But what if he really intends to pursue the outlandish plan impacting the good people working here?" Hitoshi asked.

"Mr. Hitoshi," the S-G said in a composed tone, "is your concern that we may cut back on staff? What about our programs around the world? Isn't that a bigger issue?" Rickman took the high ground in front of his subordinate and obscured his true anxiety of the impact on him of Atkinsen's intention. "He doesn't have the right to do such a reprehensible thing."

"Yes, sir, of course," Hitoshi said, bowing slightly at the S-G. "Our efforts at preventing poverty will be significantly reduced. I have no idea how it will impact our eighteen peacekeeping missions around the world."

"I want a copy of his address to the General Assembly last September. Also, obtain information on his behavior since the death of his wife." *I must do everything in my power to prevent the dismantling of my organization.*

"Yes, sir."

"Draft a letter to the President which will convey our profound disappointment at his message. We are appalled, etcetera, etcetera. I intend to meet separately with each of the Security Council members, except the United States."

A secretary entered to deliver a note to Rickman.

"Interesting. The Vice-President will make an announcement on television this morning," he said, rubbing his chin. "That's all for now, Mr. Hitoshi. I'll hold off the press until after I hear the Vice-President's remarks. Let's return all our phone calls and get together again right after lunch."

Why did Vice-President Styles choose this time to hold a press conference, Rickman wondered?

Most peculiar.

Chapter Fifteen

The press conference was scheduled for 11 o'clock. The surprise meeting called by the Vice-President had the White House press corps abuzz. After the dramatic events at the previous night's presidential address, rumors of a presidency in disarray were rampant inside the Beltway.

Clark Styles had slept very little as he struggled to mitigate a problem of his making. Unlike the President, he had no choice—it was time to resign and quit the political life he cherished.

"If I don't resign, I'll risk more than my political career," he concluded to himself. The saving grace was that Atkinsen had given him the semblance of justification.

When he disclosed to Joyce the true reason for submitting his resignation the night before, she broke down and cried. "How did you let that happen?"

"A couple of us had time on our hands in Albany. You were busy taking care of the kids. It was easy for us to get away to Utica for a friendly poker game. One thing led to another and ..." His sense of guilt controlled his emotions; another anxiety attack made him feel weak.

"Clark, tell me the truth! Did you do anything wrong to get free from your debt?" She closed her eyes.

He desperately wanted to reach out and hold her close; first, she deserved an answer, a truthful one.

"I swear to God I never did anything illegal ... and I never tried to help the guys who held the IOU's," he declared. His quivering voice sent a chill down his spine. "You have to believe me, Joyce. I prayed every day that they wouldn't show up at our door someday and harass me and my family."

Joyce stared into her husband's eyes. She held his hands in hers and said, "Okay. It's been over for years, and you've lived with this blemish hanging over your head. Don't beat yourself up any more and don't blame the President! Thanks to him you have your dignity."

His sad eyes glistened as he put his arms around her; she was his intimate best friend.

"And I still love you, Clark."

Before leaving his office to face the music, Styles wondered about a last minute invitation he received for a meeting in Chicago one week hence. *Why the hell does the Building and Construction Trades want me to attend their meeting?*

"Screw them," he snarled, as he checked his appearance in the bathroom mirror. Styles ran a comb through his hair and adjusted his tie before walking to the lectern. He looked well-groomed but pale.

How could something like this come back to ruin me? It had started out as penny-ante card games.

"Ladies and gentlemen, I have a brief statement to make." He gripped the lectern and faced the reporters. They looked as captivated as if they were watching a Hail Mary pass reach the end zone in slow time. Styles stared away from the television cameras of CNN and Fox News.

"I've been honored to have served as vice-president for three years and proud to be part of the Atkinsen administration. Without a doubt, it has been the highlight of my life in politics and public service."

He paused as a nervous cough veiled his distress. A picture had appeared in his mind of the first time he announced he was running for public office.

The short hesitation had his audience sitting on the edge of their seats.

"Unfortunately, I have been placed in an untenable position. I'm referring to the President's address last evening. The President's departure from his prepared text has troubled me deeply. His remarks have brought to the surface a wide difference between us on policy matters. These disagreements cannot be reconciled."

There was a murmur of anticipation among the newsmen. Experienced reporters had witnessed similar scenes with politicians of lesser stature all too often in the past.

"Therefore, I have submitted my letter of resignation to the President effective immediately. He has accepted it with regret."

Some reporters rushed out of the room.

"I want to thank the American people for their support. I intend to retire with my wife, Joyce, to our Florida home. Now I will take a few questions."

"Mr. Vice-President, why did the President change his speech last night?" the NBC reporter asked.

"I'm afraid you will have to ask him. Next."

"Sir, what is the major policy difference you have with the President, and weren't you going to be his running mate again?"

"I'm not getting into details about that, other than to say I do not agree with his United Nations position."

"What about the second part of my question?"

"Yes, well, no decision had been made on that, but I did indicate to the President I needed to spend more quality time with my family." Styles' throat felt dry from this deception. He recalled Atkinsen's words, "It will work out for the best." Nevertheless, his mind characterized himself as a Judas.

As Styles walked away from the lectern, a reporter shouted, "One more question, please, Mr. Vice-President. Are you on friendly terms with the President?"

Styles looked directly at the questioner and said in a soft voice, "What do you think?"

* * *

"I don't get it," said Senator Robinson. "Turn off the TV!"

Immediately following the State of the Union address the previous night, Robinson went to his office in the Richard Russell Senate Office Building to assemble his inner circle for a luncheon meeting the next day. Several members made quick travel plans to be in D.C. on time. The Senator had avoided reporters and their phone calls until he could meet with his close friends and advisors.

The hand-chosen members of Robinson's inner circle operated independent of his presidential campaign committee. They managed to stay under the radar screen during his first run for president, despite their "dirty tricks" strategy.

Refreshments were on the rectangular table in front of them as well as sandwiches on a long mahogany server against the wall, suggesting this might be an extended session.

"So, let me hear your views," the Senator invited his team of four men.

"I think its clear Styles wants to distance himself from the President after last night's fiasco."

"Why?" Robinson asked.

"He would be the logical choice at their convention to lead the ticket, if support for Atkinsen dwindles."

"No," said Robinson, sitting as judge. "I've witnessed his reactions during pressure moments. He doesn't hold a candle to Atkinsen, but wouldn't it be marvelous for us if he were their candidate?"

"Senator, I'm confused about the timing and what appears to be an impulsive decision. If he didn't resign for future political opportunities, what strikes me is that he might have known he would be dropped as VP."

"Good point," Robinson said. "A decision to replace him at the convention could be seen as disloyal, causing confusion and a negative reaction from supporters. Their campaign would get off to a bad start for sure. Styles may have done his party a good turn."

They sat quietly for several moments to ponder the implications of the resignation. A member reported, "I watched their chairman Jackman try to spin the President's remarks on ABC last night. What a bullshitter!"

Robinson stood and, in a suggestive tone, asked, "What if Atkinsen forced him out for cause?"

The senior advisor in the group stood and advanced toward the Senator. He said, "You think there may be something in Styles' past? Wouldn't it have come out by now?"

"True," acknowledged Robinson, "but we didn't focus enough on his years as state senator in the last race. For that matter we gave Atkinsen a pass last time, too. Who the hell expected him to be in the race anyway?"

"You may be right, Senator, but I'm inclined to think Styles was fed up with that bull-headed Wagner and smart-ass Harry Grant. They manipulate the president like a puppet and keep Styles in the dark."

Robinson halted the conversation for a lunch break. He sipped his third cup of coffee and weighed the views of his trusted advisors. After fifteen minutes, he resumed the meeting.

"I'm going to cut this short," he said. "First, I want someone assigned to investigate the background of Clark Styles. Let's see what they uncover. And check if Granger has put out a press release yet."

"I'll take care of it," one member volunteered. "If that sanctimonious Granger had campaigned with you the last time, you'd be President."

"Second," the Senator continued, "let's get out a statement that Atkinsen's actions were ill-conceived, unilateral, and damaging to our reputation around the world. At every opportunity I'll press him that his administration is in disorder, and his party is upset by the publicity. And don't forget to check your sources on who is in line to fill the VP vacancy!"

"Senator, what's your position on that?"

"I don't intend to urge Majority Leader Lewis or the President directly to fill the vacancy. Why give a new Vice-President and the Atkinsen ticket a PR advantage in the upcoming election, especially if it's that opportunist, Bob Allcott."

Robinson thanked everyone for their help and returned to his desk. As he reached for the phone, he thought there's more to this than meets the eye. Is the President mentally stable, he wondered? *How can he announce he's running for reelection one week and the next week act out of control?*

He called his campaign manager to receive an update on polling results on himself, Atkinsen, and "that ingrate, Granger". "I can't wait to challenge him in the primaries after his snub of my VP offer."

"Senator, there's a call from your son," the secretary said.

"Tell him I'll get back to him on my other phone."

* * *

Before returning the call to his son, Robinson reflected on how complicated his life had become. "If only I'd won the last election," he growled. *First thing I'll do when elected is propose a constitutional amendment to eliminate the Electoral College. The Presidency should be decided by popular vote! And there should be a uniform ballot, not a different one in every state.*

He took a drink of water and punched in his son's number.

"Dad, I've been trying to reach you all morning."

"As you can imagine we've been busy here because of the President's speech last night."

"That's what I'm calling about. I'm still in Mexico City working on that land deal and—"

"Bruce, I thought the transaction was signed two days ago. What's going on?"

"We ran into legal red tape, that's all," Bruce said without hesitation. "I don't know what the President has up his sleeve, but, Dad, you've got to do everything you can to keep him from upsetting the apple cart at the UN. Donald Trump must be salivating at the possibility of converting the UN building into condos …especially after they spent two billion to renovate the damn place."

"How does a reorganization of the place impact what you're doing?"

"One aspect of the arrangements I've made in Mexico for the Kansas City inland port project is based on rulings of the International Trade Law Commission of the UN. We've gained favorable rulings which will sharply reduce our liability insurance costs for transport facilities."

"Okay, Bruce, I don't fully comprehend all those details of your business, so fill me in when you return. In the meantime, I'll get the scuttlebutt on the Hill about any legislation from the administration regarding UN dues."

"I can't emphasize enough we need the status quo at the United Nations as well as the North American Free Trade Agreement. I'm required to give a progress report on last quarter's Land acquisitions and signed contracts at the Alpha-Omega Board meeting in Minneapolis next week. It's their seed money and they can be demanding, as you know."

"Are they satisfied thus far?"

"I believe so. We've been at this for less than two years, and they knew it would be a long term payback investment."

The Senator shrugged his shoulders in frustration.

"Bruce, there's a lot of controversy about the benefits of NAFTA, much of it from members of my own party. The question is would trade between us and our neighbors have increased naturally since 1994 without the tariff eliminations?"

"Dad, those arguments don't stand up to the real growth stats of the US economy. You and I agree on that."

"Right, son. Goodbye for now. Keep me informed and I'll see you in April."

"Good luck, Dad."

Robinson mused about taking political events and decisions one step at a time. He knew there's no need to be hurried so early in this political silly season.

He thought about the conversation with his son and the political inferences during a presidential campaign. *Was this the right time to become associated with a risky and unlikely business venture?* "Why did I let Bruce talk me into it?" he chastised himself.

* * *

Bruce Robinson was perspiring. After speaking to his father, he went to the hotel fitness center and exercised on the treadmill. He reflected on the call and the upcoming meeting with his partner, Charlie Zeigler. Zeigler had all the figures on recent land transactions for the Board meeting.

"Charlie, will you also get me all the info you can on the European Union? My contact at Alpha-Omega is suddenly making the US relationship with Mexico and Canada a higher priority than originally agreed to."

"I'll get right to it, Bruce."

If there was ever a time for the Senator to use the influence he boasts about, this is it. I've worked too hard and long for this deal to fall apart now.

Six years earlier.

"Let's go out tonight and celebrate," Bruce bellowed across the hall to his classmate, Charlie Zeigler.

He was in a joyous mood as he closed the door to his room in the dorm for the last time. While he was not in the top quartile of his class, he felt on top of the world with a Princeton degree.

"I'll call my girlfriend, Dottie, and she'll get you a date."

"Fine with me," Zeigler said.

They had an hour to hang out in the lounge before an evening of drinks, dinner and dancing; maybe they'll get lucky.

"Bruce, do you remember that case study on real estate and how we talked about it and made plans for the future?"

"Of course, Charlie. We thought it was a sure way to get rich."

"Well, I want to make a million fast and—"

"Hey, I want to show my dad I can become a millionaire, but not like him. How the hell did he get all his money as a politician?"

"Christ, don't complain …it got you through school." Zeigler shifted his position on the easy chair. "You know my father's in the real estate business in Kansas City. He says there are great opportunities in that part of the country."

Bruce stretched out on the couch staring at the ceiling. He thought about his dad in Washington, DC. "I'll call my mom in Louisville after dinner," he whispered.

He stood, a determined look on his face, and pointed to Charlie. "I'm going to take that job with a consulting firm in Boston for a couple of years and I'm going to marry Dottie. When the time is right, you and I can get together and explore real estate possibilities, working for ourselves."

"Great! I'll keep in touch with you while I'm working for my father."

I'm going to make it on my own, he pledged.

After a successful four years with the consulting firm, Bruce Robinson felt he was ready and it was time. He advised Charlie Zeigler to hunt for the right deal. "A sure thing," was the charge to his college partner.

"Bruce, I've completed all the research you requested on the Kansas City SmartPort project. It's the project we've been waiting for. Just like you expected."

"I'm all set to join you, Charlie. How does "Development Corp of America" sound as our company name?"

"Perfect. I'll hire a local attorney to get us organized." He paused and added, "In my opinion, with your father's position, you should be president."

"I accept," he said, chuckling into the phone. "Next week I'm introducing my dad to an interested Venture Capitalist in Minneapolis who will give us the start-up funds we need."

After he ended the call, he recalled his days growing up in Kentucky and how his dad pushed him to become an achiever, which eventually drove him out of his home.

He'll be real proud of me someday.

Chapter Sixteen

Even after one week, speculation about the State of the Union address was still the talk of Washington. Politicians of all stripes analyzed the contents of the President's speech as they would a major Supreme Court decision.

The buzz on Sunday TV shows concerned the next Vice-President. Since Clark Styles had been the presumptive running mate in the upcoming election, possible candidates were bandied about—Allcott, Childs, Quinlan, Joan Milligan, Admiral Farrell—just as sports enthusiasts select their favorite for Most-Valuable-Player. The consensus was there was no clear-cut nominee to round out the Atkinsen ticket.

The *New York Times* explored Atkinsen's behavior for the past two years following his wife's death and made an indelicate reference to the replacement of a President. The editorial read:

In accordance with the Involuntary Withdrawal clause of the 25th Amendment, the Vice-President or Congress may commence an inquiry into the emotional stability of a President to perform the duties of the Office. Since the Vice-President has resigned, Congress has the responsibility to act, albeit a remote prospect given the party in power.

A blogger theorized as fact that the Vice-President was coerced to resign. After a vigorous denial from the White House, a stealth movement to replace the President specifically for reasons of disability ceased.

Atkinsen had received a note from Harry Grant the day following the address:

Mr. President,
While I would not have dared to recommend any of your
pronouncements last evening, I respect your courage and, yes, your
wisdom. As always, I am at your service. Good instincts are a
marvelous virtue and you possess them in abundance.
                                    Sincerely,
                                        Harry

p.s. It's a shame the VP has resigned!

At Wagner's urging, a meeting with party Chairman Oscar
Jackman was held to reengage the President in discussions
concerning the bad press and status of the campaign.

"Mr. President, I can tell you that our base is sticking with you,
except for Governor Bliss of Missouri," Jackman reported. "He's
put out feelers about challenging you at the convention."

"Bliss has always been a maverick," Wagner added, smirking at
the thought. "Mr. President, he's still upset about being rebuffed in
the campaign four years ago when he questioned your candidacy."

"The bad news is you've lost almost twenty points with
independent voters," Jackman continued. "After your announcement
to seek reelection, there had been an upsurge in contributions, but
they slowed considerably since your address."

The Chief of Staff asked Jackman, "When do you think the worst
will be over? And what can we do to mitigate our losses?"

Jackman had a blank look on his face.

President Atkinsen had been listening while he fiddled with the
glass paper weight on his desk. He had ample time to reflect on his
shocking pronouncements at the State of the Union, spending three
days in mid-week at Camp David. While he had visits from cabinet
members and foreign dignitaries, he felt he was simply going
through the motions. His mood swings glided from joy to dejection,
like riding a see-saw.

"Before we get into what we have to do," Atkinsen interjected,
his face brightening with interest, "what's going on with Robinson?"

"Well, in each speech he refers to you as unpredictable,"
Jackman replied, "but doesn't even discuss the specifics in your
address. Then he uses your problem to blast Granger as unfit for the

top spot. You could say Robinson feels his party owes him the nomination since he came so close the last time. Of course, he expects the presidency to follow."

"Mr. President, the reality is he's too focused on Granger to go after you full force," Wagner said. "I've heard he's holding back his attack dogs."

"Sir, one thing you might do is tone down your rhetoric, if you don't mind me saying," Jackman opined.

"Really?" "Why?"

"People believe you were shooting from the hip at the State of the Union and—"

"Wait a second," Wagner interrupted, raising the tone of the meeting. "He can't go back on anything he said. That would show he was out of control." He clasped his hands and leaned forward toward the President. "Sir, the public expects you to be proactive, especially since Vice-President Styles' resignation."

"Frankly, Steve, I agree with you. I want to get away from the White House and meet people to explain my position."

"Mr. President," Jackman said softly, his face coloring, "please don't interpret my comments as suggesting a change in your position. I'm excited to get started and I'll coordinate with your schedule to see we get large turn-outs at each stop."

Wagner nodded at Jackman to signal he should leave.

"Thank you for your time, Mr. President."

After the party Chairman left, Wagner said, "Mr. President, about the letter we received from the UN, I—"

"Yes, I've been meaning to discuss that with you. I feel strongly about all my statements, except I will apologize for highlighting illegal immigration in the State of the Union. It was the wrong forum. Let's schedule a meeting with the Latino Council soon."

"That's a good move, sir. By the way there's a new group consisting of some UN employees and their families and friends, mostly Hispanics, calling themselves *Save the UN*. They've organized protests against you. We've alienated the Spanish-speaking community so getting their votes will be problematic compared to the last election."

"It's time I elaborate on my proposals to the Secretary-General in person."

"How about I set a date when you can address the General Assembly and meet privately with the Secretary-General?"

"Fine, Steve. Just give me time to prepare."

"Yes sir. I'll get Ambassador Kirkwood and Josh Cohen on it right away."

"Have Josh read the Volker Report. There's enough substance in it to embarrass the whole Assembly, not to mention criminal indictments for rampant corruption."

Wagner peered at the ceiling with those deep-set eyes and recalled, "Volker left no doubt of the massive fraud in the Oil for Food program. His report charged the United Nations permitted Saddam Hussein to pervert the program for personal gain, netting at least eleven billion dollars."

Paul Volker, former Federal Reserve Chairman, had led an Independent Inquiry Committee formed by then Secretary-General Kofi Anan in 2004.

Atkinsen shook his head in disgust and said, "To think the program was intended to provide food and medicine to Iraqi citizens. Goddamn injustice."

Wagner nodded in agreement.

"I blame Kofi Anan for letting it get out of control," said Atkinsen. "The public outcry forced him to investigate the wrongdoings." His shook his head in disbelief about how it could have happened.

After scribbling several notes, Wagner asked, "Anything else, sir?"

"Steve, check with Cabinet members and get views on how we might redirect the two billion dollars of UN dues and assessments that we'll save so we can achieve the same objectives much more effectively on our own."

"Will do, sir."

"That reminds me," the President said, a broad smile on his face, "Cohen had suggested that I consider throwing out the first ball at Yankee Stadium. This is the first year Major League Baseball has scheduled inter-league play on opening day. The Nationals will play their first game there."

Wagner groaned, then yielded to the idea and said, "We'll have to arrange extra security at the ballpark so I guess it will be okay. I'll let Director Harris and Ashton Williams know about it, but I know they're going to make a fuss ...for good reason."

"Steve, I've seen Williams in action. Director Harris and I have full confidence in his performance and dedication."

Wagner stared at the President as if he might reconsider the highly sensitive appearances in New York City.

"At least if you address the General Assembly that morning, we'll get both events done the same day." Wagner took a second to check his BlackBerry and say, "Opening game at Yankee Stadium is not until mid April, on a Friday."

"By the way, Steve, thanks for not prying into the Vice-President's resignation. I'll only say it was best for him. I'll let you know about replacing Styles in due course."

"Yes, sir. Styles did tell me that he valued everything you did for him."

"One more thing before you go," Atkinsen said, turning his back on Wagner. He stood and faced the French doors, waiting for Wagner to come closer to him. His hands were in his pants pockets.

"Yes, sir," Wagner said, walking past the President's desk.

"Regarding the matter of Secretary Brown."

"Yes sir, I meant to bring that subject up." Wagner removed a thin file from his briefcase.

Atkinsen turned to face his Chief of Staff. "I intend to ask for his resignation and—"

"I believe you're doing the right thing," Wagner broke in, a hint of a smile spreading across his face.

"Steve, I intend to ask for the resignation of Brown at Interior and Secretary Simon at Energy."

Although the President had spoken distinctly, Wagner seemed unable to grasp the words. His wrinkled brow was replaced by squinting; pained eyes and shock waves seemed to carom back toward Atkinsen.

The President held his ground and said, "I've given this a lot of thought, Steve, so hear me out."

"I don't know what to say," Wagner said in a shaky voice. "Is this Grant's idea?"

"Not at all ... he doesn't know anything about it."

"Can you explain it to me, sir? I've had respect for Frank

Simon's abilities in the past. Is this simply a personality conflict?"

Atkinsen motioned to the couch and they both sat.

"Well, it's true they don't get along, but there's more to it than that." He leaned forward, elbows resting on his knees, hands together. "Steve, you heard Simon at the last cabinet meeting in early December. I'm convinced he's obsessed with drilling for oil in Alaska."

"That may be true, sir, but—"

"Simon's blaming Jordan Brown for his own failure to meet DOE goals. Face up to it!"

"Sir, I'm not trying to defend Frank Simon," interjected the surprised Chief of Staff. "I recognize he sometimes pushes for energy policy changes that—"

"Right! He's delayed spending for alternative energy sources so his budget will cover testing in Alaska, which the House Energy Committee hasn't approved."

The President stood and pointed at his Chief of Staff. "Before Robinson gets hold of this information and charges me with complicity in an unauthorized act, Simon has to go. That's final!"

"Once again, Mr. President, I'm not disagreeing with you. You're obviously more familiar with this than I am," Wagner said, as he shifted his position on the couch. "I think we better be prepared for some negative press and jabs from our friends as well as Robinson and Granger. They may claim you're out of control and acting spiteful."

The President shrugged. "It's the right thing to do."

After a slight pause, he added, "Let's set up the meetings and press releases in the next few days. Senate Majority Leader Lewis knows a great candidate from Texas to head DOE."

"You really have given this a lot of thought, haven't you?" Wagner said, unable to hide his admiration.

The President continued, "We can hold a press conference in the Rose Garden to make the announcements. Then, I'm getting out of Dodge."

A smile relieved the taut lines on the President's face, despite the challenging days ahead.

Chapter Seventeen

It was almost like yesterday in Secret Service Agent Ashton Williams' memory. His investigative role in an international counterfeiting ring exposed North Korean government officials as the makers and distributors of fake $100 US bills.

"How much longer do you think he's going to be in there?" Sam Heffernan asked Williams. He yawned and sat back up in the driver's seat. "It's already after one."

Williams smirked at his young partner, who had been borrowed on temporary duty from the Forgery Section. *I can tell it's his first surveillance duty.*

"Who knows," Williams answered without emotion, reflective of nine months full time on this case. "Backup is due to relieve the team soon so be patient."

"Yeah, but the back and forth suspense and boredom are making me jumpy," Heffernan said. "Besides, this Camaro smells of rotten food or something." He scratched his head and wondered, "How long have you been in DC doing things like this?"

"This is my fourth year here. I was in our Reno field office for three years." He shifted in the passenger seat to face Heffernan and say, "You would like it there. Its fertile training ground to witness cheaters' ingenuity."

"Well, I hope I don't do this kind of work too often."

"Look, we're getting close," Williams said to reassure the young agent. He made a mental note to critique Heffernan's attitude. "The Asian man has the counterfeit $100 bills in his possession to smuggle to *Hezbollah*. He—"

Heffernan interrupted, "What makes the North Koreans so good at counterfeiting?"

"For one thing, they've acquired sophisticated equipment to etch plates with acid rather than engraving by hand. Counterfeiting profits help them support their poor economy. There are estimates that revenue from counterfeiting and drug trafficking has exceeded two billion dollars. Their government has ... who's that?"

Williams observed a tall man exiting the bar at a fast pace toward his van, a blue Chevy Suburban.

"Doesn't look like Asian to me," Heffernan whispered, "but he's carrying a suitcase."

"He's the bagman. Follow him in that van. I'll alert the others to split up the stakeout."

Heffernan drove a few blocks behind the suspect on Connecticut Avenue. The sparse traffic and street lights made it easy to keep the Suburban in sight. The van slowed at a red light and then turned onto Calvert. After passing the Omni Shoreham Hotel, it made a quick sharp left turn on 28th Street.

"Speed up, Sam!" Williams ordered. "He must be heading to his drop point at one of the embassies."

Heffernan stepped on the gas, turned the corner, and in a minute passed the Suburban, which was now crawling along near the curb.

"I'll drive to the end of the street and park," Heffernan murmured, short of breath. "I'm sure he spotted us."

"He's getting out of the car," Williams shouted through his teeth. "That's the Lebanese embassy. Jesus."

Williams jumped out of the Camaro before it screeched to a stop. He stumbled and raced toward the bagman, who was clamoring to enter the embassy at the front gate.

He'll get asylum if he gets in there.

"Stop, Secret Service!" Williams hollered, pistol in hand.

A Lebanese official appeared and approached the gate.

Williams knew he was helpless to prevent the escape.

He watched in astonishment as the bagman was blindsided by a uniformed American guard who tackled the frantic man. The guard subdued the man's struggle and secured the suitcase until Williams made the arrest.

The subsequent indictments exacerbated the tense diplomatic

relations between the US and North Korea, and the publicity led to personnel shuffling within the Secret Service. Williams was reassigned to the President's Protection Detail.

* * *

"I'll start the preparations and coordination immediately, sir," Williams said, acknowledging the call from Secret Service Director Stephen Harris. The directive made his heart skip a beat.

"The UN and Yankee Stadium!" *We'll need a lot more manpower that day.*

After graduating from Hampton College in Virginia, with top grades in a Banking and Finance major, Williams accepted a position in the Secret Service. The history of the agency awed Williams during his indoctrination period. While protection of the president of the United States (POTUS) et al is their trademark, counterfeiting detection has been their most prominent mission dating back to the Civil War.

Ashton Williams had the physical appearance of an athlete, perhaps a six foot-one wide receiver, but he only had a passing interest in sports. He loved to read, mostly non-fiction, and strum his guitar for relaxation. His girlfriend agreed to delay marriage plans until after his tour on the President's Protection Detail. Until he got to know a person, Williams seemed aloof, more out of shyness than indifference or unfriendliness. He inherited his father's penchant for hard work and reliability. Such was Ashton Williams' reputation among his peers.

Once Williams was in a position to organize a team on the protection detail, he requested a reassignment for Russell Barrett, a uniformed agent who had been assigned to guard embassies in Washington, D.C., one of the Secret Service's varied functions.

"I want him," Williams said to the Director. "I witnessed his bravery first-hand. His effort led to the discovery of a mole in the Lebanese embassy who had been cooperating with *Hezbollah*."

Taciturn Stephen Harris, Secret Service Director, adjusted his bifocals and said, "I'll consider your request."

Harris was a career veteran of the Secret Service. Over a twenty-four year period, he held just about every position in the agency, including three years on the President's Protection Detail. His appointment as Director came as no surprise—handling administrative matters and staff assignments were his forte. The agency labored to be apolitical during his tenure, reversing an unfortunate trend during the Washburn years.

Old timers had given Harris a nickname that stuck with him, except the newer breed of agents only joked about it behind his back. His physical appearance bore a resemblance to television actor, Wally Cox, who played the character *Mr. Peepers* back in the fifties.

* * *

"Guess what?" Russ Barrett called to his girlfriend, Kathleen Sullivan, as he arrived in their apartment. "I'm going to be part of the President's security team."

She dropped the newspaper. "Oh, that's great for you. It's what you wanted, isn't it?" She turned away from his fleeting hug to look out the window. "When do you start?"

He sensed her mixed feelings. Since they had started living together over a year earlier, she had become the most important person in his life. Her intellect and humor, physical attraction, and companionship enhanced the relationship for him into something more than sexual. He hated the thought of ever losing her.

"Hey, remember me telling you what it was like for me working at the IRS. Same old shit every day, sitting at a desk and handling all that paper work." *Some of those tax laws were too damn complicated for me anyway.*

"But you had regular hours."

"Sure, but you know how bored I was. That's why I jumped at the chance to work for the Secret Service. Remember how I loved the Law Enforcement Training in Georgia and the specialized training in Maryland."

"So?" she asked, waving off his macho attitude.

"So, this is what I really wanted. Guarding embassies or government buildings is fine, but I like action. Believe it or not, I scored the highest in the simulation drills on an attack on the president in a motorcade or helicopter. I had the ability and stamina to handle everything they threw at me."

"You don't have to brag to me about your stamina."

He winked at her and said, "You just like to see me in a uniform rather than a suit."

"Seriously, Russ, it can be dangerous, right? Like the capture you made of that guy at the Lebanese embassy or all the assassination attempts." She paused and placed a finger over her mouth. Brushing several strands of auburn hair off her forehead, she appeared stressed to control her Irish temper. "You'll be doing a lot of traveling, won't you?"

"Come on, what's happening to you?" he asked. "It'll be exciting."

"And I just hang out here, waiting to hear bad news I guess. Crap. I'm not your plaything, you know."

Jesus. He was jolted by the angry expression on her face.

He sat her down on the couch and kneeled in front of her, holding her hands.

"Kathleen, hear me out. You mean everything to me and I've told you how I feel about you. This job is to make a better life for both of us, not just me."

"Well, I get real scared hearing all those threats against the President." She ran her fingers through his black hair and sighed, "I wish you'd let your hair grow longer like before."

"Don't you worry one bit. I'll be okay." His reddish complexion hid a sense of guilt for the white lie.

He buried his head on her breasts; then he kissed her. He felt a pleasurable tingle when she reciprocated his kiss with her tongue searching him out.

"I really do love you," he said, caressing her teary face and leading her into the bedroom.

Chapter Eighteen

Justin Morse pranced around his living room, his curled lips showing his irritation. His cold eyes and hard features seemed more tense than usual as he pressed his hands against his temples. Pointing at the *Playboy* calendar for March, with the first ten days crossed out, he yelled, "Look, goddamit, there's only thirty days before Good Friday. We gotta settle this today."

A United Nations bureaucrat had leaked to the press that the President would address the General Assembly in April, on Good Friday by coincidence. The White House press secretary had confirmed the trip, announcing, "President Atkinsen will throw out the first ball in the opening game between the Yankees and the Washington Nationals at Yankee Stadium."

Morse was intoxicated with joy when he learned the details of the President's trip. "I can't believe how this is playing into our hands. It's a sure sign of God's will," he had asserted to his gang.

"Okay, Justin," Butch Tomlinn said, throwing his arms in the air. "Calm down. Except for Brocce, we've done our jobs. I bet we can make a decision today. What d'ya say?" He glanced at his brother, Pete, and Shorty Polski, who were gaping at Morse.

"Fine, let's just get it done then, for Christ sake!" Morse valued Butch's influence with the others. Restraining his emotion, he said, "Okay, grab a seat at the dining room table and we can lay out where we stand with the two plans."

The four buddies came together to finalize the plot as if they were organizing a fishing trip, mindless to the danger and the consequences.

"Do you think it will work at the UN, Pete?" Morse asked.

"Yeah, well I have access to the Executive dining room," he replied. "I think it'll be easy to fuck with his food and—"

"Will he be there for breakfast or lunch or both?" Morse interrupted.

Shorty piped up, "We're not sure of his schedule yet, other than he delivers a big speech at ten a.m."

Pete quickly added, "I expect my Manager will want me to help out, so I can work the room whenever the President has something to eat."

"Did you ever serve the Secretary-General before?" Butch asked.

"No, but—"

"I don't like it," Morse said. "We only get one shot at this and there are too many uncertainties."

"I kinda agree," Butch said, giving his brother a forsaken look.

Morse was silent for a moment, sitting back and scratching his head. "We're putting too much on Pete's shoulders, and I don't think it'll work. With so many people pissed off at Atkinsen, the place will be like a fortress."

Pete interjected, "Hey, remember, I'm the guy who'll be out of a damn job if the President gets his way." He tossed a dismissive scoff at his brother.

"What about the plan at Yankee Stadium?" Shorty asked.

Morse reached into a satchel and removed a glossy photograph of the bleachers and a snapshot of a refreshment stand in the bleacher's under-belly. He laid them out on the table and said, "First, you wouldn't believe how easy it was for me to get on the list to work opening day with the concession managers. I told them I was available for the season so getting the job was a snap."

Butch asked, "How do you know you'll be assigned to the bleachers?"

"I traded with some guy—opening day in the grandstands for his Friday in the bleacher's office." With a smug look on his face, he added, "Man, you gotta be smart about this."

"Tell him about the car, Pete," Butch ordered.

"Right. Well that was easy, too," he said, crimping his nose toward Morse. "I got this 1996 Mercury with clean plates. I had no problem using a fake driver's license. The tires are in good shape and—"

"Hey, will the damn thing run and where is it now?" Morse asked impatiently. *Pete's fidgeting is making me nervous.*

"Well, what the heck do you think? Don't worry. It's in my garage and it won't be moved 'til that day.'"

"Good work," Butch said. "I wish that crazy Brocce did his part in this thing like the rest of us. He just brags about screwing around."

"You're right, Butch," said Morse, "but let me handle Brocce. He's supposed to be checking with some ex-cons who had run-ins with the Secret Service." He jotted something on the back of the glossy photograph.

Shorty, with a big grin on his face, volunteered "Lay off my man, Brocce. He fixed me up with a six-foot-two broad."

"Good for you," Morse said, smirking at Shorty. "Okay, here's the make or break part. What's the latest, Butch?"

"I've done a lot of leg work so far." He leaned forward and rested his elbows on the table. "On the morning of every game there are tons of deliveries to the stadium. A few come through the pull-up doors in the old bullpens. They wheel the refreshments to the concession office under the bleachers." He stopped and smiled, saying, "I've told ya before, I went to a lot of games at the stadium as a kid."

"Who gives a shit," Shorty said, shaking his head at Butch.

"Look, you little squirt, I'll kick—"

"Take it easy, the two of you," Morse growled. "So get to it, Butch, what have you figured out?"

Butch grimaced for a second and continued. "I checked out the company that delivers the hot dog rolls. It's the Stadium Bakery Company on Jerome Avenue."

"Why?" Shorty asked.

"Wise up, Shorty," Morse said. "The boxes are big but light. Right, Butch?"

"Sure, but the main reason is the company itself and their employees. They're Puerto Ricans and just barely speak English."

"So?" asked Shorty.

Each man stared at Butch with an inquisitive look on their face.

"The boss wanted a white guy on the job, so I said I'd take it for a few months. The best part is I'll drive the truck with one of those guys as my helper. Then—"

Morse butt in, "So you have access to the boxes and entrance into the stadium. Perfect!" He sat down and scribbled more notes on the photograph.

"Not so fast," Butch said, raising both hands as a stop signal.

"Why?"

"Because security will be as tight as Brocce's new girlfriend." He grinned at his brother as he pumped his fist in and out. "The boss told me that on opening day, with the President there and everything, we'll have to show up at the Stadium about five a.m. rather than nine. Those security guys will shake us down good."

Morse thought for a second and said, "Look, Shorty's got us a terrific weapon. We hafta figure out how it can get in the box and through the metal detectors."

"That's the goddamn problem," Butch acknowledged. "Let me work on it for a few days. Hold off on this 'til the next time we meet."

"Okay, Butch, lemme know if you need help," Morse said.

Is this an insurmountable deal-breaker? Morse wondered.

Exhibiting his authority, Morse told Shorty, "Show them the weapon now!"

Shorty went into Morse's bedroom where he had hid several types of weapons. He returned with a three foot long rifle. Before handing it to Morse, he folded the stock and reduced its length to only two and a half feet.

"Isn't this a beauty," Morse said.

"It's an Armalite model AR-18," Shorty said. "The weapon's range is just right from the center field bleachers. I was told it's real popular in Europe." He looked around at his interested conspirators. "It's freaking perfect."

Butch took the rifle from Morse and said, "Feels a little heavy to me."

"Yeah, the loaded magazine adds to the weight. I think we hafta put the magazine in a separate box." Morse nodded approvingly at Butch.

"That's the way it has to be." Butch agreed, "We can't make a box of rolls seem too heavy and attract attention."

Morse let out a whoop. "How about some beers?"

They sat around boasting and drinking beer until Pete said, "You guys can bullshit about the plan all you want, but I'm going to bed."

Shorty was snoozing on the couch.

Butch pulled Morse aside and said, "Justin, you get me jittery when you act neurotic like before. The other guys don't know you got out of the Army on a Section 8 and they'll—"

"Okay, Butch, I know. I just lost it thinking about what still has to be done. Don't give it a second thought, friend. I'm fine."

"This is serious shit, and you'll be on your own inside the stadium to get the guy. You gotta stay in control."

"Thanks, Butch," Morse said, "I'll be okay." He shook Butch's hand, smiled and said, "This is great …it's going to work. Butch, you're the man now. If you can figure out how to get the boxes through security, we're in like Flynn."

"You know what they say, where there's a will, there's a way," Butch replied. "Oh, I'm going to use a magic marker and put the initials JWB on the two boxes."

"I love it," Morse said, his eyes wide open in anticipation as he strutted around like a peacock. "By the way I sent a letter to the White House addressed to that dictator Atkinsen."

"I wish you didn't do that," Butch said, shaking his head at Morse. "I bet Booth didn't do anything like that with Lincoln."

Morse ignored Butch's complaint and went to the refrigerator to serve another round of beers. As he handed a Coors to Butch he emitted a low belch and said, "They'll think the letter came from a pro-UN activist group."

"From what I've read in the newspaper, the guy running against Atkinsen seems pretty good," Butch commented. "I bet he'll be happy if we're successful."

"Maybe I'll write him a letter, too."

"There you go again, Justin. That's another screwy idea. Let's just stick to the plan."

Morse grinned at Butch, saluted him, and chug-a-lugged his beer.

Chapter Nineteen

"George, the only way you're going to beat the Senator is to dwell on his failure to win the nomination the first time," the exploratory team leader recommended. "That's where he's most vulnerable."

Granger's early attempts to garner support from party officials had met with some success. His campaign message and style had been well-received, which added to his confidence and appeal when speaking at large fund raising dinners as well as Town Hall meetings and coffee klatches.

With four months to go before the July convention, the South Carolina primary was his first big test. Granger needed to show he could hold his own with the party's titular head.

The candidates had faced each other at a small round table, with a moderator between, at the University of South Carolina in Columbia. The setting was informal, but the adversaries were tense and tight-lipped waiting for the TV cameras to go live.

"He used your own words against you, George," said Stan Flanagan, recently promoted to campaign manager. "Let's replay the final minutes of the debate."

They sat in the candidate's hotel room and watched the coverage rerun from only hours ago. Although distraught about his performance, Granger resigned himself to sit through the poor showing. He had been fooled by Robinson.

Now I know how an actor feels after a bad review.

"It's your turn, Senator Robinson," the moderator said.

"Representative Granger, I want to raise a point about the military. In the State of the Union, the President spoke of reinstituting the draft. I believe you are in favor of that position."

"Absolutely not." Granger's face appeared piqued at the question.

"I have the transcript of your speech to the American Legion a few years ago in which you clearly suggested the need for the draft and—"

"Senator, you're taking that comment out of context. That was at a time of increased hostilities around the world. We needed to protect our interests and support our friends."

"You're implying that protecting our interests and supporting our friends are not important today?" The Senator had a look of sarcasm.

"The world is more stable today," Granger said calmly.

My deviated-septum looks more prominent by the angle of the TV cameras, like a boxer's nose, Granger thought.

"Congressman, it's just another example of your position coinciding with the opposition party."

Robinson quickly removed several sheets of paper from the inside pocket of his suit jacket. He smiled at the moderator.

"Allow me to switch to American History, which was Congressman Granger's major in college." He paused to find the pertinent passage. "In your final exam, you wrote and I quote, 'Had the South Carolina delegation to the Continental Congress not been so committed to slavery, the Declaration of Independence and the Constitution would have freed the slaves. There would not have been a Civil War.' Did you not write that opinion?"

The moderator called for order as the background stirring and shouts disrupted the proceedings. Several people walked out and one man was removed by force for calling Granger a "nigger-lover". The television camera focused on a taunting Robinson and a startled Granger.

"That was written a long time ago. I was instructed to write a devil's advocate paper on the evil of that prolonged war and its repercussion for generations of Southerners." A muscle rippled in Granger's jaw, as his fist repeatedly hit the table.

The moderator stepped in for a commercial break, which concluded the program.

"George, he had you scrambling with little time to respond or justify your positions."

"You don't have to keep reminding me, Stan. I saw what the hell happened. He saved those spurious charges to the end—very clever and unfair."

"Are you kidding?" Flanagan responded. He smirked at his boss for the mild rebuke of his opponent. "The man's a snake. He wants the presidency so bad ... well ... I bet he can taste it tonight."

"So what's the damage control?"

"To begin with, you can figure we lost South Carolina," his manager concluded, scratching the top of his head. "We'll prepare a brief statement to answer questions and accuse Robinson of twisting the facts. But we have to move on and prepare for Super Tuesday."

"Okay, sounds right to me. I'm tired and I'm going to bed."

"Good night, George. Better days are ahead."

As he brushed his teeth and looked in the bathroom mirror, Granger realized he had underestimated his opponent and the toll of campaigning. Allegiances among his colleagues were fleeting and unpredictable. He recalled Stan Flanagan's words at the outset, "George, you'll have to watch your back."

Why am I diverting my energies away from my leadership position in the House?

* * *

Senator Robinson was quietly thrilled. *I guess I taught him a good lesson of high stakes politics. We're not in Kansas any more, or more appropriately, Louisiana.*

Robinson's inner circle could not contain their ecstatic reaction to the debate. "Senator, that was a masterful exchange. I think you finished the congressman's chances tonight. In our opinion Granger may drop out long before the convention. His campaign funds will dry up soon."

"I don't want to take anything for granted, but I agree and we should turn our attention to Atkinsen," Robinson said, rubbing his chin hard as if the stubble could be removed without a razor and shaving cream.

"Our view is you should simply stress your experience for the balance of the primary fight. Granger will be nothing more than a sparring partner for you to sharpen your positions for the general election. Perhaps, toss some praise Granger's way so his followers will come back to you with no bad feelings."

"I like that approach. In the meantime, let's all follow the President's address to the UN. I want each statement analyzed." He stood to signal the meeting was over. "Atkinsen's bound to say something that will be fodder for us in the general election."

Bruce is pestering me on what Atkinsen plans to say.

Robinson was confident his campaign was on the right track. No slip-ups would be tolerated. His compulsion was the presidency. "Don't lose sight of the ultimate prize," he would repeat to himself as critical decisions were under consideration.

Even in his late sixties, Robinson carried his six foot-three inch frame and distinctive gait with military-like bearing. While his bushy silver-grey hair cast him as the stereotype politician, his manner appealed to his followers as sincere. He'd move mountains to assist a constituent. His deep-set eyes captivated Town Hall gatherings, who witnessed the Senator close up for the first time.

He dialed the home number of Fletcher Jones, the acclaimed, somewhat eccentric, political commentator of the *Westchester Weekly* magazine, noting it was only 9:45.

"Mr. Jones, Senator Robinson here."

"Good evening, Senator," Fletcher said, sounding surprised. "What can …congratulations on the debate. I believe you won hands down."

"Thank you and thanks for the kind words in past columns. I'm only calling you at this time to promise I will give you an exclusive once the conventions are over."

"I look forward to that, Senator. Good night and sleep well."

"I will."

Robinson put down the phone. "The intrigue has begun."

Chapter Twenty

The circulation of *Westchester Weekly* was modest compared to DC political publications and the likes of *Time* and *Newsweek*. Nevertheless, the quality and depth of analytical reporting established the magazine as must reading for many Washington insiders. The staff was experienced newspersons who looked for a less-demanding change of pace at a smaller and more convenient suburban location. Without question, the most literate member of the staff was Fletcher Jones.

Fletcher reeked of Ivy League. His Harvard background had molded an articulate clear-thinker with idealistic visions and a sharp, sometimes brutal, pen. He was to the magazine what Andy Rooney was to *Sixty Minutes*. As a committed bachelor, he could be described as the American version of *My Fair Lady's* Henry Higgins. Except for his completely bald head and slim frame, his appearance was nondescript. At an inch less than six feet, he was happy to let his writing define who he was.

After several years as a college instructor of American and English Literature, he acceded to the constant urging of his friend, Hugh McGarry, to join the magazine as the senior political writer, with a scholarly flair in his critiques.

"I hate to bust your balloon, Hugh, but it wasn't your persuasive arguments that justified my decision," he acknowledged years later. "My motivation was that I'm intrigued by the political process and elections and legislative infighting. Now I'm a compulsive political junkie, like groupies after rock stars."

"That's obvious in your work product," McGarry interjected. "If I didn't convince you to join me, you could have been successful with your own radio talk show, assuming the audience put up with your cynicism."

"Thank you again and again for the opportunity," Fletcher said, bowing to his friend, the boss.

* * *

Today Fletcher Jones was pissed.

"I don't want to go to a lousy baseball game. Who cares if it's at Yankee Stadium?" He tossed the press pass back at Hugh McGarry, editor and owner of *Westchester Weekly* magazine.

"Get over it, Fletcher," McGarry said, ignoring his ace political commentator's rant. "The President is going directly from the UN to the opening game. Since you're covering his address to the General Assembly, you can stick with him while he's in New York."

Fletcher sank down in the large leather chair in front of his boss' desk, feeling misfit. A ballgame in any sport was not his cup of tea. Friends had heard him say many times, "Give me a game of chess and American literature and I'm set for the weekend."

"Look! I can't spare two men on a political assignment now. That's your beat." As usual, the editor would have his way.

Fletcher reached across the desk, picked up the pass, and said, "Okay, but you owe me one."

"Thanks loads," McGarry said, shuffling copy into his briefcase. "Remember, it's Friday of next week."

"How about we go for that drink you promised? I'm thirsty." Fletcher returned to his lovable self, smiling at his long time associate and friend.

Fletcher had stolen the thunder of larger publications when he finagled the only interview with Harry Grant following the election of President Atkinsen three years ago. They met in the lounge at Georgetown, both suspicious of the other, like the matador and a charging bull.

"If you don't mind, Mr. Grant, I wish to tape our conversation."

"No problem and you can call me Harry."

"Okay, Harry, can you tell me what the President intends to do about the Catholic Archdioceses that are declaring bankruptcy?"

Fletcher could tell Grant was caught off guard by the question, as he crossed his legs twice.

Grant: "It's an unfortunate situation that the church, and possibly the Vatican, must deal with. However, there is no role the President of the United States will play, directly or otherwise. He's not a Catholic as you know."

Jones: "What is his view of the status of minorities in society today?"

Grant: "Well he feels strongly that family life and the protection of children have to be emphasized. He agrees with the views of Bill Cosby that many black leaders, on a local and national level, have not helped the younger generation, young black men in particular. In addition—"

Jones: "What does he truly think of Senator Robinson?"

Grant: "The Senator has served his constituents well. On the major domestic and foreign policy issues though, President Atkinsen disagrees with the Senator's fundamental positions."

Jones: "I was searching for what the President thought of Robinson's character. His views, not yours."

Grant: Inaudible. "In any case, the President's only frame of reference is the recent campaign. You'll have to ask him that question."

Jones: "Harry, it's well known you are his closest advisor. What is his number one priority, given the evidence of corruption in the previous administration?"

Grant: "The security and welfare of the American people is his utmost concern. His policies will reflect the defense of the country. Your premise regarding the previous administration, however, is based on your opinion. If there is such evidence that I'm not aware of, I'm sure the judicial system will determine the appropriate way to proceed."

Jones: "There have been rumors of infidelity circulating about the President and—"

Grant: "Let me stop you right there! He just won an election after a tough campaign. You're beating a dead horse. Now, if you don't mind, I notice I'm late for my next class."

Jones: "Certainly. Thank you for your time."

The column in the *Westchester Weekly* reporting the interview suggested the wrong man became president. Fletcher wrote *I'm afraid we will rue the day the people did not cast their vote for John*

Robinson, a man of substance, vision and broad experience. If I had been a betting man, I'd be off to debtor's prison.

Fletcher delighted in his own reputation for pulling off a coup with this article. An upward spike in readership of the magazine gained him elite status with the likes of David Broder and George Will.

* * *

A new campaign for president was underway, and Fletcher Jones was absorbed with the strategies and barbs of each candidate. The President's State of the Union speech fascinated him to the point of distraction. *Something just doesn't add up,* he thought, perplexed at the unique harangue.

He was determined to find out what was behind Atkinsen's firing of Brown and Simon with no advance warning; and "What about Styles sudden resignation? It's all beginning to sound like a Shakespearean tragedy," he muttered to himself.

While he lamented the sudden death of Mrs. Atkinsen over two years ago, Fletcher wanted another hard shot at questioning Grant and investigating the President's background. "This time around, his record in office over the last three years is fair game," he had guaranteed his editor.

And why hasn't he filled the VP vacancy? Who will be on the Atkinsen ticket?

Fletcher was compelled to discover what makes politicians tick, what motivates them.

What a great subject for a thesis! They treat character assassination as sport, for cocktail hour conversation.

How does someone who delights in receiving simply fifty-one percent of a popular vote act so erudite and pompous, he wondered, leery of all politicians' character.

"This profession has more than its share of hypocrites," he declared to McGarry. "Profiles in courage are the exception rather than the rule."

I've got to strip away their façade with whatever tricks I can muster. The President is first on my list.

Chapter Twenty One

"Good to see you again, Russ," Sam Heffernan said to Barrett. "I've been assigned to be with you on the POTUS trip to the United Nations."

"That's fine, Sam." They shook hands. "Were you told your assignment includes Yankee Stadium?"

"It sure does," answered Heffernan, with a broad smile on his face. "I'm scheduled to be in New York the day before the speech and be at the game with you."

"I leave in a week on the Advance Team," said Barrett. "Why don't you come with me this afternoon to check the hate mail and I'll fill you in on our tactics."

This is all I need, thought Barrett. *Heffernan's a great guy and Ashton Williams recommended him, but an agent borrowed from counterfeit duty for protection detail won't be much help to me in a crisis.*

They drove a short distance from Secret Service headquarters to a building which housed a division of the Protective Research Office. The Forensic Information for Handwriting division analyzes and sorts out specific threatening or odd mail relevant to upcoming trips.

"Russ, I can't believe how much there is," said Heffernan. "Does this go on all the time?"

"Sadly, it does, and the volume has increased since the State of the Union in January." Barrett sipped his diet Coke and looked somber. "Unfortunately, that's the way it is. Forensics stays busy all the time."

"Sonofabitches," said Heffernan, reading the first batch of letters. "This guy hopes the President has a stroke when he gives his speech.

And this one wants to blow his right arm off when he throws out the first ball."

"Get used to it or you'll be knocked for a loop with this shit," Barrett advised. He raised the open palms of his hands as if to say there's nothing that can be done about it. "The UN supporters and the usual kooks are really intense about their opposition to the President. Just take notes and hold aside the ones you think require further investigation."

"Close to quitting time," Barrett said. "We'll finish up tomorrow morning. Let's start at eight ..." He hesitated as he read and reread the last letter. His curiosity was replaced by uneasiness, as he stroked the top of his head; a frown crossed his face. "Here's one that's different," he said just above a whisper. "Sam, check the date of the President's UN speech."

Heffernan turned the page on the wall calendar and said, "Let's see ... it's on Friday, the same day as Good Friday."

Barrett picked up the unsigned letter and read aloud:

Mr. Arrogant President,
> *You deserve what happens to all tyrants.*
> *You will also get yours on Good Friday.*

* * *

"What the hell's wrong with you, Russ?" asked Kathleen. "First, you didn't come near me despite my advances. Now you're up in the middle of the night waltzing around. What time is it anyway?"

"It's about three," Barrett said. He sat on the side of the bed and turned on the nightstand light.

"Here we go again," she said, raising up on the pillow and rubbing her eyes.

"Listen Kathleen, I'm worried about the President's trip to New York and—"

"What else is new?"

"I'm serious," he said. "There's a specific threat that identified Good Friday, which is when Atkinsen is at the UN and Yankee Stadium. Before I left the office, I googled Good Friday. You'd be amazed at the strange things that have happened on that day."

"Can we go in the kitchen to talk?" she asked. "I wanna get a graham cracker and milk."

As she crawled out of bed, he spied longingly at her curved hips and backside, caressed by her underpants.

She sat at the kitchen table while he poured a glass of skim milk and placed an opened box of grahams in front of her.

"Remember the Exxon-Valdez disaster?"

She nodded.

"That happened on a Good Friday. Also, the worst ever earthquake in Alaska occurred on Good Friday."

"Okay, but you could pick any date and find similar major events," she said.

"True, but Good Friday isn't the same date each year," he added.

"Well of course, I know that," Kathleen said, wiping some crumbs off her chin.

"With your Irish heritage, you should be aware of the 1998 Good Friday Peace Agreement between Northern Ireland and the government in Dublin."

"Oh my God, you're right! We never thought it could happen."

"Now you're with me." He reached across the table and kissed her cheek. "I stopped at the library on the way home and read a chapter of Carl Sandberg's *Abraham Lincoln: The War Years*. He details the assassination on a Good Friday."

"I wasn't aware of that," she said, her accent more pronounced.

"Believe it or not, I dreamt of the meeting Lincoln actually had with his security chief on the afternoon of his assassination. Since the war was over, he felt safe again and gave the security chief a new assignment to investigate the rampant counterfeiting going on throughout the South. 'I have the military with me tonight at the theater,' Lincoln said to the man. The rest is history."

"That was a tragedy, as was the assassination of Kennedy and others, but it doesn't prove a thing." She sat on his lap and put her arms around his neck. "Please don't let your health suffer about this, Russ. You're doing your best to protect the President. Let's go to bed and catch up on sleep." She rubbed his chest up and down. "You have another big day tomorrow."

"Thanks for listening, sweetheart. Maybe it's my imagination working overtime."

I'll run my premonition by Heffernan in the morning.

* * *

"You look bleary-eyed, Russ. You and your girlfriend have an orgy last night?" Heffernan poured two cups of coffee.

Barrett stirred his coffee in silence and then said, "Before we start, let me fill you in on some homework I did last night about Good Fridays." He repeated the story of his dream and research.

"Christ, Russ, this stuff is getting to you. I've heard of burnout on the Protection Detail and I'm worried about it getting to you."

"Nonsense," Barrett replied, dismissing Heffenan's concern with a wave. He held his hands behind his neck and said, "Okay Sam, it's somewhat circumstantial, but the letter has to be analyzed and I may tell Williams about my sixth sense. After all, he tried to convince the President the baseball game was a big mistake—a serious security risk. "

"That's up to you, but I think you're on the wrong track," Heffernan said, pouring a second cup for himself. "If you want to make a case for delaying the trip, why not focus on Friday, the thirteenth. More mysterious things are connected to that date."

"Yeah, but the letter referred to this Good Friday, which is not on the thirteenth. Get it!" Barrett's nose flared as he took a deep breath.

"Calm down! I was just using it as an example. Come on, everyone associates the date with bad luck. Hell, some tall buildings don't even identify a thirteenth floor."

"So what? The jinx doesn't have anything to do with this."

Heffernan paused and said, "Wait a second. I'm calling my buddy who worked on the case of Bin Laden counterfeiting US dollars. We discovered something interesting in a safe house in Afghanistan that relates to Friday the thirteenth."

They continued to examine more hate mail. "Some of these are in Spanish," Heffernan noted.

"Most likely from that *Save the UN* group," Barrett said.

The fax of the declassified recording that Heffernan requested arrived, which he handed to Barrett. "Look, here's a conversation between Bin Laden and Mohammed Atta. Notice the date!"

TRANSCRIPT TRANSLATION—Friday, April 13, 2001

B.L. *Do you have enough US dollars?*
M.A. *More than enough.*
B.L. *Have they learned to fly the planes yet?*
M.A. *Three of them are attending flight schools.*
B.L. *What about the others?*
M.A. *They are working it out. However, our man in Minnesota is having personal problems.*
B.L. *Will it jeopardize the mission?*
M.A. *No, Sheik.*
B.L. *Their ability to move around the States has worked as we expected?*
M.A. *Yes, Sheik. Without any difficulty.*
B.L. *Stick to the original plan for the second Tuesday in September.*
M.A. *With the help of Allah it will be done.*

Barrett put the fax down. A grin became a sinister laugh.

"What the hell's so funny about that?" Heffernan demanded. "It's not a laughing matter," he snarled, yanking the paper away from Barrett and stuffing it in his jacket inside pocket.

"I'm sorry, Sam," Barrett said. His tone changed to solemn as he asked, "When do you think was the last time a Good Friday fell on the thirteenth?"

"Crap, now how would I know that?"

"Would you believe it was in 2001? Bin Laden set the date for his attacks on the World Trade Center and the Pentagon on that very day ... a Good Friday."

Heffernan sat expressionless. "Hoooly shit. Maybe you should tell Williams about your theory." He leaned back in his chair and exhaled imaginary smoke.

* * *

Kathleen straddled Barrett, kissing him on the neck and ear. She massaged his penis in her hands, like she was rolling a sausage.

"What's your problem?" she snapped, as he pushed her away.

"I'm scared about this trip, that's all." Unable to be aroused, he silently cursed himself.

"Do you want me to move out of this apartment and stay away from you for awhile?"

Her question sounded to him like a plea.

"No, damn it. Can't you just bear with me on this 'til I get back from New York?" He sat up in bed and reached for the bottled water on the night stand to relieve his dry mouth.

"I hope this isn't the way it's always going to be with your job," she said, as she maneuvered to her side of the bed and pulled the covers on top of her. "Good night."

She just doesn't get it. Am I able to protect the President of the United States?

Chapter Twenty Two

"This is all you've got?" Williams said to Barrett. "You want me to alert the President because of your sixth sense?"

"It's more than that, sir."

Barrett had sent a memo to Williams asking for a meeting with POTUS, but now he had second thoughts, realizing he was the new man on the Protection Detail team.

"Like what else?" Williams demanded.

"Well, this letter was the only suspicious one that mentioned Good Friday. The handwriting and the reference to Lincoln indicated to Forensics the author was intelligent, knew the history of that assassination, and knew this trip was on Good Friday. Did you know when Lincoln was killed?"

"Makes no difference if I knew it," Williams said, casting a doubtful eye at Barrett. "Look, we've already made preparations for extra security. Everyone's aware there's a real security risk associated with this trip. You're leaving with the Advance team tomorrow so keep your eyes and ears open to the scuttlebutt in the city and—"

"You're referring to the UN," Barrett interrupted.

"Of course, and the protest rallies that go on every day outside the place. You'll be coordinating with someone assigned from the Police Department." He folded his arms across his chest and added, "We need a hell of a lot more to go on than your ...what did you call it?"

"An omen."

"Okay, something else for us to worry about. I'm not buying it, but you can come with me to this afternoon's briefing with the

President on trip details. If I bring up your concern, you better be prepared to explain it." Williams let out a deep sigh and shook his head.

Barrett nodded. He wondered if he had gone out on a limb and Williams was about to cut it off.

* * *

"Nice to see you again, Barrett," the President said, after he welcomed the agents into the Oval Office. "Agent Williams, I'm due at dinner shortly so you'll have to get right to the point."

Their meeting had been delayed for almost two hours, which explained Atkinsen and Wagner dressed in formal attire. Since the agents were not invited to sit, they stood in front of the President's desk to give their report. Barrett became more anxious during the long wait.

"Mr. President, we've received the full cooperation of UN security and New York Police. Besides a check of the Watch List, plainclothes officers have infiltrated a new organization that has been demonstrating in support of the UN since January, known as *Save the UN*. In accordance with standard procedure we have borrowed manpower from the Uniformed Division and Counterfeiting assignments. As I've indicated previously, it's difficult to protect against all possibilities at Yankee Stadium, but we—"

Wagner interrupted, "Agent Williams, your predecessor did a great job with President Bush at Yankee Stadium after nine-eleven so I'm certain your team will handle similar arrangements."

"Yes, sir. I was just about to say that. However, we do suggest as a precaution that the President wear a bullet-proof vest."

Wagner threw his hands up in the air and said, "Really, do you think that's practical when he throws a baseball?"

"Hold on, Steve," the President said calmly. "He's right, Williams. It would be restrictive for one thing and send the wrong message to the public." He opened his desk calendar and wrote a note to himself. "What else do you have?"

"I suggest we leave the game about the fifth inning or so."

"No seventh inning stretch?" the President joked. "Okay, we can leave early. Anything else?"

Barrett cleared his throat.

"Sir, Agent Barrett does have an issue to bring to your attention."

"What is it, Barrett?" Wagner asked, a grimace displaying his impatience.

"Mr. President, there was one piece of hate mail I'm concerned about because—"

"I'd like to see it," the President interrupted.

Hesitant at first, Barrett looked at Wagner, then removed a single page from the file.

Atkinsen read the short note aloud. "Mr. Arrogant President, You deserve what happens to all tyrants. You will also get yours on Good Friday."

The note pricked Atkinsen's interest in a disturbing way. He stood and glanced from one man to the other.

"What do you make of it, Barrett?" he asked. "Please, let's all sit down." All four moved to the sitting area.

"Mr. President, it's obviously a reference to Lincoln who was hated for destroying the South just as you have had numerous threats from UN supporters and hate mongers. I consider this a serious threat for another Good Friday tragedy."

"That's quite a leap," said Wagner. "There are threats all the time that cover every day of the week."

"Barrett, do you honestly believe I'll be in danger?" Atkinsen asked.

"Sir, that letter did not come from some harmless crackpot. It's a deliberate message from an angry and deranged person. The letter refers to a tyrant which is what John Wilkes Booth called Lincoln. "

"Did Forensics conclude as much?" asked Wagner, standing to emphasize his question.

"Up to a point …not exactly, but I had a dream—"

Williams cut short Barrett and said, "Mr. President, I assure you we will take every precaution for your safety."

"Thank you, Agent Williams and Agent Barrett," said Wagner. "The President is late for a dinner function."

After the agents left, Wagner said, "Mr. President, we can discuss this again if you wish. However, I see no need for a change in your itinerary."

"I agree. Why don't you go to the dinner and announce I'll be there shortly."

"Yes, sir."

"Oh, at the budget meeting tomorrow morning, I expect that the number of earmark appropriations will be reduced and the earmarks left in the budget will identify the congressmen who requested the expenditure … regardless of party affiliation."

"Right. I believe the Budget Director has worked that out in committee."

"Fine. Also, Steve, I don't think I'll go to Camp David after the meeting," the President said, gazing out the window at the oncoming darkness. "Instead, I'll take a quick ride to the Greenbrier, spend Saturday night there and return late Sunday afternoon. Have Cohen give me all his notes for the UN meeting next week."

"I'll take care of it and alert Agent Williams," Wagner said. "You haven't been there in a while so you'll enjoy it, but it may be on the cool side."

From the moment Good Friday had been mentioned, Atkinsen struggled to focus on the conversation with the Secret Service agents. He couldn't blot out the distraction in his mind from long ago. The memory was too vivid of the close personal time he and Ellen had spent at the Greenbrier at Easter time.

* * *

"What a great idea to come to a place like this," Ellen said to her husband.

Atkinsen enjoyed seeing Ellen's face light up. "I knew this would be perfect to celebrate our fifteenth wedding anniversary," he said.

"The entrance to the Greenbrier outdoes *Tara* for sure," she continued, as they exited the Coffee Shoppe and Ice Cream luncheon Parlor. "So what's next?"

"Well, we have the whole weekend and there's plenty to do. We have a horse-drawn carriage ride at 2:30."

He wanted this to be their special time together. It was fortunate he had no court cases to prosecute over the Easter weekend and she wasn't scheduled to volunteer at the hospital.

"Why don't we just stroll around the place 'til then?" she suggested, holding his hand in hers. "I feel like a kid again."

Her enthusiastic reaction to the Greenbrier and West Virginia scenery could not have made him any happier. As they walked hand in hand, he mused *she's as beautiful today as she was on our wedding day.*

She stopped and turned to him, "I love you, Herbert, with all my heart."

Time stopped for him. Forgotten were her health concerns and his transgression.

"I love you too, Ellen," he whispered in her ear, hiding his starry-eyed embarrassment. He never felt closer to her, in a spiritual as well as physical sense.

They passed the exquisite Main Dining Room and sat to rest for a moment in the grand Colonial Room where afternoon tea was served at four each day. They stared like all tourists at the five immense chandeliers in the elegant room.

"Ellen, there are bowling alleys here and I've read about the health benefits of the spring waters," he stated, hoping to spark her interest. "The water smells like brimstone, but I'm game if you are."

"Why not?" she said. "When in Rome, etcetera. But I'll pass on bowling."

"Fine. We'll do that tomorrow. Now it's time for the carriage ride."

The tour guide in tails and top hat welcomed them. "The ride will take about an hour. We follow the road surrounding the property and leading into the Alleghany Hills. Did you know we've had many Presidents visit here dating back to the 1800's?"

"Interesting," Atkinsen said. "I read that Robert E. Lee vacationed here during his retirement years."

"Yes, sah," he drawled. "Is this your first time here, Ma'am?"

"It is and it's magnificent," she said. "Driver, what is your name?"

"Ma'am, my name is Joshua and I've been driving this here carriage for fifteen years. My daddy drove it before me."

Church bells began tolling in the nearby town of White Sulphur Springs. Atkinsen asked, "Why are the bells tolling?"

"Sir, it's three o'clock and this is Good Friday. Jesus was crucified and died at this very hour." Joshua bowed his head.

They continued on a brisk pace past the towering Sycamores and Spruces, taking in the fresh mountain air.

"Joshua, I feel a chill. May I have a blanket?"

"Yes ma'am," he said, tossing one back to his male passenger.

Atkinsen arranged the blanket and put his arm around her shoulder, moving closer to her. "I'll keep you warm, hon."

The smell of fresh greenery attested to an early spring. The scenery was almost as breath-taking as in October. As they passed one of the golf courses, Joshua said, "The famous golfer Sam Snead was the club pro here for many years."

The carriage reentered the complex behind the main building. The wide, tree-lined walkway, two football fields long, between the main building and the golf and tennis pro shops was bustling with activity. Charming cottages on both sides ran half the length of the field, where hundreds of young children were enjoying the Easter egg hunt, the clowns, and games.

Ellen shuddered and looked away. "Can we go back right now?"

"Of course," Atkinsen said, signaling to the driver to end the tour. He shook his head, realizing it would take more than this great setting for Ellen to get over that she could not have children.

While Ellen rested before dinner, Atkinsen decided it was time to face her problem, no, their problem, openly. That's what the psychologist had advised all along.

She emerged from the bedroom in a bathrobe looking dejected. "Sorry, Herbert, I couldn't help it," she said. "When I saw those children—"

"I know," he said, gently pulling her close to him. Her head rested on his shoulder. "If it's okay with you, how about getting dressed for dinner, then we'll have a cocktail in the room and talk over our feelings about what happened today before we go downstairs?" He kissed her on the cheek. "We want to deal with this, right?"

"I do," she said. "I'll get dressed right away."

He poured himself a glass of Chivas Regal to relieve the anxiety, unable to predict their emotional state.

"You look gorgeous," he exclaimed as she came into the large living room, carrying her high-heel shoes. "A true Southern belle."

"Thank you," she said. She sat on the love seat and beckoned him to sit next to her. "At my last doctor's examination, the doctor explained that what happened to me a long time ago has—"

"Ellen, there's no reason to be vague about it." He shifted his position to face her. "I never told you this, but your father and I had a heart to heart one week before our wedding."

"What do you mean?"

"We met in Underground Atlanta after work for a steak dinner and a few beers. He told me what happened to you."

She lowered her head and reached out for his hand.

"He described how you were so outgoing and friendly at age fifteen … so innocent and naïve." Out-of-the-blue Atkinsen recalled, "Your father even mentioned that, as a teenager, you cried all night after reading *Love Story*. Do you remember that you even refused to see the movie?"

"I do," she said, forcing a smile.

He gulped and continued, squeezing her hand. "Those two guys took advantage of you and …" he halted. Her tears flowed crisscross down her cheeks. After putting his arms around her, he could only console her by repeating, "I love you for who you are and what you are. I always have and always will."

After a few minutes, she regained control and said, "Herbert, we knew I couldn't have children, even though I prayed I might conceive. But I never thought adoption was out of the question."

He stared into her sad eyes and touched her cheek. "Ellen, that's only one opinion."

"Because of my depressive illness, he feels it's unwise while I'm on medication. He says the stress of raising a young child may be further detrimental to my health. He hasn't diagnosed my current condition, other than to describe it as chronic fatigue syndrome." She hesitated and clenched her teeth. He held her arm when she started to stand.

"After all you've gone through, there's no way you should discontinue the medication," he said, in a low soothing voice. "So, the main thing is to manage your illness and do what the doctor recommends." He placed his hands on her face, looked into her eyes, and whispered, "We have each other. That's all that matters to me." He kissed her.

"Herbert, I'm sorry how this worked out. I wanted to be a good wife for you."

A shiver caused his teeth to chatter, which he concealed from her. *She really doesn't comprehend how wonderful she is to me and how much I love her.* He drank the last drop of scotch to ward off hoarseness in his throat.

"Ellen, we have a good life. Everything will work in the future as long as we're together."

"I'll try to take an active part in our lives and pray that God provides for us in the future," she promised.

I wish I had her courage and faith.

After a light meal and small talk, they strolled arm in arm past the specialty shops on the lower level of the main building. They laughed out loud, simultaneously reacting to a similar window shopping walk on their honeymoon, "Who would ever buy that expensive jewelry?"

Their bed was their private paradise that night. Skin touching skin, they became sensually one in a burst of passion.

"I'll always remember the Greenbrier," she said.

"So will I, Ellen," he said, short-winded. "So will I."

* * *

"I better put in an appearance at the reception," Atkinsen whispered to himself. He wondered if it were really true that time heals all wounds.

Chapter Twenty Three

"We have a problem," Butch told Morse.

"Whaddya mean? I'm depending on you, man." He was in no mood to hear bad news the day before Good Friday.

"My boss called and told me the deliveries to the stadium have to be tonight."

"So what?" Morse asked.

"That means I'll have two Ricans with me, and it'll be harder to get the boxes open without being seen." Butch slouched down on the couch with his hands clasped behind his neck. "It complicates getting through security as well."

Morse paced around his living room. The pangs of failure boiled in his gut. "Look, we can't fuck this up now. I'm all set to show up at nine tomorrow morning, and Pete is ready with the car, right?"

"Yeah, the Mercury is all revved up and ready to go. He's going to park near the McDonald's on 161st Street diagonally across Jerome Avenue from the stadium."

"Good. Shorty is checking out the stadium today and he's got a ticket to the game tomorrow. The little shit came up with a great idea for a diversion."

"You're kidding," Butch said. "The sap has some balls after all."

"So let's figure out your damn problem now and—"

"What about your weirdo friend, Brocce?" Butch asked.

Morse turned his back on Butch and said, "Forget him. He's not with us anymore. That's all I'm gonna say."

"Good riddance to the motherfucker as far as I'm concerned," Butch said.

Butch snapped his fingers and jumped from the couch. His face lit up like a light bulb. "Lemme see the other weapons Shorty got for us last month."

"Sure, they're in the bedroom."

Butch returned with a Derringer. "I have an idea and I'll need this to work it out."

"Are you sure? Butch, I knew you could handle it. Do whatever the hell it takes and call me as soon as you get back from the delivery tonight." Morse shook Butch's hand and said, "Good luck."

After Butch left, Morse stared out the front window to the driveway and brooded about his encounter with Brocce two days earlier.

Upset he had not heard from Brocce, Morse went to his apartment off Fordham Road in the Bronx. Using his key he entered the dimly lit living room and heard familiar sounds coming from the bedroom. The door was ajar. He peeked in and saw Brocce sitting on the edge of the bed stroking the head of a woman. They were both naked. She was kneeling at his groin and bobbing feverishly. Morse hesitated and watched, feeling the spontaneous rush of an erection.

Finally, he burst in and snarled, "Hey, you bastard, is this why we haven't heard from you?"

Brocce pushed the woman away, shouting, "What the hell are you doing barging in here like this? I told you your stupid project wouldn't work so—"

"Bullshit! We're all set and you let us down," Morse said, his lower jaw extended in anger.

The woman spit and said, "Who is this guy? Don't tell me he's the gang leader of your crazy plan."

"Shut up!" Brocce screamed. "Get dressed and get the hell out of here."

Morse panicked. *She knows what we're up to.*

"We needed that information on the secret service agents, you creep." To ease the tension he said, "Why don't you get some clothes on, too? Then we can talk."

Morse went to the kitchen realizing what he must do next. His plan was in jeopardy. He screwed the silencer on his Smith & Weston 9mm pistol.

Brocce came in first and a bullet pierced bone and his heart muscle. He was dead before he hit the floor.

The woman came to the kitchen half dressed and said, "What was that noise?"

Morse raised the gun aimed at her forehead and fired. She never made a sound as the bullet exploded out the back of her skull, splattering blood, bone and brain matter against the wall. Her life was over in a flash.

He detached the silencer and put the weapon in his inside jacket pocket. After wiping up each spot he had touched using a kitchen towel, he calmly walked out of the apartment.

* * *

"Juan called in sick so just take Hector with you," the owner of Stadium Bakery told Butch Tomlinn. "Load up nine hot dog roll boxes for Yankee Stadium and three for the Stadium Bar and Grill across from the bleacher entrance."

"No problem, boss. Let's go, Hector."

Butch was relieved that only one man would be in the bakery truck with him. As he planned how he could cut open two boxes unnoticed, he recalled overhearing the owner refer to his two helpers as illegal aliens.

"Hector, you have a driver's license, right?"

"I have a permit. Juan was teaching me to drive."

At midnight, the traffic along Jerome Avenue was sparse. "I'll tell you what," Butch said. "You take the wheel while I rest in the back. It's only twenty minutes or so. All you have to do is follow the elevated tracks above you directly to the stadium."

"Das great, man. No sweat for me."

Butch stopped the truck and climbed into the back. He had left the rifle and magazine clip, the pistol, and a box cutter and tape in a corner under his jacket. Hector's jacket was draped over the passenger's seat. Working quickly, he sliced open two boxes. After removing several rolls and placing the weapon and magazine clip carefully near the top of the boxes, he neatly taped them so no one would notice they had been opened.

"Watch that red light!" he called out to Hector.

"Yo man, I see it."

Butch was breathing heavy from the ominous work as he took the magic marker and printed JWB on each box. He saw they were near 161st Street so he ordered, "Pull over at the corner. I don't want the police to check you out, you know."

After Butch resumed driving, he said, "I'm only looking out for you because I know you're an illegal and you don't have any permit."

"Hey, man, I wish you wouldn't talk about dat."

The bakery delivery had been instructed to drive into the old left field bullpen and park. The walk to the office under the bleachers would only take a minute or so.

"Tonight I'll take the first two loads inside and you can take the third. *Comprende,* Hector?"

Butch handed Hector his jacket, with the planted pistol in an inside pocket, and said, "You better put this on. The temperature must be in the forties now."

"Anything you say. Man, look at all the cops here this late."

Butch unloaded three bulky but light boxes onto the hand truck and checked through security. In less than five minutes he returned for three more boxes. "Not those, Hector. You've got them the next time."

"How are the Yanks gonna to do this year?" Butch asked a police officer. The man grunted and waved him on.

Despite the cold air, Butch began to sweat. As he walked back to get the marked boxes, his legs felt heavy.

"Come on, Hector, you've got the last three." Butch stayed close to Hector pushing the hand truck.

"Hold it!" an officer at the security gate ordered Hector as a red light blinked on the metal detector. "Step over here!" He began to pat Hector down and immediately extracted the weapon from his jacket. "Sergeant, come—"

Hector pulled away from the officer shouting, "No, no." He ran out of the bullpen, crossing 161st Street. The officer gave chase but was no match for Hector's speed.

"Stop or I'll shoot!" His voice boomed out as several policemen came running. "Stop!"

A sharp sound boomed in the chilly night as the officer fired a shot into the air.

Hector stopped on a dime, as if he had been hit. He was grabbed and manhandled by four policemen.

Butch didn't wait to see what happened. He virtually ran with the unattended hand truck to the concession office where he dropped off the boxes behind the others in the large refrigerator. Leaving the hand truck behind, he moved rapidly back to the bakery truck.

"What's the problem, officer?" Butch asked a traffic cop.

"We caught a crazy kid carrying a gun."

"You're kidding."

"Get this van outta here and park it up there! We've gotta get that Budweiser truck in here next."

"Yes, sir," Butch replied. He held the wheel tight to stop from shaking. He came to a halt at the curb half-way up the street toward the 161st El train station.

The traffic light straight ahead turned green.

It's now or never.

He touched the gas pedal for the van to roll forward. Flooring the gas, he made a quick left turn onto Jerome Avenue, and sped away in the dark. After he had ditched the van in a Used Car grave off the Major Deegan Expressway, he called Morse.

"Justin, it went like a charm. It's up to you now."

The time was forty minutes after midnight. It was already Good Friday.

Chapter Twenty Four

"Mr. Secretary-General, Mr. President, and distinguished delegates, ladies and gentlemen."

The President stared out at the large audience in the General Assembly of the United Nations. He was surprised that the delegates from Iran and North Korea were in their places.

Atkinsen was aware those two governments had recalled their ambassadors to jointly coordinate a boycott of the special session. They lobbied like-minded countries hoping to demonstrate that the President was no longer respected, and to further weaken US clout in the world.

Rickman intervened by declaring a boycott as misguided. He had advised the ambassadors, "You will lose an opportunity to show the world unity against the policy of an American President. The face to face confrontation will demonstrate the resolve of UN members to resist an insult to its charter." His argument convinced them not to boycott the address.

Atkinsen waited for silence. His pronouncement in the State of the Union speech to redirect US dues away from the current UN structure remained a steadfast commitment.

"In the past I have come here to extol the efforts of UN field personnel to feed the hungry and minister to the sick. The success you have achieved in fighting AIDS and in negotiating debt relief for developing countries is consistent with the finest tradition of a United Nations. The world has benefited from this body in many respects."

Atkinsen hesitated. Glanced from right to left. Wet his lips. "Today I am here for a different purpose." His voice became tense, like the foreman of a jury announcing their verdict. "You and I have lost our way in carrying out the objectives of this organization. There is no need for me to itemize the costly bureaucratic inefficiencies contained in several independent investigations of this body, all a matter of public record. Fortunately, a dedicated program of reforms and accountability may eliminate these defects. However, there is a more significant crisis we face that can only be resolved by moral courage and self-discipline."

He scanned the General Assembly and observed the US delegation, transfixed in their attention to the proceedings.

"Terrorism has become a fact of life, destroying thousands of innocent lives to achieve an extremist agenda. The terrorists only accept their way of life and despise the legitimate aspirations of others." He focused his glare at the Sudanese Ambassador, who looked irritated.

"Yet, you have been unable to define acts of terrorism and often blame the responder rather than the perpetrator. Perhaps, the most compelling evidence of your inability to achieve the peaceful purpose of the Charter can be traced to the early days of this body. Resolution 181 divided Palestine and Israel. I dare say this larger gathering of member states today would not have passed such a meaningful edict. Furthermore—"

A disturbance broke out as numerous delegates rose in protest. Arabic expressions could be heard clearly, as delegates from Syria, Iran, Iraq, Yemen, Oman and Libya stomped out of the hall. The Saudis were seen in conference at their place, but did not join the walk-out. North Korean and Cuban delegates pounded the table with their fists, reminiscent of Nikita Khrushchev's shoe-banging exhibition. Delegates from several European countries applauded the President's allegation out of courtesy.

Atkinsen was stoic watching the abrupt departure of so many delegates. His self-assuredness on the validity of his message inspired an unperturbed countenance as he waited to continue. *They are all proving my exact point.*

When decorum was restored, he said, "Ladies and gentlemen, it is not just I who is disillusioned with the capacity of this body, noble in concept, to achieve international peace and cooperation. Just as the predecessor League of Nations failed to prevent a world war, this United Nations will fail due to timidity in the face of tyranny and terrorism. We must have the courage to fulfill the ideals of the Charter."

The US delegation applauded followed by the Australian Ambassador and other delegations.

"My government proposes the following to more efficiently achieve the goals of this world body. First, the humanitarian services should be separated into a new world organization, headquartered in Nairobi, and at least ninety-five percent of the funds will be directed to the needy. I can guarantee that American generosity will lessen the burden of member states. A satellite of the organization should be The World Bank Group in Washington, DC, which provides the funds to strengthen the economies of poor nations in order to reduce poverty."

Rickman was listening to the President and observing the delegates, with an austere look on his face. At the mention of a separated function, he leaned forward in his seat on the dais, his brow marked with concern.

"Second, we should spin-off The International Court of Justice in the Hague to operate as a free-standing legal entity to resolve disputes between states.

Last, we propose a new World Economic and Trade Organization to consolidate the hundreds of existing committees and agencies involved with trade agreements between countries, including the North American Free Trade Agreement between Canada, Mexico and my country. This unit might be housed in Paris and Tokyo." He noted a surprised look on the face of the French Ambassador.

"The newly-constituted United Nations will be once again positioned to concentrate on international security, peace, and peacekeeping missions—its original purpose. The Security Council will oversee efforts at peace, including armaments and the work of the International Atomic Energy Agency (IAEA), as well as agencies such as the United Nations Children's Fund (UNICEF).

The Secretary-General was staring open-mouthed. His lavish lifestyle was being dismantled right before his eyes. The Secretariat and its 7,500 employees, under the S-G as "chief administrative officer", would be dissected. Even before the President concluded his speech, Rickman left to await Atkinsen for the private meeting in his office.

In a firm voice the President closed, "These changes will rededicate the original ideals of a united world body whose organizational structure has become unwieldy. Further specific details of my proposals are in the report to the Security Council and the Secretary-General. Thank you for your attention and courtesy." The President was grim-faced as he left the dais to scattered, moderate applause.

Atkinsen was ushered to a reception room where he could meet delegates prior to his meeting with the Secretary-General. Unfortunately, only the British, Canadian, Japanese and Australian Ambassadors appeared to greet him along with Ambassador Kirkwood. The Danish Ambassador showed up simply for an introduction in recognition of Atkinsen's heritage. The Israeli Ambassador sent his regrets, which had been anticipated, so as not to upstage Arab countries. Atkinsen suspected that several representatives from third world countries showed up to embarrass him.

On the one hand, Atkinsen was disappointed at the poor turn-out at the reception. On the other hand, he had delivered his reasonable and forthright message without rancor. His words were now part of history.

Chapter Twenty Five

Morse jumped up in bed, perspiring from a recurring nightmare. Without a hangover, he felt hyperactive, fidgeting with everything he touched. He had a cup of instant coffee and ate two slices of buttered rye toast. Before showering, he dropped to the floor and did thirty push-ups. *I feel more relaxed now.*

He wondered did John Wilkes Booth bathe that fateful morning. Historical books and records chronicled his activities during the fateful day before heading to Ford's Theater and the evening performance of *Our American Cousin*. Morse had read them all. *What an inspirational, courageous guy Booth was.*

Standing with a towel around his waist, he called Butch on his cell phone. "Nuts," he said, when there was no answer.

After a second cup of coffee, he called Butch's brother. "Pete, is Butch with you?"

"What the hell time is it? No man, he's not with me," Pete said yawning.

"Isn't Butch going to the stadium with you? He didn't answer his phone."

"Last I knew he was going to lay low this morning in case there was a problem at the bakery so—"

Morse held the phone away from his ear and threw his hands up. "Okay, when are you leaving for the stadium?"

"We've been over this fifty times, Morse. I wanna get there before ten so I can get a parking spot near McDonalds. It's only two minutes from the bleacher exits, and then we're gone, scot-free."

"Yeah, that's great. I guess I'm just nervous today. Good luck."

Morse dressed in dark clothes for the role he would play in the plot and stuffed a black ski mask into his jacket inside pocket. Hearing the weather man on TV, he breathed a sigh of relief that the temperature would continue in the high fifties.

At seven-forty-five he drove to the 205th street Subway station on the Grand Concourse and parked on a side street. The combination of the drive and the subway ride to 161st street would have him reach the stadium by the nine o'clock work check-in time.

"I've gotta impress my new boss right away."

* * *

Russell Barrett tossed all night. At five-thirty he arose and went by rote from his bed to the shower. He ran cold water for a minute to jolt him into alertness. As he dressed, coffee was brewing; it was stronger than usual.

An image of Kathleen popped into his mind. *I can't wait to get back to DC and make up with her.*

He turned on the Fox News channel to catch any pertinent local news.

The leaders of Israel and Palestine were meeting for peace talks.

"Same old, same old," he decried.

Senator Robinson was scheduled to make a major foreign policy speech that evening.

A live picture of lush Yankee Stadium appeared on the screen as the reporter named the starting pitchers and announced that President Atkinsen will throw out the first ball to open the season.

The scene switched to St. Patrick's Cathedral and the reporter stated, "Thousands of New Yorkers and visitors are expected to flock to local churches for the traditional Good Friday services."

Barrett's dream of Lincoln had almost faded from his consciousness as he adjusted his holster and the 9mm Sig Sauer semiautomatic pistol. He looked at his wristwatch and jumped up, grabbing his suit jacket. "I better get going or I'll be late."

Williams is right. A dream is not the same as a sixth sense.

Chapter Twenty Six

Detective First Grade Mike Papperelli had started his shift earlier than usual on Friday morning. He didn't sleep well thinking of Opening day at Yankee Stadium and the President on his turf.

The investigation of a double homicide two days earlier had him bewildered. He had informed Inspector Gallagher that, "There were no drugs in the apartment and the neighbors didn't hear a shot or any noise so a silencer must have been used. It might be a case of jealousy, but the murders were too professional. One bullet. Instant kills. The place was clean, but, we were able to lift prints off the entrance door knob."

The FBI report faxed from Quantico, Virginia identified a match to prints belonging to a Justin Morse, who was discharged from the Army in 1979. Papperelli and his younger partner, Bill Davison, had searched New York Property records and the Division of Motor Vehicles on Morse.

"Bingo," Davison exclaimed. "Morse's last known address was in Riverdale in the Bronx."

"We just got the warrant to enter Morse's place in Riverdale," shouted Davison. His exuberance brought Papperelli out of his retrospection.

"Let's get going," Papperelli said. He dropped the glazed doughnut on the desk and heading down the stairs of the Kingsbridge Road precinct to their car.

Papperelli, age 49, had come up through the ranks and earned his shield several times over. Only his close friends could call him by his nickname, "the Brute." His recently-acquired broken nose, from wrestling with a robbery suspect, and strands of formerly thick black hair had altered his regular-guy appearance. The slouch in his shoulders and paunchy midsection made him unrecognizable to old acquaintances.

He and his wife lived in the Throggs Neck section of the Bronx, near their married daughter and two grandchildren. He never left home without giving his wife a hug or kiss, but always cautioned, "Not sure what time I'll get home tonight, Babe."

Papperelli's ability to ferret out clues at crime scenes was legendary among his peers. Inspector Gallagher described the talent as, "The SOB thinks like a criminal."

"Yeah, Foley, whaddya got?" Papperelli asked, responding to another detective on the car's speaker phone. He jotted notes in a pad as he listened. "Okay, put a trace on the bakery truck and keep me informed," and ended the call.

"What was that about?" asked Davison.

"There was an incident at Yankee Stadium last night. We picked up an illegal and tracked down his boss who owns a bakery shop on Jerome Avenue. The old guy got all shook up, like we were gonna put him out of business."

"Does he hire a lot of them?"

"That's not the issue. We wanted to know what the illegal alien intended to do trying to get into the ballpark with a weapon. Kid's scared shitless. Foley says he's clean. Doesn't know anything. But the bakery truck left the scene and hasn't turned up this morning. That's the real problem."

"How so?"

"The driver turns out to be a white guy just hired by the boss. This one, by the name of Smith would you believe, had asked questions about deliveries to the stadium." Papperelli stared out the window, his heart beating faster.

They turned up Manhattan College Parkway past Fieldstone Road and parked on a side street two houses in front of a two-story Tudor house. It was eleven-thirty. With pistols at the ready, Papperelli knocked on the front door as Davison watched the back of the house with waiting patrolmen.

"Open up! Police."

No answer.

After checking windows and exits, Davison smashed in a back door window and entered through the kitchen. He opened the front door for his partner.

"Check upstairs," Papperelli said. "I'll look around down here." He noted a picture hanging in the entrance way of five men in Army uniforms. Each room checked out. *Place is a shithouse.*

"Davison," he shouted, "got something."

Davison bounded down the stairs to the dining room table where Papperelli was pointing. "Hey, what a great picture of Yankee Stadium?"

"So why does he have such a big photograph? And look at the straight line drawn from home plate to the bleachers."

"Maybe he's going to the game and his seats are behind home plate," Davison said, as if his conclusion was obvious.

"What the hell is wrong with you?" Papperelli sneered, looking at Davison in disbelief. "He just kills two people and he's going to a baseball game."

A possible killer on the loose in Yankee Stadium?

"And look at this," Pappperelli said. *UN food service* was written on the back side of the photo. A line had been drawn through the words. Other scribbling could not be read.

"What the hell does SS stand for?" asked Davison.

Papperelli walked to the window. He lit a cigarette and folded his arms, motioning to Davison to keep quiet as he turned away from the window and sat on the couch, head facing the floor. Rubbing his chin, he stared at his partner, whispering, "What's happening here? A killer goes to Yankee Stadium? An innocent kid tries to get a gun inside. Why does the driver leave the scene? The President was at the UN this morning and is going to the game."

He leaped off the couch.

"Jesus Christ," he yelled, running to the door. "Secret Service. I've gotta contact the Secret Service right away. You stay here and watch for him to return. I'm heading out."

"Where're you going?" asked Davison

"I'm going to a baseball game," Papperelli grumbled with mixed emotions.

He grabbed the framed photo of the soldiers off the wall and ran to the car, his mind racing with horrible scenes of the death of a president. Snapshots of Dallas blinked on and off in his head.

Chapter Twenty Seven

Despite the troublesome warnings from Agent Barrett, President Atkinsen left the United Nations promptly at 11:30 to attend opening day ceremonies at Yankee Stadium. After addressing the General Assembly, he held a private ten minute meeting, predictably hostile, with the Secretary-General, J.J. Rickman.

"Mr. President, with all due respect, you are making a major mistake with long term implications. The influence of your country will be diminished and—"

"Secretary Rickman, pardon my interruption. I don't believe you were listening closely to my words and how funds would continue to flow to basic humanitarian services. I reiterate the fundamental issue that the UN is a bloated bureaucracy that robs the people it is committed to help."

"Sir, you're overstating the case. I have initiated reforms since the Oil for Food scandal. Your reorganization will cause the death and disease of millions without the structure we have in place. Furthermore, international credibility and harmony will be damaged."

"Hold it!" Atkinsen demanded. "Your own actions have demonstrated a bias against Israel, and you do nothing to suppress the systematic disparagement of my country. So don't lecture me on the effectiveness of your management!"

"What do you mean?" Rickman asked, squinting and flustered by the charge. His left eye twitched.

"I'm referring to the UN document that condoned violence to achieve Palestinian statehood in 2002. We now have evidence that you surreptitiously pressured your own government and the

European Union to support the document accusing Israel of human rights violations."

"Sir, I object to that. You've taken the issue out of context."

"Secretary-General Rickman, I have classified reports that many terrorists were recruited from the Palestinian refugee camps while you were the Commissioner." Pointing his finger, the President added in a loud voice, "You turned a blind eye to this problem and supported Arafat in all disputes."

"How dare you accuse me? I'm working for world peace and have the support of the Security Council." His shout refuted the conduct of a diplomat, and the scowl on his face suggested he expected an apology.

"That's the shame of it," the President piled on. "In the process you've been infected with prejudice and the power of your office with little accountability."

"I'm afraid there is nothing more to say at this time," Rickman said, the veins in his temple pulsating.

"Good day, sir." Atkinsen stood and left the 38th floor office with its gorgeous view up the East River.

As the President's entourage exited the UN building, they took little notice of the protestors across First Avenue with *Save the UN* signs. The motorcade headed to the ballpark going north on the FDR Drive, across the Willis Avenue Bridge and up the Grand Concourse in the Bronx.

"Look over to your right, Mr. President," said Steve Wagner. "That's Cardinal Hayes High School, a private all boys' school. The student body is virtually all minorities and ninety-five percent go on to college."

The distraction brought Atkinsen back to the present. "Really," he said, sitting up straight in the comfortable leather seat of the limo as it sped by the sprawling three-story building. "That reminds me. What's the feedback from the teachers union on the testing guidelines in our new Education policy?"

"Too soon to know, sir. I'll check on it when we get back to D.C.," Wagner replied, jotting notes in his BlackBerry.

"After we leave the game, fill me on reaction to my speech and those proposals."

"Yes, sir."

Atkinsen settled back and resumed his meditation on events over the last four months and since departing the White House the previous day. He had stayed overnight at the US Ambassador's residence at the Waldorf Astoria Hotel Towers. After dinner with Ambassador Kirkwood, his only visitor was Patrick Cardinal O'Keefe, head of the Archdiocese of New York. They had a pleasant chat, although the subjects were controversial—Mexican immigration policies impacting the New York archdiocese, and the future of the UN.

"I have been informed that the number of the potential unemployed will be dramatic if US dues are cut-off," the Cardinal said. "You should be aware, Mr. President, that many UN personnel, Catholic or not, attend weekend services at the Cathedral. The hardship will be difficult for some to endure. Allow me also to communicate the grave concern of the Mayor."

"Your Eminence, I appreciate your point of view and candor, as always," Atkinsen said politely.

As the Cardinal left, he wished the President, "A Happy and Blessed Easter season and good health."

The motorcade turned left on 161st Street. Wagner pointed out the Concourse Plaza Hotel as they made a wide turn. "Did you know that Babe Ruth stayed there when the Yanks played at home?"

"Really," said the President. His mood brightened as they came closer to the ballpark.

In just minutes they passed the Bronx County Courthouse and drove the wrong way on a one way street, avoiding blocked-off traffic, to reach the players' entrance to the stadium.

"Isn't it great being here for opening day," Atkinsen said, smiling for the first time and exhibiting his usual energy. This would be his third opening day game as President, the first at renowned Yankee Stadium. His love of baseball, and the home town Washington Nationals, always sparked a youthful enthusiasm in him. "If I only could have hit a curve ball," he yearned, "I could have made it to the majors."

Wagner forced a grin and said, "What would I be then—your batboy?"

"I think the Nationals have a real good chance to win the pennant this year," the President guessed. "Wouldn't it be terrific for Washington if the team got to the World Series?" Atkinsen's eyes widened at this remote possibility.

Wagner nodded and joked, "I'll tell the manager." He watched the crowd across from the entrance and was reassured that New York City's finest were ubiquitous wherever he looked. "Please be careful, Mr. President."

"Don't worry, Steve. I'm confident the Secret Service will do their job," he said, placing his hand on Wagner's shoulder. As he spoke, Ashton Williams opened the limo door.

"We're ready, Mr. President," said a serious-looking Agent Williams.

Atkinsen was surrounded by Secret Service agents and quickly escorted the fifty feet into the stadium. He probably didn't hear the jeers from the noisy crowd. It was forty-five minutes before game time.

Wagner stayed behind for a minute to observe the New York fans. As usual at sporting events one particular sign was obvious in the middle of the crowd—John 3:16—positioned so the TV audience would read it over the head of the protected President.

Wagner bit on his lower lip; the biblical allusion reminded him of Barrett's forewarning.

Chapter Twenty Eight

The President was taken directly to the Yankee Clubhouse. With most of the players on the field for pre-game warm-up, he enjoyed a hot dog with mustard and a Bud Light while talking baseball with the Yankee manager. As players came in one by one, he shook hands and wished them luck. Atkinsen looked forward to watching the game from the owner's box located in the back of the mezzanine.

Fletcher Jones and several sports writers were permitted to enter the clubhouse. "Mr. President," said Fletcher, his hand raised to be recognized first, "How do you evaluate the reaction to your address at the UN?"

Atkinsen long felt exasperated by this political analyst who had belittled his victory over Robinson years ago. He had been warned by Grant to be cautious even in incidental meetings with Fletcher Jones. "We can't get in a pissing match with someone who buys ink by the barrel," Grant wisecracked.

"I believe the delegates at the UN will give my proposals serious consideration and—"

"But, Mr. President, there is an unconfirmed report that the Secretary-General feels you undermined his position and were discourteous to him."

"First, you should confirm the reliability of your source. The main point of my visit was to deliver a hard, long-overdue message. My proposals are in the best interests of the recipients of UN humanitarian assistance and to secure world peace. Now it's time for America's favorite pastime. Nice to see you all."

Fletcher took notes and grinned at the President.

The President ambled through the narrow passage from the clubhouse to the Yankee dugout. His nerve endings tingled with excitement. As he twirled his right arm around to prepare to throw sixty feet to home plate, he said to Mickey Strong, the catcher, "I may bowl you over with my high hard one, son."

"I'll be ready, sir," Strong replied, his lips curled in a broad smile.

* * *

Shorty Poliski's seat was in the upper deck in right field. At 12:40 he left and walked back down the ramps to the lower deck. He joined many fans scurrying along the walkway in each direction, parallel to the field, between the box and reserved seats.

As he neared the Yankee dugout, Shorty became tense. His head jerked right and left as if he were watching a tennis match. He wondered where the hell to set-off the firecracker and should I do it before or after the National Anthem?

"Get out of my way!" he yelled at a fan watching a few players on the dugout steps to observe the crowd.

The public address announcer blared out the starting lineups.

"This is it," he whispered.

He stood directly behind home plate, removed the three-inch flash powder firecracker set of three from his cigarette pack, lit the string and rolled it down the aisle. Popping sounds could be heard like the rat-tat-tat of a toy gun, as all heads turned toward the aisle. Shorty didn't wait. He moved quickly to the exit ramp, but fans rushing up the ramp for the start of the game slowed his getaway.

"Lemme through," he shouted, pushing people out of the way as he ran for the exit. His heart was pounding in his chest and perspiration ringed his forehead.

"Where're you going, pal?" A stout policeman, close to the grandstands to hear what sounded like gunshots, spied Shorty dodge like a halfback past fans, stumble and knock over a child as he rushed toward the exit.

Physically drained, Shorty offered little resistance, as the officer grabbed him firmly by the collar and called for assistance.

* * *

Ashton Williams staked out his position in the corner of the Yankee dugout that led to the clubhouse. He had assigned two agents to stay with the President in the clubhouse prior to game time. Although he couldn't convince Wagner to encourage the President to forego this event, all precautions were taken to protect the President. Yet, he felt more apprehensive than customary.

"Report on your status." Williams heard the order from the Command Post communicating with agents in all sections of the stadium.

"Position secure," was the common response.

Williams reflected on new information from a Detective Papperelli received only minutes earlier. A photo was distributed of a Caucasian male linked to a possible threat against the President. *Even if there is a connection, how do we locate him in this crowd?*

The Command Post issued an order, "Barrett, stay in center field and send Heffernan to meet up with agents at the old right field bullpen! And you can expect a Detective Papperelli of the NYPD to join you shortly."

Williams heard Barrett respond, "Yes, sir."

There was a disturbance in the right field bleachers as a small group chanted, "Save the UN," over and over. One placard read *THE PRESIDENT MUST GO.*

"Keep in touch with the counter-sniper at the base of the back wall below the Hess Oil sign," Williams added.

"Will do."

An agent in the bleachers reported to Williams there may be a problem at the concession office. "Vendors can't get in the place."

Williams ordered the agent, "Take a cop with you and get there right away! Report back to me on the problem."

Williams stood on the top step of the dugout and scrutinized the crowd. *Omigod, this is a freaking hopeless situation.* He stared up at an agent in the press box who had the best panoramic view of the stadium.

"All agents. Watch your positions during the National Anthem!"

"What was that?" Williams shouted. He bolted up the dugout steps onto the field in time to see spectators behind home plate leaving their seats and others cranking their necks to discover the source of the noise. One man picked up a fizzled-out firecracker and showed it to onrushing uniformed men. In less than a minute Williams heard the news that the police apprehended a man who they believed was responsible for the firecracker. A Secret Service Response Team was on the scene to interrogate the man.

Too many odd circumstances, Williams thought, as he labored to connect the dots. *POTUS will be a sitting duck.*

Williams greeted the President arriving in the dugout just as the incident with the firecracker had been resolved.

"So it was just a prank?" Atkinsen said, after hearing a status report from Williams.

"Mr. President, we have to determine if the suspect acted alone. Perhaps, he's a crackpot, but the threat is still out there. I wish you would reconsider—"

"Come on, Agent Williams!" Atkinsen said, loud enough for the Yankee players in the dugout to gawk at them. "The crowd, the TV audience, they all know I'm right here. I can't back out now."

Williams could not argue the point.

Steve Wagner rushed into the dugout from the clubhouse, stopping short when he saw the President. He stammered, "I heard there was a problem. Someone fired a shot at you."

Williams didn't wait for Atkinsen to respond. "Jesus, no, Wagner. The President was not in any danger." He responded with annoyance in his voice. He raised his hands to signal everyone to calm down.

"There's no problem, Steve. Everything's under control," the President said, nodding to Williams.

Now the damn rumors are starting, Williams thought. The firecracker incident might be a tactic to lessen their vigilance or worry, like the First Officer on the deck of the Titanic concerned that the iceberg they just missed may not be the last one as the liner continued at the same speed, on the same course.

"Please stand for the singing of our National Anthem."

Atkinsen, Wagner and Williams remained in the dugout as the players stood on the top step, their caps over their hearts.

Chapter Twenty Nine

Russell Barrett and Sam Heffernan were assigned the center field bleacher area where no spectators were permitted. A sweep of the entire bleachers had been carried out in the early morning hours. Their assignment commenced at nine.

As a member of the Advance Team, Barrett had visited Yankee Stadium twice before Friday. He covered the entire stadium with members of the Office of Protective Research's Technical Security Division, experts at electronic surveys. He watched as the Command Post was set up in a protected area behind the lower grandstand where communications equipment was installed.

This is cool, he had thought as he sat in the Yankee dugout during one of the reconnaissance visits. *My father should see me now.* He didn't understand why they were tearing the place down. But now, he had more important things to think about.

By noon a hazy sun cast a bright glow above the stadium roof behind home plate. Peering in from center field, Barrett was almost blinded by the glare even with sun glasses. Nevertheless, he spotted sharpshooters on the stadium roof.

Drowsy from little sleep, he decided to walk within the fenced-off area toward the left and right field bleachers to keep alert. "Sam, hang out here while I get some exercise and do some routine checks of the area."

"Sure thing, Russ," Sam said. "I love the excitement of all of this."

"Actually, it can get pretty boring at times," Barrett answered with a wave and a yawn. "I'll be back in a few minutes."

He had taken only a few steps when he heard a voice in his

earpiece. "Yes, sir," he said, acknowledging the Command Post order. "Hey, Sam. Head over to the right field bleacher wall near the old bullpen. Help out some agents there. You can see that group from here protesting against the President."

"I'm on my way, Russ."

Barrett strained hard to focus but felt jumpy. He poured water on his hands from his water bottle and doused his face. Repeating the motion perked him up as did the announcement of the starting lineups.

He heard Williams' voice say, "An incident behind home plate has been secured. Maintain your positions and be alert!"

Barrett's breathing was heavy as he squinted at the spectators in the right and left field bleachers, now rising for the National Anthem. Staring down from the top row of the bleachers, he noted two policemen in position at two of the three ramps, but only one at the ramp directly below him. "Where the heck is the other one?" he grumbled.

The jet fly-over took his breath away, sounding like thunder rolling across the sky. As the aircrafts' roar faded into the distance, he stepped down a couple of rows to get a better view of the ramp.

"Welcome to the opening day game between ..." The words trailed off in Barrett's consciousness.

"Why has the other cop left his post as well?" he uttered to himself. That old sixth sense kept gnawing at him.

A voice from the Command Post screamed in his ear. "Code Five Three. Code Five Three. Conduct a row by row search of all persons in the left and right field bleachers."

"Good God," he stammered. *A killer*!

Taking two rows at a time, Barrett literally vaulted down eleven rows of empty benches to the railing overlooking the ramp.

* * *

Justin Morse squirmed in the prone position as he focused the telescopic sight on the President waving to the crowd. "Keep on moving, hot shot," he whispered. *In another minute it'll all be over and I can make my getaway.*

* * *

An uptight Barrett scowled, "Where the hell are those two cops?"

Jesus Christ. Guy's got a gun. He's gonna shoot the President. Oh God.

Acting on fright Barrett stepped up on the railing and jumped the seven feet down onto the would-be assassin's back.

The crack of bone and thump of bodies was no match for the thunderous applause at the sight of the President waving to the crowd. The force of the glancing blow squashed Morse's head into the concrete and sent his weapon clattering ahead to the bleacher outfield wall.

Morse quickly recovered as a stunned Barrett bounced off his enemy.

"Bitch," Morse growled, pulling off the hood. A cut above his eye bled profusely, as he pushed his attacker aside.

Barrett leaped at Morse and tackled him around the waist as the would-be assassin attempted to creep down the ramp and run. The two men rolled down the ramp like children playing a game. Barrett jammed his fingers into Morse's neck to hit a nerve and disable him, if only for a moment. A raging Morse broke free and twisted Barrett's arm behind his back.

"Oooo." Barrett screamed from an immobile left shoulder as Morse stood and limped as fast as he could the forty-five feet toward the roll-up metal door blocking his escape to the street.

On all fours and writhing in pain, Barrett lifted his head to see Morse draped on the door's pull chain, his arms extended to raise the ten-foot high heavy door. *Bastard only needs two feet to crawl under and escape.*

Barrett groaned as he reached for his weapon. Although his right hand trembled, his aim was true.

He saw Morse grab his thigh and cry out. But the wounded killer continued to drag down the pull chain far enough for a body to slither under like a snake.

"Stop or I'll shoot!" Barrett shouted to Morse who ignored the warning. He steadied his aim and fired.

Barrett watched as Morse crumpled to the ground, one arm outstretched under the door to the street. Purely a reflex action.

Justin Morse was dead.

As he adjusted his earpiece, Barrett felt a high he had never experienced before. The surreal scene ended abruptly for him when the loud crowd noise penetrated his ears once again.

The entire action had taken no more than thirty seconds.

* * *

"*Shortstop* will be on the field in a moment," Williams advised the team. He gave the President a reluctant nod to proceed.

I can't do anything to stop him. For the first time he noticed his hands all sweaty and a trickle of blood from a scratch on his knuckle.

As the President emerged from the dugout followed by Mickey Strong, Williams concentrated on the spectators in the box seats. His eyes caught someone standing in the press box. Fletcher Jones was pointing to center field. Turning his head in that direction, Williams searched for Barrett.

I don't see him.

"Barrett, report in. Barrett!"

Williams lunged out of the dugout and ran toward the President, who stopped his wind-up.

"Williams, I got him," Barrett's voice boomed in his ear.

He hesitated for a moment and then continued at a normal pace toward the mound. Stopping at the first base foul line, he cupped his hands over his mouth and shouted, "All secure, Mr. President. Let your fast ball rip." *And then we're getting the hell out of here.*

"Thank you, Agent Williams," the President said. A look of uncertainty turned to a broad grin.

Atkinsen went into his wind-up like a veteran pitcher and threw a perfect strike to the catcher.

Chapter Thirty

Rector Guzman was delighted to welcome the President to Easter Sunday services.

The Rector proclaimed at the start of service, "Alleluia, Alleluia, the Lord is risen. And, Lord, we are grateful that the President is safe and sound with us today."

Atkinsen responded along with the congregation, "Alleluia."

Unlike his last visit to St. John's Episcopal Church at Christmas, the President's attention and devotion to the service went without temptation. He felt tranquil in mind and spirit as he listened to the Rector's sermon on the intercession of the resurrected Christ. "In a letter to the Romans 8:38-39, St. Paul said, 'For I am convinced that neither death, nor life, nor principalities, nor present or future things, nor powers, nor height, nor depth, nor any other creature will be able to separate us from the love of God in Christ Jesus our Lord.'"

"Your words were inspiring, Rector Guzman," he had said after the service. "Thank you." He imagined Ellen expressing a similar belief.

As Atkinsen walked away from the church to the waiting limo, he had a flashback to his childhood. Each and every Sunday he attended church services with his parents—a close family unit. He remembered the Church vs. State debate at Georgetown and questioned if politics had separated him from his religion. *How did I allow myself to lose the inner comfort of my faith?*

"Lord, thy will be done."

"Excuse me, Mr. President?" asked Ashton Williams from the front seat.

"Oh, nothing. Just talking to myself." Atkinsen sat back and wondered if this is what it means to be born again.

On the drive back to the White House for a meeting with Grant and Wagner, Atkinsen rehashed in his mind the outcome of Friday's trip and his activity on Saturday.

Based on Agent William's determination that Yankee Stadium was a crime scene and a serious security risk, they left the ballpark immediately once the President returned to the dugout. A number of Secret Service agents stayed behind until the FBI assumed responsibility for the investigation. The police had detained a Roberto Morales, the leader of the group called *Save the UN*, for a disturbance at the game, but released him for lack of any evidence connecting him to the assassination attempt.

Atkinsen smiled as he read the box score of the Nationals 5-2 win over the Yankees.

He was secluded all day Saturday in the White House while the FBI accumulated evidence of the plot with the Secret Service and the NYPD. He read the transcript of the FBI interrogation of a Shorty Polski, who had been held in custody for suspicious behavior and the firecracker incident.

After Polski was read his Miranda Rights and the interrogator jawed with him about his role in the assassination attempt, he denied any wrongdoing and explained that, "the firecracker was just a prank." Polski finally broke down when he was told that Morse was dead.

FBI: Let's start over. Somebody give him a cigarette. Who was in on this with you?

S.P.: Me and Justin Morse. We were Army buddies. He lives in the Bronx.

FBI: What did you expect to accomplish by killing the President?

S.P.: Morse hated all authority and was upset by the President's UN speech. He had a one-track mind; knew everything about the guy who assassinated Lincoln. Just plain crazy.

FBI: How did he get the weapon inside the ballpark?

S.P.: I don't know.

FBI: Come on! We know he worked in the concession office. He killed the manager.

S.P.: I still can't believe he did that.

FBI: It's going to be tougher on you if you don't cooperate.

S.P.: Okay. They were hidden in the hot dog roll boxes.
FBI: Give us a name!
S.P.: Butch Tomlinn.
FBI: Where is he now?
S.P.: I swear I don't know.

Interrogator's comment—Mr. Polski confirmed information we had developed. The NYPD has an APB out on Butch Tomlinn and his brother, Pete, and a Brocce, no first name.

On Saturday morning the *Westchester Weekly* distributed a special editorial edition on their website under the Fletcher Jones byline. Atkinsen bristled at the concluding paragraph, which read, *There may be an unfortunate tendency for the President to exploit the attempted assassination for political advantage, given his ratings since January. Shades of ancient English kings!*

Although the facts of a possible assassination attempt were unclear, Jones' scoop of the national media had the White House press corps in an uproar. Wagner had told the press secretary to understate the incident with a preliminary report to White House reporters.

"The President was never in any danger. There had been a scuffle with a Secret Service agent which led to the arrest of an assailant. The assailant was killed attempting to escape."

The President made several phone calls Saturday afternoon to congressional leaders to assure them he was unharmed. He was informed that Agent Barrett had suffered a separated shoulder and was admitted in Columbia Hospital overnight due to hypertension.

Meanwhile, my reorganization proposal at the UN isn't getting the coverage and attention it deserves.

* * *

"Good afternoon, Mr. President," Wagner said, as Atkinsen arrived in the outer office.

Grant and Wagner followed the President into the Oval Office. Coffee and Danish and Easter candy were available on the credenza. The atmosphere in the office was as gloomy as the gathering dark clouds over the Nation's Capital.

"Thank you for coming in on a Sunday, Easter Sunday at that," the President said, making eye contact with the two men sitting opposite each other on couches. Atkinsen sat in his favorite arm chair and crossed his legs. His usual congenial manner was not evident.

Wagner inquired, "Mr. President, if you don't mind me asking, what exactly does John 3:16 say?"

Atkinsen's face lit up. "As a matter of fact, I read that Gospel passage the other night. *For God so loved the world that He gave His only Son, so that everyone who believes in Him might not perish but might have eternal life.*"

He was lost in the thought for the moment as his advisors looked at one another.

"Let's get down to business. I would like your thoughts on how we proceed from here." The charge to his advisors signaled a no-nonsense agenda for this meeting.

Wagner spoke first. "Sir, I feel it's an opportune time to build momentum for the campaign. Jackman and I believe you should nominate someone to fill the Vice-President vacancy. He could be out front campaigning while you handle the nation's business, acting presidential."

The President stared poker-faced at Wagner. "Do you both have someone in mind?"

"Yes, sir. We feel Governor Tom Bliss would help the ticket and make a great VP. It would definitely unify the party."

"What to you think, Harry?" asked Atkinsen, testing the political logic of their selection.

"Sir, my inclination is to consider it a bad idea."

"Why?" Wagner shot back in a flash.

"Give me a chance, Steve," Grant said; his tone was composed. "To begin with, it would appear we're rewarding a potential opponent in the primary. Bliss has made it clear he will contest the nomination. The President doesn't need a contentious former rival as a running mate. Second, the VP should come from the West Coast and—"

"Wait a minute!" Wagner said, raising his voice a notch. "That hasn't been decided and it's only your opinion. I can list several fine candidates from other regions of the country."

"True, it is my opinion," Grant replied. "But you and Jackman have put the cart before the horse. The convention in August is the time to unite the party, and the platform has to generate real enthusiasm, including the selection of a VP." He looked at Atkinsen for a resolution.

The President had been listening intently to the exchange. "I tend to agree with Harry on this one, if for no other reason than Bliss seems stuffy and a blowhard. With four months before the convention, a lot can happen that may influence our thinking. Besides, the Hill is no longer complaining about the delay. Naming a VP at this time is tantamount to confirming my running mate. It gives the congress a chance to make a circus out of the confirmation process. So then, what's next?"

Wagner's teeth protruded over his lower lip for a moment. He clasped his hands together and said, "I think we should focus on a few key states and meet with party leaders. Fund raising appearances will give the President the occasions to expound on his views of the UN." He hesitated and said directly to the President, "It's the strategy we followed during the last general election."

"I agree," said Grant. "This will give the UN and Rickman time to analyze your proposals more fully."

"At the same time we can challenge Robinson on statements he's making about your campaign now that he seems to have a lock on the nomination," Wagner added.

"Good point, Steve," the President said. "Get with Jackman to work out the schedules and tell Cohen to develop the themes he and I have talked about."

"Yes, sir," said Wagner, looking content again.

"Mr. President," Grant added, "I believe you might consider holding a special ceremony to honor Agent Barrett. I've been told the assassin already had you in his sights before Barrett obstructed his aim and killed him."

"I don't think that's a good idea," Wagner said frowning. "The agents don't like too much public attention."

"That's true," said the President.

"It's not unprecedented," Grant continued. "Several agents received recognition after the Kennedy assassination as well as after the attempt on Reagan."

Atkinsen thought for a second and said, "Well, if Director Harris and Agent Williams are okay with it, let's do it."

Grant said, "I've already cleared the idea with Williams."

The President noted the shifting moods of his Chief of Staff as Wagner raised his hands in surrender. *He seems to be taking everything too personal.* Atkinsen wondered if the constant pressure of the job and confrontations were getting to this tough marine.

"Steve, I'd like you to set up a meeting at the White House with congressional leaders. It's time I use the bully-pulpit to get some stalled legislation moving on the Hill."

"Yes, sir," Wagner said, taken aback.

"Good idea, Mr. President," Grant interjected. "That'll stop the talk of a lame duck presidency. The lobbyists are trying to run everything."

"I want you both to know that, although I may have waffled on my decision to run again, I'm totally committed now and I expect the team to be likewise. If you know of any reasons or anybody who does not feel the same way, I'd like to hear about it sooner rather than later." Atkinsen looked hard at the two men to emphasize his determination.

"I've already advised the University I'm taking a Sabbatical from June to next February," Grant responded.

Wagner simply nodded to denote his commitment.

"Good," Atkinsen said. "Now we can move ahead as a team."

Chapter Thirty One

After Grant and Wagner left the Oval Office, Atkinsen mused about his new-found enthusiasm. *Will it last throughout the campaign? Who'll be on the ticket with me?*

"Damn that Clark Styles," he spoke his thoughts. "We worked so well together and he had to screw it up." He hesitated and added, "I'm still not convinced that Bob Allcott is the right pick. Jeez, is he presidential timbre in the event of ...?"

As he changed for bed that night, he came across another photo of Ellen outside their first house, after five years married, in the Buckhead section of Atlanta. He pictured in his mind her bliss as she danced around the lawn in bare feet on an emotional high.

"Try and catch me," she said, in a playful mood.

"Stand still so I can take your picture."

"Oh, Herbert, I'm so happy. You'll see what I can do in this house. I have a thousand ideas for the decorations." She scanned the front of the house and said, "I always wanted a white picket fence. It should start right here. Let's do that first."

"Slow down, Ellen. We're going to live here a long time." Her zeal was catching. "How about we have our first picnic in the backyard? I'll cook burgers and hot dogs on the grill."

"Wonderful," she whooped, as she skipped toward the side of the house and almost tripped into the rhododendrons.

"Take it easy or you'll hurt yourself. You know what the doctor said about getting stressed out with a new house."

She put her arms around him when he reached the back of the house. "I wasn't sure this day would ever come for me." She pulled him down gently on the large blanket spread out on the grass. "I've never been happier. I love you very much, Herbert."

"And I love you too." He kissed her hard and long.

Looking up at the Wedgwood blue sky, she said, "Do you ever think back to how things were here, say a hundred years ago?"

"Wow, I guess I may have every once in a while."

"It must have been so simple and friendly, like in the movie *Somewhere in Time* with the enchanting Rachmaninoff melody."

"Ellen, you are a true romantic."

"I wonder if you'll ever change jobs."

"That's the furthest thing from my mind, honey," he said. "What in the world made you bring that up?"

"Because I'm proud of you right now and all you've accomplished. I want to make this house into a home ... our home. I hope we never leave."

As he buried his head on her bosom, she whispered, "Don't worry. It'll all work out. We can get help and do one room at a time."

"Ellen."

"Yes, dear."

"It's not the furniture or the decorations that will make it a home for me. It's having you with me, now and forever." His body trembled as he held her close. He wished this moment and their intimacy would never end.

"Of course, it's the same for me having you here," she said, looking into her husband's eyes with an angelic smile.

They were quiet for a few moments, lying side by side, looking up at the two story house and the sky. His toes touched hers. It gave her the giggles, but he felt a sensual tease.

"Stop, Herbert, it tickles," she said, hardly able to speak.

"You're gorgeous when you smile," he said grinning.

She sat up, pointed to a corner of the house, and said, "That's the room I want to furnish when we adopt ..."

Atkinsen threw the photo to the floor, no longer lost in memories. A shiver passed through him as he slouched down on a couch, accidentally knocking a lamp off the end table.

"Is everything all right, Mr. President?" asked an attendant from the hallway.

"Just a minor problem. It's okay now."

This is the life I have to endure.

He sighed and said, "Why God, why her?"

Chapter Thirty Two

"Mr. Ambassador," Rickman pleaded, "you must see the danger in the American President's proposals."

The Secretary-General had invited the Russian Ambassador, Sergei Sirkov, to his residence in Sutton Place for a private dinner. He had crafted a plan to forestall the adoption of Atkinsen's UN proposals.

"If the proposals are carried out, Russia or China would not be able to reign in any future aggression of the United States. The United Nations, as we know it today, would become a weak organization and, therefore, have no power to arrange dialogue and compromise on major issues between countries." Rickman hesitated, hoping that Sirkov would recognize the benefit of counter-balancing or opposing US meddling in the international body.

Sirkov had been silent, periodically swirling the glass in his hand and sipping vodka. He said, "Sir, you realize there has been talk that the proposals make sense and require serious consideration. The American Ambassador has been lining up support."

"Yes, and I'm prepared to accept an autonomous International Court in The Hague. But, the larger issue relates to super-power independence so—"

"Mr. Secretary-General, pardon my interruption, but are you prepared to use the good graces of your office to overcome the proposals?" Sirkov put down his glass and folded his arms

Rickman recognized the stare of a diplomat, as he had on numerous other occasions in his career. *He wants to judge my commitment so the Russians can be viewed as supporters rather than leaders in efforts to defeat the proposed changes.*

"I assure you and your government that I will work to oppose change. However, my efforts will be behind the scenes for the most part." Rickman held one argument back as he waited for Sirkov's reaction.

"My government has always resisted the influence of a single country or bloc to dominate the decision-making process," Sirkov said. "Likewise, the decentralization of many UN operations does not appear to be in the interest of world stability and progress." He raised his glass as if to toast the final word on the subject. "One more thing, however, President Atkinsen has announced he is running for reelection. The recent assassination attempt has increased his ratings in the polls. He has strong impetus for you to overcome, does he not?"

"May I speak frankly and confidentially, Mr. Ambassador?" Rickman asked, extending the hook.

"Of course."

"I have it on good authority that the President's health is impaired."

"Really. Go on!" Sirkov shimmied forward on the couch.

"Perhaps, it has to do with the death of his wife over two years ago. He has been depressed to the point of exhibiting confusing behavior. One day he's locked in his office, the next he's in a jovial mood, pushing his cabinet to action with new or unusual ideas."

Rickman stopped to fill their glasses with vodka. He watched the diplomat absorb this medical information.

"How can he handle a political campaign?"

"That's a good question," Rickman said. "He has been duped by his advisors for the purpose of defeating Senator Robinson, who is known, by the way, to be a UN advocate. During the campaign I believe Atkinsen will be exposed as unqualified to be president again."

"So his poor public showing will make his UN proposals moot," Sirkov concluded.

"Exactly."

After the Russian Ambassador had departed, Rickman was content he had laid the foundation for formal opposition to Atkinsen's proposals to shrink the United Nations. "His tampering would repeat the mistake of dismantling the League of Nations," he reasoned out loud.

Rickman knew he only needed one veto from the five permanent Security Council members to thwart any changes to his domain.

Tomorrow I will have Hitoshi arrange a meeting with candidate Senator Robinson. It will be a pleasure to watch Atkinsen self-destruct as the campaign unfolds.

At Rickman's request, a security manager investigated the individual detained by the police at Yankee Stadium during the assassination attempt. The manager had given a verbal report to the Secretary-General and Mr. Hitoshi.

"His name is Roberto Morales and he is one of the organizers of the *Save the UN* group. I believe he's from a Latin American country, but that hasn't been confirmed as he is not well known."

Rickman decided he could use this person for his advantage. He instructed Hitoshi to contact Morales and offer him $5,000 from the Emergency Fund to finance peaceful demonstrations.

"Mr. Secretary-General, the man is quite brazen," Hitoshi reported. "He not only demanded more money, but insisted he speak to you regarding this matter."

Rickman punched in the number of Roberto Morales on his cell phone. "Mr. Morales, this is the Secretary-General of the United Nations. I agree to advance Ten Thousand US dollars to your group to protest the changes proposed by the American President."

"Do you object if I deliver the group's message directly to the President?"

Rickman hesitated. "No objection."

"We accept your generosity," a condescending voice answered in broken English. "It will be done."

Chapter Thirty Three

"We've been cooped up in this place for a month," Pete Tomlinn growled to his brother, as the porn movie he had watched just ended.

Butch put down the *Daily News* and shot back, "What the hell do you want me to do about it? You know the cops and the FBI are looking for us." He opened the refrigerator for a cold Bud Light. "I don't like it any more than you."

"How about my idea to pack up the Mercury and drive to Alabama? I know a lot of places near Fort Rucker we could hide out in."

"Pete, it's been over thirty years since you were stationed there, so don't be so sure we'd be any better off," he said, smirking at his brother. "Besides, we wouldn't fit in with all those rednecks. You wanna be a dirty peanut farmer?"

"Look, we've got to do something to get money and it ain't gonna happen here so—"

"Where's your girlfriend?" Butch broke in.

"She's out buying more food for us," Pete said, looking out the second floor apartment window onto Woodlawn Avenue. "I have to tell you she was bitching to me last night about us staying here and doing nothing. It's costing her a small fortune."

Butch held back a snicker. "You're nuts. She loves sharing the two of us in bed. I think she's a nympho. She even hinted at making it a threesome some night."

"Well I don't like the brotherly sharing any more, get it," Pete said. He went to the bathroom and slammed the door closed.

Butch continued reading the newspaper. "The Red Sox are on TV tonight playing the Yanks," he shouted toward the john. As he flipped pages, he noted a headline; *UN head criticizes Atkinsen's proposals.* On the bottom of the page was a caption, *President to Visit Bronx.* The short article made known *President Atkinsen will give the Commencement address at Fordham University in June.*

"Sonofabitch," he yelled, bounding off the couch. "Listen to this, Pete. The President's going to be here again in two weeks. This is our chance."

Pete came out of the bathroom zippering his pants. "No shit," he yelled. "That means that agent Barrett may be with him."

"You got that right and we're going to get him. Let's take another look at the tape of the President giving him a medal," Butch said.

This is payback time for killing Morse, Butch thought. *I never thought we'd get the chance again.*

Pete turned on the TV and a scene appeared of the President with Agent Barrett in the East Room of the White House. The President was speaking. "For service above and beyond the call of duty, our thanks are extended to you for your heroism. On behalf of the country and with my personal appreciation, I award you this Presidential Citizen's Medal for distinguished service." The President turned to pin the medal on Barrett.

"Stop the tape!" Butch cried out. "Leave it right there. Take a good look at his face, Pete. He's a marked man." Butch hadn't felt this angry since he read newspaper reports on how Morse was killed and the capture of "that piss-ant Shorty."

"We owe it to Morse to get him," Pete added, "no matter what."

"What the hell has got you two so excited?" Lily asked, entering the apartment with the groceries and glancing at the TV screen.

"We'll tell ya later," Butch said. "Here's what I want you to do for us, Lily. Bring home everything you need from that beauty parlor you work in to change our appearance. We've got a job to do and then we can get out of here and head south. Okay?"

"Sure, as long as you take me with you. I don't wanna spend the rest of my life in a stinking apartment in the Bronx."

"Can you change Pete's hair style and color it and his mustache gray? You can give me a haircut like I got in the Army and color my beard gray also."

"No problem," she said.

"Thanks, Lily, you've been great," Pete said, giving her a hug as he unbuttoned her blouse.

"Keep your pants on 'til tonight," she said, teasing him as she pulled her hair back. "Then you two studs can have some kinky fun my way."

* * *

"Jesus, the President's going to be here again next month," Detective Papperelli announced to his partner.

Since the attempted assassination, he had been assigned fulltime to coordinate with the FBI on the whereabouts of the Tomlinn brothers. While the FBI interviewed all known people who might have knowledge of their location, Papperelli started from the beginning.

"So far, I know the older brother, Butch, went to work at the bakery with a fake identity card," he recounted to Davison. "We know he was discharged from the Army the same time as Morse from Fort Campbell."

"Right. And we know his brother, Pete, was employed at the UN until the day Morse was killed." Davison said. He seemed bored at another rehash of the scenario.

"Hey, one step at a time," Papperelli said, annoyed at his partner's lackadaisical attitude. "We know Brocce and Shorty Polski were involved in the plot and, for some reason, Morse shot Brocce and his girlfriend. At least we solved that one."

"Okay, Mike, I'm with you," Davison said, pouring his second cup of coffee. "I wonder about Polski's story to the FBI that Morse planned to escape by going down the subway and getting lost in the crowd."

Papperelli nodded and said, "I'm having trouble with that too. Suppose he was actually going to meet someone in a getaway car." He paused to speculate on Morse's thought process in organizing his escape. "What were the Tomlinn brothers assigned to do that day?"

"Butch Tomlinn most likely would hide out after the illegal immigrant was caught and he got rid of the bakery truck so—"

"And we don't know what Pete Tomlinn was up to." Papperelli stood and walked around his desk and sat on the corner of Davison's desk.

Davison added, "We checked out their sister who lives in Jersey, but she hasn't heard from them in years."

"Let's get the Robbery Squad to give us a list of stolen cars the last three months," Papperelli said. "In the meantime you and me will check out all the Used Car places with the Tomlinns' pictures."

"There's a call for you, Papperelli," the front desk Sergeant called out to the exiting detectives. "It's the Secret Service from Washington."

Papperelli picked up the phone in a private room and said, "Detective Papperelli, may I help you?"

"Detective, this is Agent Barrett on the President's Protection Detail regarding President Atkinsen's trip to Fordham University. I've been told I could coordinate with you."

"Sure thing, what do you need from me?" Papperelli asked; he had been advised by the Inspector to expect the call.

"I'm arriving in the Bronx the day before the ceremony and I'll be checking out the perimeter of the campus where I'll be assigned. I need someone who knows the area."

"Did you say your name was Barrett? Yeah, I saw you on TV with the President. Great work getting that prick, Morse. Sorry I couldn't get there in time to help out."

"There are still two members of the gang on the loose. You're on that investigation, aren't you?"

"Yeah, well, we're following up on leads but nothing so far," Papperelli replied, detecting a sense of urgency in the tone of the question.

"I can't believe all you guys haven't even picked up a trace of the two—"

"Wait a second, Barrett! I know the FBI is totally involved. This case is priority one for the NYPD, and I'm full time on it. Shit, I haven't had supper at home in weeks."

After a pause, Barrett said, "Right. I'm sorry, Detective. I guess I've been too close to the whole thing."

"Understood," Papperelli said; he lowered his voice. "Do you want me to stick with you while the President's here?"

"Absolutely. The President will arrive by helicopter on a ball field at the campus and depart immediately after his address."

"Okay, Barrett. I'll expect to see you in two weeks. You can call me Mike."

Despite a long career with the NYPD, Papperelli had been engrossed in this case like no other he could recall. Now his adrenaline rose at the thought of his role in the visit of the President of the United States.

"Come on, Davison, we've got work to do!"

Chapter Thirty Four

Senator Robinson was uneasy about the secret meeting requested by the UN Under-Secretary, Kato Hitoshi. He knew he could not refuse, since Atkinsen had created a political hot potato for him to exploit. As he waited in the hotel room outside DC in Fairfax, he wondered what benefit he would obtain from the encounter.

Do they expect me to repudiate the President's proposals?

After welcoming Mr. Hitoshi, he said, "If you don't mind, I need to keep this meeting brief so I wish you'd get right to the point." His undiplomatic opening seemed to catch the UN official off guard.

"Senator, we have been grateful of your support of the United Nations in the past and hope, if you are elected President, that we will enjoy a close relationship on the goals of world peace and fighting poverty."

"Mr. Hitoshi, I assure you I share those aims. I do have concerns about the UN's bureaucracy, but my priority is that the peace-keeping missions are carried out effectively by an increasing number of UN forces, not just American."

"Senator, sir, I believe you accept the current structure and will provide equitable funding for our operations and humanitarian efforts."

"That's true," Robinson answered, becoming impatient at the relevance of the conversation. "However, I don't want the US military to take any role in nation building."

We could have done this on the phone. He's just another glib diplomat.

"Then you must have reservations about the proposals of President Atkinsen," Hitoshi said.

Here it comes. Robinson almost said out loud what he was thinking.

"What about them?" Robinson asked, as an innocent question.

"I believe you and I agree that they may be detrimental to the goals we share."

"Perhaps."

"Secretary-General Rickman is committed to the UN structure and the reforms he has enacted. He sees your election as the guaranteed way to maintain the status-quo. Stated another way, your defeat will be unfavorable to the future of the United Nations."

"I know you're not suggesting direct involvement in our election," Robinson said, anxious to hear what's next. "What can the Secretary-General do about it?"

"Since he is so opposed to the proposals, he may use his office privately to encourage each Ambassador of Latin America and South America to inform their countrymen of the situation."

"What good will that do?" he asked, a puzzled look on his face.

"If the citizens of those countries alert their friends and relatives in America to speak against the proposals or ...or vote against anyone supporting the proposals, we can be certain of your victory."

Robinson's facial expression went blank at this unexpected development, which converted a potentially antagonistic ethnic group to a new constituent for his election. He sat motionless as he digested the implication of outside interference in an American presidential election.

"If Rickman wishes to pursue that plan, why are you telling me?" he asked. The question concealed his sanction of the approach.

"Senator, consider this a courtesy call that we understand your position and—"

"I will not agree with the plan he concocted and I will deny this conversation took place," Robinson exclaimed to the diplomat, raising his voice. "However, I cannot tell the Secretary-General of the United Nations what he should or should not do to complete the organization's mandate and carry out his responsibilities."

Mr. Hitoshi smiled as he bowed and said, "Good night, Senator."

I'll convene my inner circle in due course to get their feedback on this meeting. Meanwhile, I'll steer clear of this issue in all speeches and press releases. He mouthed, "And I'll let Majority Leader

Lewis know I'm strongly opposed to any interference by this administration in UN operations, so any Senate action on dues will be tabled until after the election."

"This should satisfy Bruce when I see him tomorrow morning," he said to himself.

* * *

"Dad, you won't believe how great the business has been going so far," Bruce said to the Senator. He sat back in the armchair, right hand on his chin and legs crossed. "We've acquired land all along the route or have contracted to manage key facilities. As a matter of fact—"

"Are we moving too fast with finances and do you have qualified manpower?" the Senator asked, skeptical of the progress.

"The investment from the Venture Capitalist is holding up and we've collateralized the facilities we've purchased," Bruce replied, exuding confidence. "Charlie Zeigler and I have hired many of our MBA classmates who know how to wheel and deal." He laughed as he said, "Believe it or not, we had a case study at Princeton that involved similar transactions. Our rental income and capital gains on sales will be enormous."

"Have you run into eminent domain issues yet?" Robinson searched Bruce's facial expression, proud of his son's grasp of such complex business arrangements.

"Not yet, but we've stayed abreast of local politics in major cities besides Kansas City to steer clear of getting stuck with such land and—"

"What about in Mexico?" the Senator interrupted.

"No problem to date, Dad. The opportunities for us with the increased trade are outstanding. The NAFTA Railway will eventually cover twenty-five thousand miles linking Mexico and Canada. Imagine—new Distribution Centers, Warehouses, Malls, truck stops, Intermodal facilities, etcetera! I want to get licensed in Canada next, and start in Manitoba Province. And I have my best negotiator watching developments on the plan for a Super Highway through Texas."

"Yes, the potential is huge."

"Dad, the best thing is the North American Union is becoming a reality."

"You're jumping to conclusions much too soon, son," the Senator warned. *Bruce doesn't comprehend the politics of this undertaking in an election year.*

"But, Dad, the Alpha-Omega Group accepted our business plan with the ultimate expectation it would lead to a North American Union ... with your political influence. They foresee an economic boom from a US population explosion and the elimination of trade barriers. It's their capital, and they forecast an above average return on their money once our stock goes public. In effect, they're betting on your election."

"I know. I've been laying pipe with my recent votes and public statements regarding the implications of a global economy. I've had to explain my change of heart on some bedrock positions." Robinson rubbed his forehead, concealing his eyes.

"I understand, Dad. We knew that when we formed our company and sought out the Alpha-Omega Group."

Senator Robinson felt a knot in his stomach. *It's a choice I had to make and there's no turning back now.* "I never suspected they had a political agenda as well as financial ties to European Union bigwigs," he had confided to an advisor.

His one meeting with the Group Chairman, Enrique Martinez, was, in hindsight, too smooth and well-organized. Martinez said, "It's a great honor to participate in this project with you and your son. We look forward to a close relationship to assist you to achieve your objectives."

Further on in their business dealings, Robinson complained, "Martinez's Spanish and Mexican government connections should have raised a red flag that they concealed their true goals."

Bruce continued, "The Alpha-Omega people expect that Kansas City will become a sanctuary city for illegals just like Minneapolis and—"

His father hit the desk with his fist. "That's something I can't promote or support! You get that?"

"Yes, sir, that's quite clear."

"Let's get back to the transactions in Mexico, okay. I'm suspicious about local Mexican officials being obstacles along the way."

"Dad, I've spoken about our operations to a Commerce Minister who has the ear of the Mexican President. That's why your importance here in the states is critical to keep everything on track."

"I have the support of both senators in Missouri and Kansas for the KC SmartPort project as well as one senator in Texas. I've made promises to them when I'm elected president, either for positions in my administration or a new Distribution Center in Wichita. But its Mexico that concerns me politically and legally."

"I have several Mexican attorneys working with us, so don't worry." Bruce hesitated and added, "I also have an in with someone at the UN Trade Law Commission which handles disputes and can control the limits of insurance liability for operators of transport terminals and insurance costs."

"What do you mean? An in?"

"Stay out of this part, Dad. He's on our payroll."

"Goddamnit, son. You can't get mixed up in that stuff. You—"

Bruce raised his hand to interrupt and exclaimed, "That's the way they operate down there. It's done all the time."

Robinson stared at his son, shaken by the news but trying to focus on the big picture.

"Now you know why Atkinsen's UN reorganization plans must be thwarted. You can't let it happen, Senator!"

"I know, I know."

Chapter Thirty Five

"I'll be back in two days," Barrett said to Kathleen. He stroked her wavy hair and kissed her neck.

"I'm nervous you're going back to New York again so soon," she said, peering into his eyes, like a baby looks at a doting mother. "It might be dangerous with those UN fanatics. And don't be a hero this time, you hear me, Russ?"

He laid down his traveling bag and laughed. Caressing her close, he teased, "Are you going to miss me?"

"You know damn well I will, so don't make a joke about it." She turned away as her eyes began to tear.

"Don't worry, Kathleen. I'm not assigned anywhere near the President and—"

"You weren't the last time either."

"Touché. Really, my job is to mingle with the crowd at the entrances to the campus. I probably won't even see the President." He smiled again as he picked up his bag and said, "Williams told me he owes me, so he gave me an easy one on this trip."

"Will the citation from the Mayor be on television?" she inquired in a meek tone.

"I'm due at City Hall at four tomorrow afternoon," he replied, as he put on his suit jacket. "The President will be long gone to the White House by then. I guess the ceremony will be covered on the six o'clock news." He kissed her on the cheek and said, "Aren't you proud of me?"

"You big ox," she said, half-frowning. "If loving you includes being proud, you know I do." Her expression changed to a blush.

He opened the door to leave for the airport. Winking at her he said, "Maybe I'll pick up a nice ring when I'm in the *Big Apple*."

"Oooh," she squealed.

* * *

Detective Papperelli invited Agent Barrett to dine at Mackenzies in Manhattan that night. They had driven around the outskirts of the Fordham campus in the afternoon, checking each entry and exit point and the immediate neighborhood.

"Unfortunately, I can't be with you tomorrow," Papperelli said, after they were seated in the restaurant.

"Not to worry. I'm meeting up with other agents at nine. Thanks for scouting the campus with me anyway."

"I read the Mayor is presenting you with a special citation. Congratulations!"

"Oh, right. Thanks."

"Would you like a drink?"

"No way," Barrett said. "Strict orders from the Director. I'll have the veal," he said, handing the menu to the waiter.

"To the best of my knowledge the FBI hasn't made much progress on the investigation yet," the Detective reported, sipping his Merlot. "After the search of Morse's home, nothing else was helpful other than to confirm the guy was a weirdo about the Civil War. He killed four people we know of and you stopped him from getting the primary target."

"I'm not surprised he knew history, but his involvement in a John Wilkes Booth gang does classify him as a nut," Barrett said. After taking a bite of a roll, he said, "So, we have no idea where the Tomlinn brothers are hiding out or in what state?"

"That's right. Even with a manhunt on the lookout for them, they've just disappeared." Papperelli ate his strip steak, wondering how the Tomlinns could escape detection if they moved around. *I'm convinced they're holed up somewhere local.*

When the meal was finished, Barrett said, "Before dropping me off at the hotel, could we stop in the Jewelry district in midtown for a minute?"

"For a hero like you, it'll be my pleasure," Papperelli said, a broad grin on his face.

* * *

"Pelham Bay is the next and last section to check out but there aren't many used car dealers in this area," Davison said.

"Yeah," Papperelli acknowledged. "It's too residential."

He pondered the complexity of the President's visit that afternoon. The strain from a perceived impending disaster, without any evidence, showed on his weary face.

"You get much sleep last night, Mike?"

He let out a deep breath and said, "I'm okay. Hey, isn't that our first stop on the next corner."

They pulled in directly in front of the sales office. "Where's the boss?" Davison asked.

"Who wants to know?"

"Police." Davison showed the man his shield.

"Sorry. I own this place. What can I do for you?" His tone was conciliatory.

"Do you recognize either of these two guys?"

The owner studied them for a minute. He said, "I've never seen this one, but ... this one looks familiar. Yeah. He's the guy who jewed me down for my 1996 Mercury."

"Get out your records on it!" Papperelli ordered.

They followed the owner into his office. He located the invoice with notations on it *WRONG ADDRESS,* but a phone number was verified belonging to a Lily Fleming.

Davison used the office phone to call the telephone company. In a matter of minutes, he had an address on Woodlawn Avenue.

"Let's go!" Papperelli shouted.

The drive to Woodlawn Avenue took thirty-five minutes. Davison called ahead for a patrol car to wait for them at the scene and watch for a black 1996 Mercury.

Papperelli, Davison and a police officer climbed the stairs to the apartment, with their guns ready.

"This is the Police. Open up!" Davison yelled, pounding on the door. He hit it again. No answer.

"Awright, I'm opening it," a woman's voice responded.

The three men burst in past the woman and searched each room.

"It's all clear," Davison confirmed. He directed the woman to sit on the couch. "Mike, there's men's clothes in the bedrooms."

"Okay, lady, where are they?" Papperelli demanded. He didn't want to waste anytime with niceties. His face contorted to a mean-looking boxer and repeated, "Tell us what we want to know right now!"

"They went out," she cried, hiding her frightened face. "I don't know anything."

Davison grabbed her by the arm and said, "You're in deep shit, lady. These guys were involved with an assassination plot and—"

Papperelli interrupted, "We know you had nothing to do with that, so don't become an accessory and make things bad for you." He had spoken in a calmer voice, checking his watch. *The President's almost finished the commencement address.*

Lily broke out crying.

"Did they go to Fordham University?"

"No," she said, brushing away tears, "they left about an hour ago to go downtown."

"What are they gonna to do down there?" Davison shouted.

Papperelli walked to the window, holding his hands together on the back of his head. *What the hell is going on downtown today?*

"Omigod." He approached the woman and jammed his hands into her shoulder blades. "I'm going to ask you just one time, lady. Have you heard them mention the name Barrett?"

She gulped for air. After staring at the other detective for help, she stammered, "Yes. I've heard them say that name. So what."

Papperelli pushed her back on the couch and told the policeman, "You stay here with her. Davison, let's get the hell out of here!"

The drive from the north Bronx to lower Manhattan down the Bronx River Parkway and the East River Drive took forty minutes, with flashing lights on their car all the way. Davison called to alert Inspector Gallagher in Manhattan South of the danger.

"Faster!" Papperelli shouted at his partner.

Those bastards want to avenge the death of their buddy. They don't give a shit about the President.

Davison drove up the curb and parked on the sidewalk a block from City Hall about 3:45. He ran ahead and arrived just as a limo with Agent Barrett pulled up near the twenty-five steps leading to the entrance to City Hall. The Mayor was at the top step to greet the honoree. Applause broke out as Barrett came into sight.

Out-of-breath, Papperelli shoved through the cheering crowd. He could see Barrett starting up the steps.

"Barrett, get back in the car!" he screamed at the agent.

Barrett automatically looked around at the sound of his name, but continued up the steps.

Papperelli thrust toward the front of the roped-off area. "Get out of the way!"

Who's Davison wrestling with?

Pete Tomlinn was on top of Davison as Butch took aim at Barrett.

"Stop or I'll shoot," Papperelli barked. His hands trembled as he stood firm, feet apart.

Spectators ran or fell to the ground, all screaming. Policemen ran to Barrett's protection, spread out and lying face down on the steps.

Papperelli saw a man he didn't recognize gape at him and redirect the pistol.

I've got to do it, he determined.

He fired twice at his target. Butch slumped to the ground, landing hard against his brother. Davison flung his adversary off and twisted his arm behind his back. He placed handcuffs on Pete Tomlinn, who sobbed on his dead brother's chest.

The crowd quickly dispersed in panic. The Mayor had moved inside out of harm's way and, after learning the situation was under control, awaited the honoree inside the building.

As Barrett stood to survey what had happened, he spotted Papperelli. He saluted the detective and mouthed, "You are my hero." He went up the steps two at a time and entered City Hall to receive the citation from the Mayor.

Papperelli smiled and waved to his new friend.

Thank God we got here in time.

Chapter Thirty Six

"Let's be realistic," Granger told Stan Flanagan. "Our Finance chairman says we won't be able to pay our bills. My support has dwindled ever since the South Carolina debate." He was calm as he nodded to the distraught advisor and reached out to shake his hand. With only weeks to go before the July convention, he decided to call it quits.

"What do you intend to do, George?"

"I'll prepare a statement that I am withdrawing my candidacy. Why don't you alert the press that I'll have a statement to make, say, tomorrow morning."

"Sorry, it turned out this way, George. You did so well in Iowa and New Hampshire. I still think you're head and shoulders above Robinson." Flanagan hung his head in defeat.

"Ladies and Gentlemen, thank you for coming. First, I want to acknowledge my hard working campaign committee." Granger looked around the room, smiling at his supporters, who clapped in a subdued, automatic reaction.

"Let me also express my appreciation to those of you who have covered my campaign. You have been cordial to me and my wife, Mary Jo." He left the lectern to kiss his wife, who appeared numb by the proceedings.

"I have had the unique honor to address the American people regarding my views on the future of our great country. I have stuck to the issues that matter for the common good and national unity. I believe I have had a positive influence in the dialogue on major questions impacting domestic and foreign policies."

He hesitated to clear his throat and cough. He saw a dejected Stan Flanagan leaning against the back wall.

"It is clear from the polls that my party prefers a contrasting direction to mine and I feel obligated to accept their position. Therefore, I am withdrawing my name as a candidate for my party's nomination for the presidency. I will attend the convention and lead the delegation from Louisiana."

There were mild boos of disappointment and cries from the audience.

"Thank you for your interest and I'll take a few questions."

"Congressman Granger, do you think that your platform regarding UN dues, similar to the President, hurt your chances with the party base?"

"That's an issue that requires broader discussion on a bipartisan basis. So I can't say it was a deciding factor."

"Will you accept a Vice-President spot on Senator Robinson's ticket?"

"As a practical matter it's unlikely to have the national ticket include nominees from the same section of the country." Granger felt there was nothing more to say, resigned to be an also-ran. "One more question."

"There have been rumors of bad feelings between you and the Senator. Will you support Robinson in the general election?"

"One decision at a time, if you don't mind." He started to leave then stopped to face the questioner. "Don't believe everything you think you hear," he said with a chuckle.

* * *

"George, I watched your press conference and admire your position," Robinson said to Granger, calling from his campaign headquarters. "You orchestrated a fine operation and conducted yourself well."

"Thank you, Senator."

"I'm sure you agree it's now time to look ahead to the general election. Our party must take back the presidency and I want to work with you to insure that it happens."

"Well I'll be back in the House as Minority Leader doing my job again."

"Yes, and I'd like to talk to you about that." Robinson held the phone away as he referred to the prepared notes on his desk. A notation at the top of the page reminded him "do not gloat."

"First, I don't believe you should let out of the Ways and Means committee Atkinsen's proposed bill on UN dues elimination. Since the chances are it just may pass in the House, let's not give him a victory on that or anything else prior to November."

"Senator, I'm not sure we can stop the Majority on that issue. I will speak to Allcott about the timing of a floor vote. The President's proposal on UN reorganization has picked up steam with the pub—"

"Err, do the best you can. George, what I really wanted to ask was for your endorsement at the convention. I feel we must let bygones be bygones and show strength for the good of the party. What do you say? Can I count on you?"

"Look, John, you know I've been a party loyalist and I'm ready to do what I can. I'm sure the vote at the convention will be unanimous. But I want to know who your VP pick will be and I'd like to know the tone of your acceptance speech when presenting your ideas for the future."

"Well of course. I'll provide you with anything you want to know at the start of the convention." He felt upstanding by the magnanimous gesture. "In the meantime it's important that you and I show we're together, especially with Governor Bliss challenging the President in the primaries."

"Senator, I'm not prepared to issue any statement before the convention and—"

Robinson's stood, gripping the phone tight, as he squirmed to control his anger.

"George, you opposed me once after I offered you a chance to be my running mate and I didn't take to kindly to that so you best consider who your friends really are and pick the right side." He stopped to catch his breath. "Don't be so sure you'll get the Speaker's position when I'm elected and we win the House back."

"I hear you loud and clear," Granger shot back. "Thanks for the call."

* * *

"Friends, I want to thank you for your hard work and energy up to now. It has paid off. I will win our party's nomination for President unopposed at next month's convention."

The small gathering of campaign workers and party officials gave Senator Robinson a standing ovation.

"Thank you again. Now we need your absolute dedication as we enter the home stretch in the general election. Polls indicate the country is dissatisfied with the status quo. Our opposition will spare no effort to continue in power. We have the message and the will of the people on our side to achieve our goal, which is …?"

He placed his hand to his ear and listened.

"The White House," arose a vociferous cheer.

"Now I'm going to let you in on a surprise. The number one man on my list to be Vice-President is standing in the wings in the great state of Michigan. He's my good friend and a great American. I am thrilled to announce I will put forward my nominee for Vice-President, former Governor Frederick J. Hughes."

I hope Granger eats crow on my choice of Hughes. They've been at odds for years.

There was a buzz of surprise and mild applause that turned into wild glee.

"The Governor is due on television within the hour to indicate his willingness to join the party's ticket. As you know he is a distant relative of Senator Arthur Vandenberg who, with Charles Lindbergh, fought for an isolationist policy in the Nineteen-Thirties."

Robinson paused to sip water and gaze at the captive audience. This was his stage; it was an occasion to be at his flamboyant best.

"Governor Hughes and I see eye to eye to reverse Atkinsen's foreign policy and close all our military bases around the world. We are committed to putting America first in all matters to protect our homeland. Our slogan will be *No Foreign Entanglements.*"

The reaction was muted at first but gradual acceptance became evident with prolonged applause.

"Let me remind you all that George Washington espoused the theme of avoiding permanent foreign alliances in his Farewell Address in 1776. Finally, I must say this about the incumbent. Herb Atkinsen is unfit to be President any longer. His erratic behavior, if unchecked, will eventually harm the country. His administration is in disarray. So it is imperative that we fight as hard as we can to win the presidency. Are you with me?"

The room erupted into roars of support, chanting *Robinson and Hughes--Give them the Blues.*

Robinson was elated. He moved about the room, shaking hands with everyone.

Herb Atkinsen won't have it so easy this time. It's my turn.

Chapter Thirty Seven

Tom Bliss of Missouri was known as a non-conformist and he liked it. The President's State of the Union had ignited a spark in him that he had the wherewithal to carry-out a serious challenge to Atkinsen's run for a second term. *They can't shun me aside like the last time.*

At a party caucus prior to the last convention four years ago, Bliss had interjected a vigorous objection in the discussion of the party's nominee. "I don't care what Atkinsen's reputation is in Georgia. He doesn't have the charisma or experience of Craig Washburn."

"Be reasonable, Tom," said the party chairman Jackman. "This is going to be a tough race against Robinson and we have to be together on our candidate. Come on, Herb Atkinsen is considered a dark horse already by the pundits so we've got to get behind him."

"All the more reason I can't back him," Bliss said, blowing out cigar smoke and raising his hands in a stop position. "I want Washburn to tell me directly he's unable to run."

The chairman snickered, "You're carrying your state slogan a little far, aren't you?"

"Maybe, but Washburn's the one who put us back in the majority and I wanna make damn sure we're not stabbing him in the back."

Following the convention and Atkinsen's nomination on the second ballot, Bliss pledged a so-so endorsement for the party's candidate for President. His support didn't last long.

After the first debate with Robinson, Bliss was infuriated. "Why did Atkinsen vow to cancel that trade agreement with the European Union?" Bliss demanded. "It was a feather in Washburn's cap after tedious negotiation. Not only that, Atkinsen ends up on the same side of the argument as the opposition."

"Hold it, Governor," Wagner said, getting red in the face. "We're under pressure from the peanut lobby in the Southeast. That's where our priority is."

"Well you can tell him I think it sucks and I guess I'll have to heed my own priorities in the future."

Shortly thereafter, Bliss failed to show at a rally for Atkinsen in Independence, including a visit to the Truman Library and Museum, which conveyed a firm snub to the candidate. His adversarial position was irreconcilable.

They haven't heard the last of me. Whether Atkinsen wins or loses, I'll be ready for the next race for president.

* * *

"Welcome to the one and only debate of the Majority party before next month's convention. My name is Jim Lehrer."

After introducing President Atkinsen and Governor Bliss, he acted as moderator while the candidates spared with one another on domestic issues for thirty-five minutes.

"Let's move on to foreign affairs," Lehrer said. "Your turn, Governor."

"I'm delighted to discuss the administration's failure in foreign policy," Bliss said, staring into the camera. "The President's own words about the UN are evidence of his lack of judgment in diplomacy. In particular, he sent the wrong message to China."

"Which is, Governor?" asked Lehrer.

Bliss referred to his notes and said, "China has been handed a way out of UN membership so they can pursue their military growth without accountability. The UN has been an impediment to their strategy of becoming the world's superpower."

Lehrer motioned to Atkinsen. "Mr. President."

"It's obvious the Governor has not read my proposal for a continuing peacekeeping force that is independent of the UN layers of bureaucracy. His charge that China is opposed to the UN as a world body is false and reckless. Their trade would suffer if they were outside the international community."

"Mr. President, how do you view our position in the world

today?" asked Lehrer.

"I believe that the treaties on economic and military issues we have negotiated have strengthened our position in global markets. It is for that reason I am convinced that my proposals to reorganize the UN are timely and efficient. The current peace requires vigilance. Like Ronald Reagan said, 'Trust but verify.'"

Bliss swung his arms and shook his head in disbelief. "First of all," he stated, "this president has weakened the achievements of his predecessor, President Washburn. His mistaken economic treaty with China did nothing to reverse the demand problem and price escalation on cement exported to China, which cost American jobs and hurts our—"

Atkinsen interrupted, "China's economy is growing just like we want our economy to expand."

"You have failed to see the threat and their power. What happens if they put a sell order in on the US government Bonds they're holding?"

"Our objective is to increase imports to the Chinese marketplace to come in line with their exports to us. The fact is, economically, we and the Chinese are tied together."

"Mr. President, that expectation is a far off dream that could become a nightmare."

"Excuse me, Governor. You seem paranoid about the Chinese. I'm curious—have you ever visited China ...and what's their capital?"

Bliss had a blank look on his reddened face. "You've gotta be kidding."

"While we're at it, who is the number two man after Hu Jintao and what's the name of their prime minister?"

Bliss fixed his eyes on the moderator and snapped, "This is not a game of *Jeopardy*. I've made my point."

After several seconds of strained silence, Lehrer announced, "We'll take a commercial break and be right back."

Atkinsen could be heard in the background saying, "It's Beijing."

* * *

"What's the verdict, Harry?" Atkinsen had removed his suit jacket and loosened his tie before taking a swallow of his bourbon.

He sat with his elbows on the armrest and tapped his fingers to get his advisor's take on the meeting.

Grant took his time to respond, making himself comfortable in a corner of the couch opposite the President, who was gently rattling the ice cubes in his drink.

"I rate the first part as a draw. Bliss did have a great line on affordable health care."

"Right," Atkinsen acknowledged. "I thought he was one up on me."

"Unfortunately, you looked a little stiff and tentative on TV at the beginning."

"Uh huh."

"He started out well on foreign relations, with his booming voice, but lost it when you challenged him on China. Honestly though, he has a point about our long term relationship with the Chinese."

"I attempted to downplay it, but, you're both right. It is a concern."

"Where did you come up with the idea of asking him those questions?" Grant's facial expression transposed from solemn to joy.

"Spur of the moment kinda thing," Atkinsen answered. "Hope I didn't humiliate him."

"Here's the bottom line, okay." Grant said, sounding in-charge, "The convention is anti-climatic. You're way over the top with the committed delegate count." Laughing, he said, "Now we know Bliss' ulterior motive four years ago was to be the candidate instead of you. He's finished, and, Herb, you ended up looking presidential for the first time in a long time."

A relieved smile gradually formed on Atkinsen's face. His buoyed spirits lifted him off his chair to shake Grant's hand.

"I have to say that the contest with Robinson will make Bliss seem like a pussy cat," Grant warned. "So it's time to get serious about your VP and the Atkinsen ticket."

"I've given it some thought," Atkinsen said, turning business-like. "Since you had suggested we should choose someone from the West Coast, I've indicated I like Speaker Bob Allcott."

Grant hesitated and poured a diet Coke from the bar. He took a sip and said, "Well, he's not exactly what I had in mind. He seems arrogant. Perhaps the power has gone to his head and—"

Atkinsen interrupted, "Wait a second, Harry, I've met with him on policy matters and he's always been constructive."

"Sure, he's taken your administration's victories as his own. Allcott is good at form and posturing over substance."

"Shit, Harry, we must be talking about two different people," Atkinsen said, frustrated at their disagreement. "I wish you had expressed your opinion long before now."

Grant crossed his legs and clasped his hands together. "Herb, you may be one hundred percent correct. Allow me to do some homework on this and get back to you with more than an off-the-cuff reaction. If I can't come up with an alternative, I'll certainly go with your hunch."

"That's fine, Harry. However, it's a hell of a lot more than a hunch." Atkinsen stood to leave, glared at his advisor and said, "I'm late for a scheduling meeting with Steve Wagner. Let's resolve the VP spot as soon as possible."

"Yes, Mr. President. I'll get right on it."

Chapter Thirty Eight

Harry Grant had a dilemma.

I have to find out more about Allcott fast. Maybe I've misjudged him.

From the Congressional Record he located the only reference Bob Allcott made on the House floor to the President's State of the Union address. In early February Allcott had responded to quips by Minority Leader Granger that the President's own party had not demonstrated support for his ideas. Grant scrolled to the meaningful exchange between the two men.

"Is the Majority leader ashamed or simply reluctant to demonstrate support for the unexpected words and manner of the President in his State of the Union address?" charged Granger.

"Let me inform the Gentleman that President Atkinsen does not require or seek my approval of his remarks at any time. We are proud of his administration and his personal leadership on matters involving the State Department. His legislative initiatives which have passed this House have benefited the American people.

Due to other pressing matters, it is our intention to take up the issue of UN dues after the election this November. Similarly, we respect the President so we will hold off judgment on the unfortunate dismissal of Frank Simon at the DOE and his proposed replacement."

"Et tu Brute," Grant thought. "Rather disingenuous of the Speaker."

"Like in all other matters, we will cooperate with President Atkinsen for smooth coordination between the administration and this House," Allcott concluded.

"I'll be damned!" Grant scratched the top of his head.

He reread the entire transcript of the session which was conducted to an empty House chamber, except for the leaders on both sides of the aisle.

"Rather than prop-up Atkinsen at a tough point in his presidency, Allcott does a two-step," he deduced.

Grant checked Bob Allcott's biography which disclosed he was an eight term congressman from Washington State. Further research revealed he won his first term by defeating the corrupt mayor of Seattle, who was subsequently found guilty, in a tainted election. When Washburn became president seven years ago, Allcott lobbied hard among his peers and was voted to the powerful Speaker of the House of Representatives post.

Granger seems to be giving the President the benefit of the doubt on the State of the Union address and, at the same time, pushing Allcott to confirm he stands with the President.

"But where the hell is Granger coming from?" he said aloud. "What's his motivation?"

Grant shoved the chair away from his desk, clasped his hands behind his neck, and stared at the ceiling. He went to the bathroom to throw cold water on his grumpy face. He walked the twenty-five paces from one side of his office to the other, periodically shaking his head.

The wall clock showed it was almost midnight, which surprised him. Despite feeling exhausted, he returned to his desk and wrote on a yellow legal pad: *one, running mate should be from West Coast based on recent polling data; two, Allcott not on board with Pres on new initiatives or UN position; three, Country is desperate for unity; four, ...*

He stopped to question how to thwart the dangerous isolationist policy of Robinson. "We'll go backwards more than seventy years to Fortress America if he's elected," he whispered.

Grant felt his career behind the scenes in national politics would be based on this recommendation and this moment in time.

With renewed energy, he googled on his computer the name George Granger. Once satisfied, even impressed, with his profile, he studied Granger's voting record in Congress and the Louisiana legislature. "I'll be darned," he blurted out at Granger's stately positions on national issues.

After making decaf Green tea, he decided to review his class notes and lesson plan on Amendments to the Constitution. His specific interest was the Twelfth Amendment, ratified in 1804 a mere thirteen years after the first ten amendments, and the Electoral College. "This is too important to trust to memory," he realized. Intense concentration on the subject followed. He removed his glasses and rubbed his eyes, wondering if his mind were playing tricks on him. The intermittent pain in his left arm drove him to focus harder on his assignment.

He said aloud to the empty room, "Since the electors vote for Vice-President separate from President, thanks to the Twelfth Amendment, is it too big a hurdle to expect our slate of electors in each state to vote for someone from the opposition party?"

It took two more hours but he knew what he had to do. "I'm going to that reception tomorrow night for a retiring congressman and cajole a meeting with Granger."

* * *

"Good evening, George, I've been trying to get you attention all evening," Grant said to Granger, as he pointed in the direction of a quiet sitting area outside the main reception room.

"You're looking good, Harry," Granger said smiling. "Hanging out with the college crowd is working miracles on you."

Grant laughed and abruptly turned earnest. "Why are you opposed to the President's anti-crime bill?"

"Did he send you to ask that?" Granger asked, with a quizzical look.

"No. He doesn't know I'm talking to you."

"Since you ask, the bill has too many loopholes. I'm all for adding more police in the inner cities, but, I believe, the administration has lost focus on the judicial system and the jail population. There's no appropriation for new jail construction and the DOJ is playing hardball on our amendments."

"I don't want to argue with you but—"

"Who's arguing?" asked Granger.

"I've been meaning to ask you why you became a candidate."

"The stock answer is all politicians have ambition for higher office, and I'm no different."

"So how did you feel about pulling out?" Grant leaned slightly forward in his chair to hear the answer and observe Granger's mannerisms.

"If Robinson wins the election this time, I expect to be the Speaker and I'll be able to achieve programs that are important to me."

"What do you think of Robinson?"

"What the hell is it with you and all these questions?" Granger shifted in his chair as if to leave.

"Suppose I answer my own question and you can nod your head one way or another," Grant suggested, continuing the cat and mouse game.

"I'll listen for another minute," Granger said, sitting back and folding his arms across his chest.

"I don't think you like Robinson's isolation policy. I don't think you agree with him on the UN." Grant paused and added for maximum effect, "And I don't believe you like him."

"What's the point of all this, Grant? I'm not sure I should give you the time of day, let alone tell you things you could manipulate against me or my party."

"Fair question. First, I assure you I'm not here to trick you or take advantage of this conversation." He moved closer to Granger and spoke in a slow cadence, "I've studied your record in Louisiana and in Congress. I've heard your policy differences with Robinson. I've read your views on the UN and your withdrawal speech emphasizing unity." He hesitated as he checked their privacy.

"Go on," said Granger, squinting as if he were in a dark room.

"Now I'll let you in on a secret. Your views on America's position in the world and broad domestic issues of long term consequence are not much different than the President."

The blood seemed to run out of Granger's face.

"I'm smart enough to see that you and Atkinsen are compatible in temperament and character, besides having a vision of how you'd like things to be." Grant waved to a waiter and ordered two double scotches, neat.

They sat mute until the drinks arrived. They touched glasses.

Grant said, in a barely audible voice, "I remember a point you made on your first national exposure on *Sixty* Minutes. I quote,

'President Atkinsen's supporters can say we are on the right path toward a new order bringing the country together. I can lead us one step further to achieve the unity we all desire.' I know you meant every word, didn't you?"

Granger asked in a faltering voice, "Exactly, what are telling me … or asking me?"

"This conversation is off the record, but I intend to discuss with the President the possibility that he select you as his running mate."

"As Vice-President?" Granger gasped.

"Yes," Grant said. "If you don't hear from me again, you'll gather this discussion never took place."

Neither man noticed several congressmen exit the reception and wave goodnight in their direction.

Granger stood to leave. "You never asked me what I think of Atkinsen."

Chapter Thirty Nine

"I cut short the Cabinet meeting when I heard you wanted to see me," the President said to Grant. He wondered what had taken him so long to offer his advice on the VP nominee.

Grant nodded and said, "Since you're leaving for the convention in two days, I knew you expected my views on the choice for Vice-President. Sorry I couldn't get to you any earlier."

They sat facing each other in the Oval Office, without engaging in the usual small talk. Atkinsen took note of the arched eyebrows of Grant, who squinted at the Bible conspicuously placed on the table behind the President's desk.

Grant said, "I promised I would take an objective look at Bob Allcott. Here's a one-page summary of my evaluation."

Atkinsen read the brief report, unhurried, and concealed his emotion. After removing his reading glasses, he said in a deliberate tone, "You're saying Allcott has distanced himself from my views on the UN."

"Yes, sir, without question."

"I've heard rumors he's upset about the firing of Frank Simon, but there's been no attempt to speak to me or Wagner." The President stood and walked back to his desk, allowing time to think before the next step. He pulled a manila folder from the center drawer.

"I've thought about the next name on my short list, Senator Childs of California. He can get us needed votes and my relations with him have been cordial." Atkinsen glanced at Grant to observe his immediate reaction to Michael Childs. "And there's Congresswoman Joan Milligan of New York to consider."

Grant shifted his position on the couch to face the President. He scratched the back of his neck and said, "Sir, I really don't know too much about Childs' record, but he does have a good reputation as a reliable, conscientious worker. He's a good party man."

"Twice good, Harry? Childs is good but not good enough, huh." The thought hit Atkinsen he may not be able to propose a VP at the convention. *When was the last time the VP spot was open to the convention floor?*

"As for Milligan, mark my words, Mr. President, she'll be a strong candidate for higher office four years from now. She's a very principled, astute political strategist. Unfortuneately, when her name was included among the contenders, a New York paper made a rude reference to her being "Atkinsen's new girlfriend.""

"Shameless press," Atkinsen said, gritting his teeth. "So let's advance her into more high profile positions to insure she receives national exposure. Right?"

"Absolutely. And that's when Admiral Farrell might decide to enter the race. He's clearly the most popular war hero since Eisenhower and Norman Schwartzkopf, who simply didn't have the stomach for politics."

Atkinsen waited for more from his advisor. Finally, he watched Grant stand and rub his chin. "What's on your mind?" asked the President.

"Instead of identifying available individuals who meet your qualifications to get elected, maybe we should focus on your long term agenda and direction for the country, and who can best help you reach that goal."

The President was perplexed, as he absorbed Grant's drift. He slouched down on the couch and crossed his legs. "Fine. So where does that take us to select a VP? Do I just throw out my damn list and leave it to the convention delegates?"

Grant's furrowed brow seemed like ridges across his forehead as he wet his lips and sat next to Atkinsen.

"Mr. President, I have a recommendation of who might help you get elected and develop a new agenda for the country that achieves a united leadership for the future. That's what you've said you wanted."

"Yes. So who would that be?" asked Atkinsen. A wide-eyed look of anticipation defined his appearance.

Grant held back a stammer. "Minority Leader George Granger."

The President sagged on the couch as if a haymaker had landed on his jaw. He pulled himself up and rested his elbows on his knees, hands under his chin. He glared at Grant and proclaimed, "Are you kidding me?"

"As a matter of fact, I'm quite serious," Grant replied.

The President sat straight up, shaking his head, and said, "Then you're just plain crazy or getting senile." He slapped his forehead and ran his fingers through his hair, wondering how this bad dream would end.

"If you're willing to listen, I can explain and—"

"Harry, we need help," he blared.

"I've researched Granger's background," Grant said. The intonation in his voice rose two levels as he ignored the President's plea. "The man has been a moderate in his party and a champion of change from extremist positions. Believe it or not, his views on foreign policy are in synch with yours, and I've seen the same compromises on domestic issues as I've observed in you over the years."

"I hardly know the guy, for God's sake. He seemed thoughtful and non-combative at White House meetings, but—"

"All right. I've spoken to both Senators from Louisiana about a made-up lecture for class on the character traits of honorable politicians. I used Granger as one example. They gave him high marks on fairness and honesty. He's tenacious on getting the important things done ... always puts aside personal or party politics, and his approach is mild-mannered but firm. His FBI background check was clean. One thing for sure, he's not a windbag."

"He wanted to be his party's nominee for president, didn't he?"

"Herb, he was motivated to obstruct Robinson," Grant pointed out, now sounding calm. "The best of all reasons."

"Even if he is a good man, or the right man for that matter, why would we do such a thing?" Atkinsen had the vanquished look of someone sentenced to jail.

"Two interrelated reasons," Grant said, speaking as a friend. "The polls are not in your favor. After the convention, when Robinson starts to harp on your performance since your wife's death as well as the State of the Union conduct, it's only going to get worse." He paused, seemingly searching his memory. "Besides, history is on his side. Jefferson, Jackson, Harrison, Cleveland and Nixon all became president after a previous unsuccessful run for president."

"You conveniently forgot Adlai Stevenson," the President said, smirking at history's relevance.

"By the way, Vice-President Jefferson and President John Adams were in different political parties," Grant offered, planting a seed in the President's mind. "Oh, I didn't mention that Granger is a practicing Catholic which will help in the Midwest and Northeast."

"So, this is purely a political maneuver." Atkinsen's retort conveyed his disenchantment with Grant's idea.

"Of course it's a consideration in order to win the prize. But, Mr. President, let me go to my second reason. The course of the United States will be changed forever if Robinson is elected. He'll carry the Senate and House with him. You, better than anyone, recognize the danger of that happening ... and so does George Granger." Grant emphasized Granger's name as if it were introduced for the first time.

Atkinsen was awed with the fervor of Grant's defense of his recommendation. *The old codger would have fit in nicely with Franklin and Jefferson and Adams and Madison during the drafting of the constitution.*

"Wouldn't he mitigate the impact of a Robinson presidency as Speaker?" Atkinsen inquired.

"Robinson would be much too powerful, and my sense is there's no guarantee Granger gets the leadership post based on his entry in the primaries."

Atkinsen stood and walked to the French doors. *The implications of this are too staggering to imagine.*

Grant continued, "The way I read the tea leaves is that the country would turn away from Robinson if there were broad opposition to his candidacy."

Atkinsen was silent for several minutes, folding and unfolding his arms. *I've never challenged Harry before but this is different.*

"Before you reach a decision, Mr. President, I must tell you I've spoken to Granger and he didn't reject the possibility."

The President turned and looked dumbfounded at his advisor. *Jesus Christ, he's deadly serious.*

"Herb, you know I've always admired you and respected your political judgments in the past. All I can suggest now is for you to follow your instincts."

Once again Atkinsen was quiet as the thought of those words stuck in his throat. He visualized Ellen speaking those words to him.

Atkinsen stood next to his advisor, looked him in the eye and asked, "Harry, have you thought ahead to cross the t's and dot the i's if this were announced?"

"I believe I have, Mr. President. You're familiar with the Miller Center of the University of Virginia, a nonpartisan public policy group."

"Sure."

"They issued a Commission report in 1992 that recommended the nominee should meet the test of suitability for becoming President as well as personal compatibility and political considerations."

"Does Granger meet the test?"

"I'm convinced he has the qualifications and you and he can work well together. Also, the Commission considered an interesting option that the presidential nominee proposes two names for VP at the national conventions. Neither party has entertained that option up to now, of course."

"Isn't there a major risk the delegates will rebel against him?"

"I've taken one other person into my confidence."

"Oh God. Who is it?"

"Bill Frick, your old campaign manager. Because he trusts you and you trust him, he agreed to try to head off any discord on the convention floor about your VP selection."

Atkinsen stretched out on the couch with his head on the armrest. Once again he wondered how other presidents gleaned wisdom in the Oval Office.

After staring in space to gather his thoughts for several minutes, he sat up and ordered Grant, "Tell Wagner to see me and inform Granger I'll call him in the morning."

"Yes sir, Mr. President. Thank you."

Chapter Forty

"Do you know why I'm calling?"

"Yes, Mr. President, I do," Granger said.

"Why would you agree to do it?"

"After Harry Grant spoke to me, I felt I had been hit by a two-by-four. It took a sleepless night for the quandary to crystallize in my mind." He paused.

I think he may be hyperventilating, Atkinsen conjectured.

"It would be easy to point at Senator Robinson to justify my reaction. The man has hijacked the principles of my party. It would also be easy to sound magnanimous by proclaiming I'm doing it for the good of the country. But it's more fundamental than that."

"Go on," the President said, engrossed in the explanation.

"Mr. President, I would accept the VP spot on your ticket simply because you ask me." Granger expressed his rationale with passion in his voice. "With all due respect, sir, I would ask why of you."

"I'll call you back in five minutes."

Granger's right. He only has to answer to his constituents and the party leaders. I admire his clear thinking. Grant's assessment of the man appears accurate. Wagner has good things to say about him also, but disapproves of the whole idea as irrational. "I'm the one who must articulate the reason for an abnormal choice for VP," he whispered.

Atkinsen tasted his second cup of coffee. It was cold. He debated with himself if he should call Harry Grant, but abandoned the idea realizing that his advisor had done everything expected of him. "This decision is my alone to make," he stated.

Funny thing. Granger is superior to Styles in experience so my administration is stronger right off the bat. Grant vouches for him. However, everything depends on whether we can function together as a team. That's the big question I have to address.

"Wait a minute, I'm getting ahead of myself," he mumbled. "We have to be elected first."

He closed his eyes for some moments and then pushed away from his desk to stretch. He dialed Granger's private number again.

"Congressman Granger."

"Yes sir, Mr. President."

"You're correct to want to hear my reasons for calling just as it is of necessity I understand you better."

"Thank you, sir."

"Following your reasoning, I could boil down a complex issue into blunt statements to explain why I would choose someone from the opposite party to be my running mate. It would be easy to say I'm putting the country's harmony above party unity, or I need all the help I can get to beat Robinson." He shifted the phone to his right ear. "As a substantive symbol, starting at the top, I want to diffuse the rancor in Washington. By the way, Wagner tells me you have not engaged in the backbiting for political gain."

"Thank you for saying so, sir," Granger interjected.

"What appeals to me is political integration. I don't mean to end the two-party system, in fact I encourage Independents as well, but there's got to be something more dynamic to convince the American people the political process is working inside the Beltway. Do you know what I mean?"

"I think so. It sounds like a tall order ... and a worthy objective."

"Too many people are making a living from the polarization." Atkinsen could hear Granger swallow. He continued, "So many elected officials act as if their position on issues were ordained by God. Here's what's interesting. When you place the country's big priorities above all else, you discover there's more we agree on in order to get the little things done that can have a major impact."

"Yes, sir, I concur."

"For example, let's start promoting American history at the lower grades so our children will grow up to be better citizens. That's something we can agree on for the benefit of the country. And how are today's young parents not as well off as their parents going to pay for the escalating cost of college in the future?"

"May I suggest the prevention and enforcement of violent crimes against society is another example?" Granger introduced.

"Absolutely. Reasonable people have to come to grips with achieving more safe and secure living conditions for everyone. Furthermore, we've got to provide opportunities to all who seek to advance themselves. Our economy is the envy of the world, and it's being emulated, the result of capitalism, despite its flaws."

"I'm in complete agreement with you on that point, sir," Granger said, sounding more enthused. "Also, if I were privy to all your military briefings, the need for a draft would probably be more plausible to me. One matter that upsets my constituents is the interpretation of laws based on a judges' beliefs rather than right or wrong."

"True, but let's agree to disagree about the subject of abortion for the moment," Atkinsen added, biting his lip. "Grant says it's still the third rail of politics."

Harry and Wagner were on target in their appraisal of the man.

For the next five minutes the President was silent as Granger described his family background, college activities at Louisiana State University, and political leanings. "I believe I live my life according to my religious faith," he stated in conclusion.

Impressive! He's kept his faith during his political career while I almost lost my soul.

"George, I'm prepared to nominate you for Vice-President at the convention."

"Mr. President, I—"

"We can spend time afterwards developing a meaningful role for the Vice-President during the campaign and in my administration, if we are successful. However, there is one situation or condition for which you must give me your word."

"Sir, I'm honored beyond words to be on your ticket," Granger said, a noticeable quiver in his voice.

"I want your word as a Christian gentleman that, if I die or leave office before my term as President is up, you will carry out our mutually-agreed upon policies without caving in to influences from your old political cronies or special interests."

"Mr. President, you have my word, so help me God."

"Furthermore, I make no promises to you about my support four years from now."

Atkinsen held the coffee cup to his mouth, but didn't drink. He had lunch by himself in the Oval Office. A thousand thoughts were swirling around in his head after his choice of George Granger. He grimaced at one thought that he was playing with fire. He put the cup down using both hands to avoid spilling coffee on his desk.

"I haven't felt this low and lonely in a long time," he said to himself.

Chapter Forty One

The band was playing; banners were everywhere and balloons were hanging from the rafters. The delegates were in a festive mood on the last night of the convention in Madison Square Garden. When the assemblage sang the National Anthem, the spirit of patriotism was as if a gigantic wave transported the crowd in a euphoric frenzy.

As the President rehearsed his terse message in a private room, Grant watched the proceedings on the convention floor and commented on his many years observing the gatherings of both parties.

"Herb, up until the last convention, this event was like a wild party with parades up the aisles. Pent-up energy was released to get the general election started with a bang. When you won the nomination on the second ballot last time, the old practice has become more serious about the platform and promises, and ..."

Although Grant continued to speak, Atkinsen didn't catch a word. He mused on the reception his selection would receive, beginning with party insiders. He was rightly pleased his acceptance speech the previous night had been received with jubilation by the delegates. All the disappointment with his State of the Union speech was forgotten. Now his preference for Vice-President might be setting politics back over two hundred years, perhaps to how the Founding Fathers wished it to be.

Here we go again, Ellen. I wish you could hold my hand like the last time as we faced the unknown.

* * *

"Thank you very much, thank you," the President said, raising his arms to silence the rousing delegates. "Once again my sincere thanks for your trust in me to be the party's nominee for a second term as President. Special thanks to the Missouri delegation and Governor Bliss for casting a unanimous vote for my nomination last evening."

Hooting and applause broke out in the Missouri section.

"My remarks tonight will be right to the point. I intend to meet with each state delegation leader in the caucus room immediately following the closing of the convention tonight."

Atkinsen stared out at the delegates who seemed taken by surprise at this unusual ending. Since the rumor mill concerning the Vice-President nominee was epidemic, another uncertainty added to their tense wait.

No turning back now.

"The American people want solidarity in their government with a moral foundation. They deserve unity. I don't believe our citizens would be satisfied if the person in the Oval Office is a divisive Senator Robinson. I commit to preventing that from happening."

Shouts of agreement and incessant clapping were scattered throughout the Garden.

"The Founding Fathers understood the importance of unity when they wrote a constitution for a United States of America. For the country to survive and prosper, we must abide by the Constitution as a living document throughout the twenty-first century. To achieve the ideals so desired, my vision is a shared political responsibility at the federal level, a political integration to give it a name."

The stirring among the delegates signaled to Atkinsen they were uneasy about the new nomenclature.

"I feel strongly that political integration at appropriate times in history should start at the top. This is one of those times."

He searched the crowd for Harry Grant without success. *God help me.*

"Therefore, I put forward a man of high integrity, Congressman George Granger, as my Vice-Presidential running mate."

A stunned silence quickly erupted into shouts and boos. Cries of betrayal were heard from sections of the Garden. Chairman Jackman, looking befuddled, banged the gavel repeatedly as he begged, "Order, please, order! Clear the aisles!" He restored control after ten minutes of pandemonium.

Television commentators were too shocked to speak, allowing the public to witness the angry disturbance on their television screen.

"The Chair recognizes the delegate from Georgia."

"Mr. Chairman," Frick screamed, "we are proud of Herb Atkinsen's years as President. His judgments in domestic and foreign policy have been sound and his record is impeccable against attacks from the opposition. His courage in the face of personal travails is undeniable. Only yesterday we nominated him unanimously to lead our party and run for a second term."

Grumblings of disapproval continued from all sections of the floor.

House Leader Allcott stood at first, fists clenched, with members of the Washington State delegation. He flopped back in his seat, head shaking. His anger contorted the tremor on his flushed face, symptomatic of Parkinson's disease.

Frick held the microphone tighter as he announced, "We have all trusted President Atkinsen's judgment. I move we accept his nominee for Vice-President. Simultaneously, I move that at our next general convention the presidential nominee must submit two names for the delegates to consider and to approve one for the VP spot. Furthermore, that there is forty-eight hours between the nomination of the President and the approval of a Vice-President nominee."

"Is there a second?" shouted Jackman.

The Mayor of New Orleans jumped up to be recognized. "Mr. Chairman, as head of the Louisiana delegation, I second the motion and endorse George Granger as an honorable man with proven experience who would never disgrace his state or his country. We respect the choice of President Atkinsen."

Once again the outburst was deafening, although many cries of support now filtered through the unruly opposition. The beleaguered Chairman appeared flustered as he checked with the Parliamentarian not once but twice.

The catcalls were numerous.

Jackman hit the gavel three times and called the question. "All in favor say aye."

The noise rivaled that of any sporting event ever held at this famous arena.

Jackman proclaimed, "The ayes have it."

The convention ended in mass confusion amid cries of parliamentary rule blunders.

Tim Russert reported in his closing commentary to the TV audience, "This convention is a throw-back to the way things were in the Eighteen-Hundreds—rowdy, raucous, and with unrestrained resentment. Yet, despite everything, a new dynamic in American politics has burst upon the scene. Time will tell if the Atkinsen ticket can withstand the flak from diverse sides."

While Granger, who was in his DC office, was prepared to deliver an acceptance speech on the large screen behind the rostrum, the reaction of the delegates was too explosive. His statement was released to all the delegates in lieu of his appearance.

I am honored to be a candidate for Vice-President on the Atkinsen/Granger ticket. I guarantee him and you my wholehearted support.

At this critical time in our history I pledge to work with President Atkinsen to define and achieve America's priorities. My country is first. My party is second.

Now it's up to me to satisfy the state party leaders of the viability of an integrated ticket, Atkinsen thought, as he moved to the caucus room surrounded by Secret Service agents. He relied on Grant's expertise with respect to the constitution, and the 12th Amendment in particular.

He played over in his mind Grant's unequivocal words of warning. *It's essential that party loyalists who become electors in each state stick with Granger as your Vice-President. You've got to convince them it's best for the country. If you get a majority of electoral votes and he doesn't, the decision goes to the Senate and puts Robinson in the inconceivable influential position of dictating who your Vice-President will be.*

"God help me avoid a calamity for my party and a public revolt against our political system," Atkinsen muttered under his breath.

Chapter Forty Two

Fletcher Jones was astounded. "I've got to start my column right now while this bombshell is fresh in my mind." He pushed his poodle out of the way and sat at his computer, itching to interpret the incredible outcome of the convention.

Not since the early days of this republic has there been a maneuver like the one President Atkinsen pulled off this evening. It is a matter of urgency that the American people request an MRI on his brain.

The President offered a simplistic view of the future that borders on naiveté, despite three years in office. His selection of a running mate (I dare not mention his name) portends a challenge, perhaps sinister, to the constitution he has taken an oath to protect.

Does he wish to end the two-party system as we know it? And replace it with what—political integration? Pure semantics. Better yet, poppycock.

For whatever reason President Atkinsen has lost his sense of practical politics and, therefore, his ability to be an effective leader is nullified. He's Popeye without his spinach or Samson without hair. Worse still, the world will see us as rank political novices.

Not only did "Mr. Smith go to Washington", he became the President of the United States.

As for the drama of the upcoming campaign, I expect we will see a real ...

Fletcher stopped to read his first draft. His nostrils flared at the taste of the cognac poured hours ago. *Should I sleep on this first before sending it to McGarry?* He decided to hit "Save as draft" and moved to his favorite armchair.

He punched a number into his cell phone. "Hello, Hugh, I wonder what you're up to?" *I don't guess he'll catch my humor.*

"I'm up to my eyeballs trying to comprehend what the hell happened at the convention, as if you didn't know." McGarry sounded disturbed. "What's the matter calling at this hour and when do I get your piece?"

Fletcher snickered into the phone and said, "Can you imagine what our friends at the *New York Times* and the *Washington Post* are going through right now?"

"Yeah, real comical. But I'm more concerned about getting your commentary out first. Where is it?"

"I'm working on it, Hugh. Don't push me."

"Whaddya mean, don't push," McGarry bellowed. "This is the news event of the year and we have to get our side of the story out."

"I hear you," Fletcher said nodding, as if his boss were in the room. "It's just that it's not the way political analysis works. My immediate viewpoint might be different in the light of day."

"Bullshit, Fletcher. Get the story to me tonight!"

Fletcher went back to his computer. He stared at his draft for several minutes. *I won't change a thing and I'll just continue from where I left off.*

"Nuts. Let me get McGarry his damn story."

I expect we will see a real life personal tragedy for Herbert Quinton Atkinsen. It is regrettable and will not be pleasant.

He hit Send.

Fletcher changed his position in bed umpteen times. He wondered about reactions to the VP candidate from the press, radio and TV commentators, and Senator Robinson.

"Should I admire or quiz Atkinsen's self-confidence and motive to have an opposition party member at the highest echelon of his administration?" he asked himself.

Maybe I can retract the editorial.

He went to the kitchen for a diet Pepsi and sat as his computer again. He said aloud his follow-up notes as he typed:

"One, the decision to open up the VP spot at future conventions is a remarkable breakthrough, no more rubber stamp;

Two, regardless of what I wrote in the editorial, there is an indisputable honesty in the President's openness. It's refreshing;

Three, a case could be made that Atkinsen has displayed statesmanship, and courage to boot;

Four, is this ticket an alliance of convenience or integrity?

Five, have I overlooked the strength of George Granger? How does the Electoral College process handle this anomaly? How will the President's message resonate with the public? Check Zogby poll results."

I'll dwell on these points in the morning and discuss the options with McGarry.

Sleep came easy this time.

Chapter Forty Three

"That f'ing turncoat," Robinson snarled to his inner circle. "Granger will live to regret his switch."

His uncharacteristic rage subsided when his senior advisor said, "Let's consider where we go from here, J.B.?" This elderly friend was the sole confidant to take this liberty

Before responding, Robinson took time to calm down and scheme. *What can we do to discredit the two of them?* He had a pessimistic feeling about Atkinsen and Granger becoming allies.

"Have you come up with any information about their backgrounds that we can use in the campaign?" he inquired.

"I've learned who the President's psychiatrist is. We might be able to discover what medication he's been taken."

Robinson nodded, "Keep on that. I'm convinced he's had a problem. In fact, isn't it reasonable to assume he's taking something to control moodiness? I've witnessed some strange behavior."

Another said, "I've looked into his Atlanta home. There's a housekeeper by the name of Sanchez who may be an illegal alien. We can get that out on a blog and let him squirm out of it."

"Do it!" said Robinson. "At the very least, it will be a distraction from his stump message."

"Senator, the reason for the firing of Frank Simon has never come to light. We could insinuate that energy companies paid kickbacks to the Department of Energy for contracts, and let the chips fall where they may."

"Okay, but don't come on too strong against Frank Simon."

"We could try a forged letter like we did in Pittsburgh the last time and—"

"Forget it!" Robinson interrupted. "That was sleazy."

"Senator, the problem we have is that Atkinsen has been above board in his dealings with committee chairs and—"

"That's bull," Robinson shouted. "He's not that lily white. Wagner handles the dirty work. Now what else can we do?"

"Sir, how about we investigate the sudden resignation of former Vice-President Styles?"

"A valid vulnerability to probe," Robinson acknowledged. "I'll handle that one myself."

The youngest member of the group raised his hand and smiled. "No need to fabricate anything for what I uncovered."

"Really."

"Remember the "rubbergate" banking scandal back in 1992," he said to the curious onlookers. "Well, George Granger was one of the House members who overdrew his checking account. While he got away with it because it was legal under House rules, it would be an embarrassment to publicize this again and point to his poor judgment and character."

"I like it," Robinson said smiling. "Make a big issue of it on talk shows, etcetera."

"J.B., how about we use some of our war chest to woo their party officials who will become electors in the Electoral College to jump ship? There's a lot of majority party activists disillusioned with the Atkinsen ticket."

"Sonofabitch, that's a great idea to divide them. Allocate funds to our strongest states, but be discreet." He paused and added, "Let me tell you all that I've encouraged, secretly of course, a write-in movement for Admiral Farrell. He's expressed serious concern for the administration's military deployment policy. He'll take votes away from Atkinsen." He glared at each man and said, "Remember, keep it quiet!"

"Yes, sir. Actually, it's only a matter of time before the Admiral gets the bug for politics."

Robinson checked the time and said, "I'm due at a Commerce Committee hearing. Thank you, gentlemen. Let's meet again in one week."

I'm not going to tell them about my meeting with Hitoshi.

* * *

"Fletcher Jones here."

"It's Senator Robinson."

"Yes, Senator. What can I do for you?"

"I'll get right to the point. I told you several weeks ago I have some information for you that should be brought to the attention of the public. It concerns the President." Robinson paused, certain he had piqued the journalist's interest. "By the way, I thoroughly enjoyed your editorial on the President's choice for Vice-President."

"Sure thing. Let me get something to write on ... ready."

"Mr. Jones, ever since Atkinsen's wife died, it's obvious that his behavior has been strange at times. I'm not going to rehash what is general knowledge, but I've become aware that Atkinsen is taking an anti-depressant."

"Got it," Fletcher said. "Senator, why don't you get this salient fact to the news media yourself?"

"If I or my staff did, it would smack of mean politics. My obligation here is to see that the electorate is aware the President is on strong medication before they decide how they're going to vote."

"I'll consider how to make known the information."

"Fine. I had promised you an exclusive, but now I also have a scoop for you. A dependable source in the administration informed me why the Vice-President resigned."

There was silence on the other end. "Did you hear me?"

"Senator, this isn't off the record, is it?"

"You handle this anyway you see fit, okay. The inside story is Styles wanted to be president and demanded Atkinsen step aside for health reasons. He—"

"Pardon me, but that's the first I've heard of anything like that, whether in the news or on talk shows. If true, your two stories taken together paint a devastating picture for the President."

Robinson detected astonishment in Jones' voice. "I suspect you have your own means of verifying the facts. Good night, Mr. Jones."

Robinson hung up. He felt smug.

When the firestorm starts, it'll be the end of Atkinsen and Granger.

Chapter Forty Four

The White House
President Herbert Q. Atkinson
Press Release

President Atkinsen held a two hour meeting this morning with the Vice-President nominee, House Minority Leader George Granger. This was their first meeting since the national convention earlier this month. It has been described at a strategy session for the general election and an exchange of views on the roles each would assume on the campaign and in a second term.

The President has communicated his appreciation to National Committee Chairman, Oscar Jackman, for resolving all disputes and grievances following the national convention. "A viable party is essential to defeat the opposition," the President wrote to Chairman Jackman.

President Atkinsen issued a statement: "I'm pleased to have such a distinguished and highly qualified individual as George Granger as my partner in this critical election. For the next two months we will focus on presenting a new approach to government in order to eliminate the partisan malaise that exists in Washington today. In addition, we assure our Allies around the world that we will honor our commitments. Our team is positioned to achieve the goal of my reelection as President of the United States. I look forward to the challenge and responsibility."

Congressman Granger released the following: "It is an honor for me to work with President Atkinsen at this important time in history. While we have established a new kind of bipartisan partnership, the goal of responsible government is our highest priority. I acknowledge the good wishes of support I have received since the convention and promise to perform to the best of my ability on behalf of the President and the country."

The Atkinsen/Granger ticket has posted their campaign trip schedules on their websites, which commence on Labor Day. The President will attend an AFL-CIO dinner in Tampa, Florida, and Congressman Granger will march in a Labor Day parade in Detroit, Michigan.

The website includes a photo of the two men, arms raised in a demonstration of unity.

Chapter Forty Five

"What the hell were you thinking?' the President screamed at Wagner. Atkinsen had marched down to the office of his Chief of Staff, expecting the few minutes would cool his temper. "How did you let this happen?"

Wagner looked flustered. "Mr. President, I'm not sure I know what you're referring to," he stammered.

"I'm referring to the TV campaign ad about Senator Robinson and a date rape charge," the President said, in a slow, deliberate voice.

Wagner searched through files on his desk as he replied, "Mr. President, we got that information from the *Lexington Herald-Leader*. His name was identified in a police report about a possible rape of another student at the University of Kentucky."

"So without verification you hinted strongly in the ad at his bad character ... based on a possible misdeed." *This is incredulous.* He stomped around Wagner's office.

"Well the consulting firm felt it reflected on his character and the public should make its own judgment about the incident," Wagner said.

"Goddamnit, Steve. I just got off the phone with Robinson. That story was blown out of proportion and later retracted."

"But he pulls those kinds of things all the time with you and Granger and—"

"Let's stop this right now!" Atkinsen shouted between his teeth. "First of all, you know how I feel about negative campaigns and dirty gossip. I'll be damned if I have to sacrifice my principles to win this thing. We agreed on that guideline four years ago. Right?"

"Yes, sir."

"Guess who the girl in question was?"

Wagner shrugged.

"It's his wife. They were married during junior semester over forty years ago."

"Oh no," Wagner exclaimed, grabbing the back of his neck with both hands.

"I apologized to Senator Robinson and told him the ad in all markets would be pulled immediately. The shit will hit the fan tomorrow when the story will be reported in the press and on TV. You better hope the story doesn't have legs."

The President shook his head in anger and walked to the door. Turning back to face Wagner he said in a restrained voice, "The campaign had been going great up to now once the party leaders saw the wisdom of the ticket. We've had big crowds at our rallies. None of Robinson's dirty tricks have hurt us. The polls show that our integration message is gaining acceptance."

Face flushed, Atkinsen strode to Wagner's desk, pounding it once with his fist. "You blew this one, Steve. With only one month to go before the election, you just stick to operating the White House."

Atkinsen backed away and added, "While I'm at it, don't be so abrasive with your staff and the reporters. I'll speak to you about all this again when the election's over."

Wagner was speechless. He acknowledged the President's departure with a subdued nod.

As Atkinsen walked back to the Oval Office, he reflected on the trauma Ellen must have faced with her seduction and the subsequent publicity.

* * *

Fletcher Jones entered the bar in Alexandria about 10:30. He allowed his companion to choose this out-of-the-way location for a nightcap before retiring to the young man's condo. Fletcher had ordered two Sambucas on the rocks when he glanced to the far end of the bar.

I don't believe it! It's the President's Chief of Staff.

"Sonny, something has come up, so why don't we call it a night and I'll catch up with you some other time," Fletcher said. *Get lost, kid.*

He picked up both drinks and casually moved past a few customers. "Mind if I sit next to you, Mr. Wagner?"

"It's a free country," Wagner said, louder than was necessary. "Oh, I know you," he continued, squinting at his uninvited bar partner. "You're Fletcher Jones."

"Right you are."

"What brings you doing down here?"

"I covered the VP candidates town meetings in DC and—"

"So what didya think?"

"Hughes had his talking points down pat, but got a little windy with his responses," Fletcher replied. "Granger labored to explain his cross-over, but I admired his candor. There's a certain selflessness about him that's appealing."

"Hey, that's good news."

He's inebriated. His combative nature mellows with booze.

"And what are you celebrating in this godforsaken place?" Fletcher asked, stimulated about this chance opportunity for an exclusive. *Carpe diem.*

"Does it look like I'm celebratin? Of course. Bartender, another scotch for me and my friend."

"I already have two."

"Then two more for me so I can catch up," Wagner called out.

"Wagner, you deserve a break after all that has transpired this year, starting with the State of the Union."

"Isn't that the truth?" Wagner said, imbibing the last drop in his glass before the new drinks arrived.

"The President has certainly startled many of us with his unforeseen actions. You—"

Wagner jumped in, "I didn't know a damn thing about what he said in the State of the Union address. I felt like a punching bag after it. And it resulted in an assassination attempt no less." He burped. "Excuse me."

"What about Brown and Simon?" His journalistic knack was roused by a talkative insider.

"The President outsmarted all of us on that one. Those changes in his cabinet were the proper moves to initiate."

Fletcher raised his glass to Wagner in a silent toast. Wagner reacted in kind.

"Off the record, what's behind his selection of Granger for VP? It's a compelling and curious, even mysterious, ticket."

Wagner took a sip of his drink and rested his right elbow on the mahogany bar. "He wouldn't have been my choice, but my opinions don't carry a lot of weight these days."

Do I detect he is irritated with the President?

"The scuttlebutt is that Grant had something to do with the selection."

"That old fart," Wagner chimed in, spilling drops of his drink on the bar and his suit jacket sleeve. "Pompous old man thinks he knows everything."

"I always respected Clark Styles," Fletcher said, hoping to elicit the inside scoop on his resignation. "Too bad his political career ended that way."

"Yeah, well the President put himself on the spot the way he handled that situation," Wagner sighed, sounding wary.

"My sources tell me Styles wanted Atkinsen to step down so he could run for president."

"Bullshit," Wagner shouted, causing the bartender and the only couple at the bar to stare at them. Wagner motioned for Jones to come close and slurred, "The President protected his VP from something I'm not aware of. In any case Styles holds Atkinsen in high esteem."

"Really," Fletcher said, dubious of Wagner's opinion in his condition. "I have pretty reliable contacts for my information."

"This much I know. The President did a special favor for his VP. You can take it to the bank." Wagner looked at his watch and swallowed half his drink.

"Can I give you a drive home?"

"Naw, a taxi is picking me up in ten minutes," Wagner answered, looking like he could use a deep sleep.

"You can tell your boss I'm sorry for my column suggesting he should have an MRI."

I don't think he heard me.

"Thanks for the company and I'm sure I'll see you on the campaign trail," Fletcher said louder, finishing the one snifter of Sambuca.

"Maybe."

As Fletcher walked to his car, he wondered which story to believe and the status of the campaign. "McGarry thinks Robinson is a shoo-in to win the election," he whispered. "So did I."

His car accelerated at a fast pace and went through a stop sign at the end of the long parking lot.

"Somebody's lying to me and I'm going to find out who it is," he resolved, pitching the unpaid parking ticket in the back seat.

Chapter Forty Six

"Thanks for joining me for the next couple of days, Harry," the President shouted to his advisor, above the noise of the whirling helicopter blades. "When was the last time you were on a campaign swing?"

"I remember it well. It was one day four years ago when you alerted the Teacher's Union that the retirement benefits of their members may be reduced similar to corporate America." His voice quivered as the ride turned bumpy.

"Don't remind me of that fiasco."

Atkinsen let the newspaper fall on his lap, after reading Robert Novak's column, and said, "I should be mad at you, Harry, for suggesting I even mention the repeal of the Seventeenth Amendment. Nebraska legislators got wind of it and are upset because it casts William Jennings Bryan in a bad light, among other things."

"Sorry about that, Mr. President, but I'm convinced its day will come. Senators will consider—"

"Just drop it, okay, Harry! This is politics, not academia." The President flipped the newspaper to his advisor and friend, sensing for the first time that Grant was showing his age. "Let me give you some personal info to chew on," he said, anxious to change the subject. "It'll make you wonder if destiny is playing a hand in my reelection."

"I'm listening, but I'll be glad when we're back on the ground," Grant grunted, looking like he had seen a ghost.

"You knew Woodrow Wilson's wife died during his first term, but did you know her name was Ellen?" A rhetorical question. "Did you know she was from Georgia, same as my Ellen? Wilson's biography says his wife was concerned about the poor and had an angelic personality. Remind you of anyone?"

Grant perked up and said, "Fascinating! Wilson won a second term so it may be a sign of things to come." He steadied himself in his seat and added, "Herb, I wasn't aware of those coincidences, but I'm sure you also know Wilson remarried a year after his wife's death."

"Well I have no intention of getting married to achieve a similar fate. It's just not in the cards."

"We're almost there, Mr. President," Williams called out from the front seat.

"Thank you, Agent Williams," the President acknowledged, echoed by a comforted Harry Grant.

The heliport at Newark/Liberty International Airport came into sight, glistening from the bright sun on a beautiful, cloudless early October afternoon.

* * *

Roberto Morales, leader of the *Save the UN* movement, sneered at the report the President had reversed his statement on the flow of illegal immigrants. He told his followers that, "The American President panders to Hispanic voters. We must show up in full force at his rally in Newark." He was disappointed he couldn't get closer to the President at Yankee Stadium.

"Roberto, we have almost ten thousand dollars to last until the election, more than we need," his underling, Miguel, said.

"I know. Our cause has generous supporters," Morales said. "And stop staring at my blonde hair!"

Rickman is a fool. I could care less about the UN.

"The United Nation's issue has been a perfect cover for me," he whispered out of Miguel's earshot.

Miguel asked, "Should I order more *Save the UN* placards for the protest in Newark? And I think we need more box lunches."

"Don't be so concerned with manpower at the rally or the number of placards. There's enough." Roberto blew cigarette smoke at Miguel, as his beady eyes reread the *Newark Star Ledger's* article of the President's visit. "The rally is outdoors so I'm changing our plans. You and I will mingle with the crowd at Prudential Plaza and—"

"But what about our people? Who will direct them so they are heard?"

"Miguel, you worry too much. They have flyers telling them what to do and where to assemble. You and I have a bigger mission. Meet me in the lobby in thirty minutes."

Roberto Morales had a dark reputation in the sinister global underworld as another Carlos. Drug cartels in South America had paid handsome sums for his clandestine missions against law enforcement agents, who were getting too close to their heroine and marijuana operations. Always working alone, Morales was a master at infiltration and disguise, which earned him the nickname *the Chameleon*. He was fluent in several languages. A modest beach home on the island of Majorca was his safe refuge.

After a summit meeting of South American leaders with President Atkinsen, a new initiative to "go to war" against drug traffickers had been adopted. Atkinsen promised military and economic support for the plan. "I'm committed to reduce this plague on our young."

Morales unlocked the carrying case which had been mailed by diplomatic courier to the embassy and hand-delivered to him at the Comfort Inn in Newark the previous evening. He read the communiqué from a South American government: *In accordance with your instructions, $500,000 has been deposited in a Swiss bank account. As discussed, your assignment is to weaken the US President politically or physically to prevent his victory in November. The enclosed is one method you may wish to employ. We expect the same success as on previous assignments.*

"The American President brought this on himself for being overly belligerent against the drug cartel," Morales stated out loud. "He should mind his own business ... and let buyers enjoy themselves."

Morales removed two hypodermic needles and a vial of curare. *If I can get close to him, just a small amount of curare will paralyze him in minutes, which gives me time to escape.* He removed the cap from one needle and plunged the syringe to five cc of curare. *Amazing how medical science has used this deadly poison as a safe muscle relaxer.* He replaced the cap and put the covered needle in his shirt pocket. Before leaving the room to meet Miguel, Morales lit a match and set the communiqué on fire.

"This may be my only opportunity to come in close contact with the President," Morales mouthed. "It's worth the chance."

* * *

Russell Barrett and Sam Heffernan were in the back seat of the lead car in the motorcade to Prudential Plaza.

"Sam, take a look through these pictures of people in the Trip File," Barrett said, as they sped by a slum area on the outskirts of Newark. I wonder if he'll notice there are three pictures of the same guy.

"Okay," Sam said. After a few minutes, he handed the pictures back and said, "Hey, I forgot to congratulate you on your engagement."

"Thanks. I figured I can't do any better than Kathleen so why not …I'm only kidding," he laughed. "She's a wonderful person and I'm a very lucky guy." Barrett thought of his return to DC and then remembered, "After this rally, we have one more stop in Cherry Hill."

Kathleen will be happy to know I'm requesting a transfer to counterfeiting duty after this trip.

The motorcade turned off Broad Street into the open plaza in front of several tall office buildings. Newark police cordoned off the crowd away from a make-shift stage where the Mayor and the Chairman of the Latino Progressive Association would greet the President. An extra detail of Secret Service agents were on hand stationed throughout the plaza.

Barrett and Heffernan observed the crowd as the President exited the limo, while Grant stayed behind for this brief, symbolic rally.

Atkinsen bounded up the steps to the stage. He was met with polite applause and some boos from the small gathering of Hispanic leaders from Northeastern counties of New Jersey. A larger crowd could be seen across the street from the Plaza, including a noisy protest group chanting *Save the UN*. A convoy of Post Office trucks lining the sides of the Plaza shielded the stage from the protestors.

For ten minutes Barrett heard parts of a stump speech in which the President promised that those who work to help the American economy and pay taxes will be legal and on the road toward citizenship. His standard ending that, "America is a nation of immigrants, which makes us great," resulted in shouts of *Viva el Presidente.*

"Oh crap," Barrett said, as he saw the President shaking hands and giving high fives to the line of people along the roped off area. Rather than go directly to the limo, Atkinsen veered off to the crowd and was "pounding flesh" as politicos were compelled to do.

Barrett noted that Ashton Williams was at the President's shoulder urging him to keep moving. Williams waved to him to stay ahead of them. Barrett was about fifteen feet in front scanning the faces and movements of people who were waving and shouting, *Aqui, por favor.*

Last time Shortstop was this close to a crowd, someone almost took his watch, Barrett recalled. *Where the hell is Heffernan? Sonofagun, there he is right behind the President, pushing outstretched hands and arms away.*

Barrett felt his nerve endings tingling. Feeling like he was getting the shakes, he wondered if he should he see a doctor.

Near the end of the line, he noticed the forth man ahead along the rope, a short stocky Hispanic, shifted places with a taller handsome dark man with wavy blonde hair. The tall man was leaning over the rope with his arms folded across his chest, peering at the oncoming President.

I've seen that guy before.

Williams had picked up the pace with the President at his side, like they were joined at the hip. They were only two arms-lengths behind Barrett.

Staying focused on the tall man, Barrett watched him unfold his arms and hold his right hand on his chest with his fist cupped. *Is he holding a pen? Is it a ...*

"Knife," Barrett shouted into his microphone.

He lunged at the man, who raised his right hand to fend off the attack. Barrett felt a scratch across his hand. They wrestled to the ground as spectators were pushed away amid pushing and screaming.

Barrett was kicking away at air.

Morales ended up on top of Barrett's back and jammed his face on the asphalt. *"Diablo,"* grunted the *Chameleon.*

Bleeding from a gash on his cheekbone and a broken nose, Barrett felt the weight lift off his back. *He wants to stand and escape.* He grabbed the man's jacket and held tight, in the face of a spreading weakness. Footsteps and a struggle surrounded him, drowning out loud screeches. As he started to black out, his grip on the jacket was loosened.

The tall man's getting away.

He heard Williams' voice say, "Get the cuffs on the guy and carry him to the car. I'm going with the President in the limo and get out of here."

I can't breathe!

Artificial respiration?

I'm coming home to you, Kathleen.

"You'll be okay, Russ."

Heffernan's words were the last thing he heard before losing consciousness.

* * *

"Are you Kathleen?"

"Yes."

"I'm Ashton Williams."

She nodded, seemingly in a daze. The early diagnosis of Russ' possible paralysis caused her deep distress.

"He's been asking for you."

"How is he?"

As Williams led her to a private room of Newark General Hospital, he said, "You'll see for yourself."

She looked in the room. The bed was vacant.

"Surprise!" Barrett yelled, as he emerged from a hiding place behind the door. He twirled her around and hugged her.

"You scared me to death," Kathleen shrieked, bursting into tears. "I thought you were going to die."

"So did the doctors. It took four days for the poison to leave my system." He placed both hands on her face and said, "If I didn't get to see you soon, I definitely would have died."

"You handsome brute," she cried, touching his nose.

"Not so hard, Kathleen, it still hurts."

He picked her up in his arms and kissed her on the lips.

Although his manner was characteristically playful, she felt elated by his display of tenderness. "I've missed you, Russ, and I was worried sick." Her head hung down as she whispered, "Just miserable."

To cheer her up he said, "Williams told me I've been transferred to a desk job at headquarters as a Global Terror analyst and—"

"I'm so glad," she announced, finally able to smile.

"He also passed along a message from President Atkinsen wishing me well and wondering 'if I find trouble or does trouble find me.'"

"You must be real proud," she said, spoken like an adoring fan.

"They're releasing me from this place in an hour and we're going to be busy the rest of the day."

"Why? What are we going to do?"

"We're going to your church to set the date for our wedding, don't you know."

"Oooh, Russ. Can I call my mother and go shopping for a wedding gown?"

"Absolutely, but I'd marry you in your bathing suit."

She gave him her best Maureen O'Hara look and sighed, "I don't know why, but I love you with all my heart."

Chapter Forty Seven

Senator Robinson read the newspaper reports of the attempt on the President's life. "If this keeps up, he'll get a sympathy vote for sure," he mumbled to himself.

The ups and downs of the campaign were frustrating him. Nevertheless, poll numbers gave the Robinson/Hughes ticket a six point lead over Atkinsen/Granger with less than a month to go to Election Day. Analysts attributed the President's lost ground to the false rape charge, despite his genuine apology.

Robinson's staff had prepared talking points for the lone debate with Atkinsen next week. The negative impact of the President's UN proposals was highlighted as well as foreign policy differences, most notably on the Middle East. He planned to introduce a non-intervention initiative.

The Senator had cut short campaigning in Wisconsin in order to attend a Senate Commerce Committee meeting. Several resolutions relevant to the Kansas City SmartPort project were on the agenda for vote.

The Commerce Committee of the Senate consisted of eight members of the Majority party, including the Chairperson, and seven members from the opposition Minority.

For the first twenty minutes of the meeting an Under-Secretary of the Commerce Department recited statistics on trade between the US and Mexico since the North American Treaty Agreement, which had eliminated most tariffs, except for agricultural products.

"Senators, trade between our country and our two neighbors now amounts to two point four billion dollars per day, that is, per day."

"Pardon me," the senior Senator of the Majority from Maine, Phillip Vogel, interrupted. "Mr. Chairman, I believe we can read the data and we're wasting time listening to the Under-Secretary recite a series of numbers."

"Mr. Chairman," Robinson called out. "While I agree with the gentleman's point, suffice it to say that NAFTA has resulted in a substantial increase in trade between the two countries, particularly for automobiles and computers. Our economies have increased above average since it was adopted. Furthermore,—"

"May the respected gentleman yield for a point of order?" Vogel asked.

Seeing a nod of approval from Robinson, Vogel said, "I'm delighted to hear the comments from the esteemed Senator. Some of us have a long memory and can recall in 1993 that Senator Robinson was a vociferous opponent of the NAFTA negotiation. Perhaps, we may get the benefit of his newfound good sense ... over a cup of coffee."

Robinson looked away without comment, although he observed the arched eyebrows of his colleagues. *Not the time for me to get into a hassle.*

Once the Chairman noted that Robinson was not baited into a response, he checked the agenda and stated, "We'll now take up the resolution concerning the Kansas City Custom Port, currently under construction, for Mexican officials. As you know this Custom Port is a necessary aspect of the KC SmartPort project. The resolution is to recommend to the State Department that the land be designated as Mexican territory."

Again Vogel was first to speak. "I recognize the need for Mexican officials to inspect cargo from the Kansas City transportation network for export to Mexico and the Pacific Rim countries. The cost savings are substantial indeed. However, I'm not convinced that it is necessary to cede the land."

Robinson's colleague in the Minority was next to comment.

"It is encouraging for me to see the senior Senator from Maine disengage himself from the position of his party. We hope that he may influence his colleagues accordingly. It is not in our best interest to permit Mexican territory right in our heartland. The reasons are clear, that is, border security issues and more illegal immigration. There are no uniform standards of cargo inspection and employee background checks. In fact, this entire Kansas City project may lead to dissolution of the borders between us, Mexico and Canada."

Supporters of the resolution raised their hands to be heard. The Chairman said, "Regarding the opinion of my colleague from Maine and the opposition party, this resolution simply recognizes that the location and legal rights of the officials should be deemed Mexican territory, similar to an Embassy, and subject to their government's direction."

The Minority committee members looked to Senator Robinson, who remained silent.

The Minority spokesperson continued, "Mr. Chairman, there are cultural and immigration issues that threaten our security and—"

"Sir," the Chairman interrupted, "Homeland Security is fully apprised of the KC project and coordination is underway to assure safe border crossings."

Members of his party stared at Robinson with incredulous looks. He was quiet, seemingly more interested in taking notes.

The Chair announced it was time to vote on the resolution, which would be referred to the full senate. "Majority Leader Lewis wants to bring the resolution out of committee to the senate floor," he reported.

A show of hands counted eight in favor and six opposed. The Chairman would vote only to break a tie. The resolution passed.

Immediately following adjournment, the Minority members held a caucus and questioned Robinson. He could feel the resentment in the air. Curses could be heard in the ante-room. The usual decorum was disregarded.

"Senator, first, you give them a gratuitous endorsement on NAFTA, which has cost American jobs. Inroads to gain AFL-CIO support may have been reversed. Then we lose the argument on the Custom Port because of your silence and your vote in favor. Your position is both disappointing and outrageous. We expected you would be with us against giving Mexico sovereignty on US soil."

"Sir, don't be so insolent!" Robinson's retort was unequivocal. He stood to address the group. "Gentlemen, can't you see that my vote, whether a No vote or Abstain, had no bearing on the outcome. You know the Chairman would vote in favor to break the tie. I'm now in a position to ask for reconsideration to change my vote."

He hesitated to see if he were softening their annoyance.

"Frankly, my vote was also to remove a ·charge that Atkinsen could make against me in our debate. You have heard him say that my policies would hinder world trade and slow our economy." He paused and, with a grin, said, "Besides, I'll make sure that there's no senate vote until after the election."

Robinson enjoyed a late night cognac.

I still have their support. Bruce should be happy.

Chapter Forty Eight

"George, I want you to watch *Sixty Minutes* tonight."

"Yes sir, Mr. President, I will," Granger said. He had taken took the call in a private conference room in the Cleveland hotel.

"It's an opportunity for me to clear the air before any more wild rumors get out and hurt our campaign."

Atkinsen worried about how the interview would be received by the public, but realized he must be seen as straightforward. He was aware the bloggers were having a field day with innuendos. *It'll be all over national news and talk shows tomorrow.*

"I want you to know that Chairman Jackman is working hard to get pledges of support for the ticket from my party's state electors."

"I know that was your biggest concern," Granger acknowledged. "It would be the first time the Electoral College might vote to split the top spots since the Twelfth Amendment was adopted. A tough challenge for Jackman!"

"Meanwhile, how are the rallies in Ohio going?" the President asked. He had heard that the initial response to Granger at party member gatherings was "tepid, at best".

"I do sense the public accepts our team. Certainly, there's less antagonism than before and larger crowds. Curiosity about the ticket has generated a lot of interest."

"Well, that's some progress anyway. Robinson and his people aren't letting up on that issue. He's trying like hell to drive a wedge between us. Those zingers over our difference on my Supreme Court nominee, Melissa Danbury, have hurt a bit. On the other hand, even anti-Atkinsen journalists have dropped the coverage of Robinson's accusations I've been too cozy with lobbyists."

Atkinsen checked the time and organized papers on his desk at random while Granger reported that high gas prices was the hot topic at each campaign stop, and union leaders are still upset at our position on NAFTA.

"Grant has informed me that the UN matter is no longer a negative with the public and, in fact, is trending in our favor," the President interjected.

"Mr. President, I've always thought you were absolutely right on about the UN corrupt administration so that doesn't surprise me," Granger volunteered. "Here's another thing I'm hearing on the stump. There seems to be a disconnect between the public's understanding of isolationist policies and the message from Robinson himself. Even his running mate made off-the-cuff remarks to a reporter that spoke well of a North American Union with Mexico and Canada."

"George, if you and I avoid distractions and stay on point, we can change a lot of minds. Stick with it."

"Yes sir."

"Oh, George, soon as you're back in DC, let's get together at the White House. There are a few matters that have bothered me that we have to clear up."

"Really, Mr. President," Granger replied in an uncertain tone. "Yes, I look forward to meeting with you. Good luck tonight."

"Thanks. First, I'll handle the Allcott problem. Then I have to resolve an unavoidable distraction on *Sixty Minutes*."

* * *

"Allcott speaking."

"Bob, President Atkinsen."

"Oh, yes, Mr. President. I didn't expect—"

"I don't have much time with my TV appearance and all."

"Of course, sir. Good luck."

"I want the bad-mouthing of my ticket to stop. I know how you felt about not knowing in advance my selection for Vice-President."

Allcott said in a hoarse voice, "I was extremely—"

"I know, but get over it. Look at the big picture. If Robinson wins, you're out as Speaker."

"Sure, but—"

"Let me finish. If I'm reelected and carry the House, how do you think our party members will feel about you as Speaker again after your negative attacks against the ticket?"

"It's a matter of principle with me. Picking a running mate from the opposition party is contrary—"

"Stop! I understand your position. For that reason I won't use my influence to derail your bid to hold the Speaker spot. Do we understand one another?"

There was a pause. Allcott cleared his throat.

"Okay, I'll keep my criticisms to myself. Thank you for the call, Mr. President."

"Thank you, Bob."

* * *

No sooner had the call with Allcott ended, Atkinsen's secretary buzzed and said, "Mr. President, the producer for tonight's interview is here to see you."

"Already." He instinctively checked his watch, sensing that time had become his enemy. "Give me five minutes and show him in." *What was his name again …?*

Without warning or reason, Atkinsen felt apprehensive. He wondered if it were the unpleasant meeting to be held with George Granger that setback his good mood; or was it the inquisition expected from the cunning Mike Wallace?

Chapter Forty Nine

"Mr. President, this is Mrs. Sanders. She—"

The visitor interrupted. "Mr. President, my name is Sandy Sanders. I'm the associate producer for the telecast."

Atkinsen stood and walked to the front of his desk to greet the woman. "Good afternoon. Mrs. …Mrs. Sanders, is it?" He was taken aback by the petite lady and her abrupt entrance. "You're early, aren't you?"

"Yes sir, the arrangements take much longer when we're on location." She pointed to the knot on his tie. "Oh, it's a great pleasure to meet you."

"Yes, right, my pleasure as well," he said, as he sized her up and straightened his tie. "Sandy Sanders …sounds whimsical. People must have fun with your name. I guess you can blame your husband for that." When he saw her arched eyebrows, he felt sheepish for his comment.

"Yes, well, things like that happen in life."

"True." Looking at her poker-face, he thought that was a stupid thing for him to say about her name.

"Mr. President, I'm sure you're familiar with preparations for appearing on camera, but I would like to review the interview format with you."

"Let's do it."

"Oh, I've left something outside," she stuttered. "I'll be right back, if that's okay."

He nodded. As she reached the door, he called out, "How about the Oval Office as a Green Room?"

She surveyed the office and replied, "Fantastic," smiling for the first time.

Wow! What an engaging smile. She's very attractive.

He only glanced at the list she gave him. He thought of the interview and the guile of Mike Wallace. *I'm ready for him.*

There was a soft knock on the door and she returned. "May we continue, Mr. President?"

"Sure thing. Mrs. Sanders, is everything all right?"

"I suppose its nervous energy. I've—"

"Why don't you have a seat?" His tone was solicitous.

Before she could respond, he motioned to the sitting area. She moved to the couch as he sat in the armchair to her left. As she covered the few simple details of the interview, Atkinsen interrupted, "Why haven't we met before when I've been on *Sixty Minutes*?"

"Actually, we met briefly. As associate producer I normally play a support role, you know, behind the scenes. My producer came down with a stomach virus yesterday so I'm flying solo for this telecast. Truthfully, I am a little nervous because I've seen too many things go wrong on the show in the past." She looked at the ceiling and said, "I can't believe I'm saying all this. Thank you for your patience, Mr. President."

"You're doing fine …relax.!"

"I also sat several pews behind you at St. John's on Christmas and Easter Sunday."

"Oh." The occasions flashed before his eyes.

Sandy stood to leave.

He asked, "What does your husband do?"

Facing the door she answered, "My husband had been a labor lawyer here in Washington. In fact, he worked in the same firm as Mr. Wagner."

"Really."

She turned to face the President and said, "My husband died six years ago from—"

"I'm sorry …I didn't know." His face reddened from his earlier silly remark about her name.

"Thank you. He died suddenly from a heart attack. Never even had a problem before that." She shrugged her shoulders as if there were nothing more to say.

"I know how devastating the loss of a spouse is. If you don't mind me asking, how are you adjusting to life without him?"

She appeared surprised at the question and then reclaimed her seat on the couch. "I'm doing okay …not much of a social life, but work is a wonderful diversion. I travel to New York City quite a bit."

"How did you become a television producer?"

She made herself comfortable and said, "I was a Communications major in college and worked as an intern at a local TV station in Nashville for three summers."

As he listened to her describe her background and living in the Nations Capital, he was taken by the soothing sound of her voice not evident in her business persona.

"After years of part-time employment here in DC, the station asked me to stay full-time when my husband died with the promise of a promotion to producer. I accepted, of course."

"That's great. I bet you do your job well." He paused and asked, "Can I offer you something to drink …some soda or water?"

"No, thank you." She glanced around the room and said, "I love these paintings."

"Do you? I don't get much chance to visit the National Gallery here in DC. I sure miss it."

"My parents taught me to appreciate artistic work, and it was my minor in college. I try to visit each new exhibition at the museums."

"Uh, uh, interesting." *What else can I ask her*? "How do you like working with that rascal Wallace?"

"Mr. Wallace is a wonderful person as well as a smart reporter." Her response sounded defensive.

"The people he's interviewed might not feel the same way."

"Mr. President, if you don't mind, I do have some matters to attend to." She stood to leave again.

"Of course."

"I'll stop by fifteen minutes before the telecast." She stopped at the door and said, "By the way, my maiden name is Taggert." Out the door she went.

Omigod. Was she really upset with me?

Atkinsen's mood had reversed to upbeat. The remaining time before the telecast went by quickly and included phone conversations with

Wagner and Grant. He decided to openly address the question of his mental history and let the chips fall where they may. For sure, Wallace will be ecstatic to have the facts come out during his interview in front of a national audience. *Did I disturb Mrs. Sanders by my unfavorable reference to Wallace?*

"Welcome back, Sandy Taggert Sanders."

Sandy bit her lip and smiled. She had returned five minutes earlier than expected in order to escort the President to the East Wing.

"Mrs. Sanders, I want to apologize for my inappropriate wisecrack about your name."

"Mr. President, that's not necessary. Frankly, I'm used to hearing funny reactions." She paused and added, "The only reason I mentioned my maiden name was you appeared embarrassed by our introduction."

She wanted to ease my discomfort!

"How did you get the nickname Sandy?"

"Gosh, that's goes back a long time. It started with the color of my hair …then, not now. My father, Scottish to be sure, played golf and his favorite was the professional, Sandy Lyle. So it was inevitable I'd be called Sandy rather than my given name, Sandra."

While she continued speaking, he took note of her light color hair pulled back in a bun. Her brown eyes were sparkling. It seemed to him she used make-up sparingly, except for lipstick, which highlighted her smile and natural beauty. Her thin nose complimented her petite frame, although a business suit hid her body features. I guess she's around fifty or so, he thought.

"Do you mind if I call you Sandy?"

She squinted and said, "Well, no sir, if you wish."

They walked down the hall to the East Wing following Agent Williams.

Should I or not? "Why not?" he mumbled to himself.

"Sandy, Thanksgiving is less than a month away. I wonder …do you have any plans for Thanksgiving dinner?" He had the same feeling in his stomach as a boy asking for his first date.

Sandy looked flabbergasted. Her jaw hung down as she labored to catch her breath. "Eh, no, eh, I really haven't thought about it."

"Thanksgiving at the White House is fabulous," he exclaimed, causing Williams to turn around. "I expect to be alone and I would truly love for you to join me."

"Well, may I let you, I mean, your staff know if I'm free ...that is, if I have a conflict?"

"Certainly, but I'd appreciate it very much if you can make it."

Sandy stared straight ahead as they neared the television set-up. She stopped and said, "Mr. President, no matter what, I want to thank you for the gracious invitation."

They could see Mike Wallace as they entered the room. He whispered to her, "I better get my act together. This is show biz time."

Sandy whispered back, "I'm sure you'll handle the interview well. You have great instincts."

Atkinsen halted, like he was frozen in place. He couldn't believe his ears. Staring at Sandy for a long second, he said, "Thank you."

Chapter Fifty

"Thank you for meeting with us again, Mr. President," Mike Wallace said. "Four years ago, as a candidate for the presidency, you appeared on *Sixty Minutes* and indicated you would cope with the pressure of the job with the aid of strong advisors. Now your Vice-President has resigned over policy differences, two members of your cabinet resigned, and there's hearsay that your health is problematic. Are you capable of a second term in the White House?"

"I welcome the opportunity to speak about my ability to carry on the duties of President. Right off the bat let me say I had been on medication for a posttraumatic stress disorder prescribed by my doctor ever since my wife died almost three years ago. The doctor took me off the small dosage of medicine last December."

"Sir, could you tell us what your medication was?"

"Yes, it was Zoloft, an anti-depressant. I have instructed my doctor to release my treatment and medical records."

"Mr. President, you better than anyone knows the stress of the job. I'm sure you are aware that recently former Senator Thomas Eagleton of Missouri died. The country's reaction to his mental illness in 1972 caused George McGovern to remove him as the VP nominee. Do you believe the public is ready to accept someone with your history?"

Atkinsen glanced at Wagner and Grant standing behind the camera. *Harry insisted I do this interview and expect tough questions from irreverent Mike Wallace.*

"First of all, Senator Eagleton, God rest his soul, had a more serious illness, including hospitalization and electroshock therapy. It was reported he was undergoing counseling for nervous exhaustion at the time."

Wallace added, "And McGovern made the mistake of proclaiming that Eagleton was "one thousand percent fit".

"Indeed," said the President. "In my case the incidents of short term depression following the death of a loved one is not uncommon." His lips quivered ever so slightly as he paused. "Besides loneliness, the only evidence in my behavior was a limited detachment in group meetings, only occasionally at that. I will admit to feeling inadequate for the job at times. In the end I believe the public will judge me on my policies and my character."

"If I may inquire, Mr. President, some have questioned your mental state for your unforeseen and surprising remarks at the State of the Union address earlier this year. What about that?"

"My comments and proposals that evening were designed to incite the Congress to action and to promote needed change in the United Nations. While I did become momentarily emotional, I knew exactly what I was saying, regardless of Vice-President Styles' reaction. The UN must be restructured in order to be most effective. I believed then as I do today that the Secretary-General has abused his authority. As you know I retracted my point on illegal aliens after promises from congressional leaders they will address the problem. I can assure everyone that I am fully capable of conducting a vigorous campaign and hope to receive the people's support on Election Day."

"I'm sorry, Mr. President, but in all candor one must question you're decision to campaign for a second term given the tragedy in your life and your health problem. What can be your motivation?" Wallace had leaned forward and spoke in his unique fatherly tone.

Atkinsen glared at Wallace. *Disrespectful old curmudgeon.* "Last week you interviewed Senator Robinson on this program. Quite simply, I do not want the United States to retreat inside our borders and ignore the technological and communication and economic components of a global society. That's why I'm running against the Senator."

Wallace sat back, hands folded on his chin. "Exactly what do you mean by political integration on the Atkinsen ticket?"

"It's simple in concept, applicable only at the Federal level, and, admittedly, difficult in implementation. That's why it must start at the top, akin to corporate structures. Extreme points of view from either party cannot dictate the direction of the country. Let's face facts; each party has its own divided factions. As far back as Washington's Farewell Address, he warned of political factionalism that ignites animosity."

The television camera caught his hand shake as he sipped his water and allowed his point to linger.

"The polarization in Washington must be diminished by focusing on the country's needs, not powerful special interests or personal agendas. The uppermost core value at the top must be America's interest first, overriding intrinsic party platforms and positions. With direction from a fusion head, politicians can work together civilly on the nation's priorities and maintain core values. One political party should not be viewed as owning an issue that's important to the American people."

"You appear quite passionate about this paragon, but is it practical?"

"Perhaps, Mr. Wallace, we should look back to the Founding Fathers, a Thomas Paine for example, for the lasting import of his *Common Sense*. Today, we must come together behind a common purpose and articulate it for all Americans."

"Mr. President, I would be remiss if I did not refer to your recent outward demeanor," Wallace said. "Those who see you everyday say who seem more patient, more unruffled ...more at ease, all in the face of the travails and vindictiveness of the campaign. Some use the words born-again. How do you respond?"

"Well, I acknowledge a more positive feeling about things and a better sense of tolerance." He stopped, and then raised his hand. "Let me add, for years I focused on my education and my career. So it's not a matter of being born-again, rather I've rediscovered my Episcopalian upbringing."

"One last question, sir. Why the selection of House Minority Leader George Granger as your Vice-Presidential running mate?"

"Our criteria were a devout American first, with incomparable political experience and reputation. I wanted a leader who could bridge the gap between extremists' ideologies. Congressman Granger met those qualifications."

"Interesting use of the word devout," Wallace said. "Thank you, Mr. President."

Atkinsen continued to look at the television camera until the light went out. Out of the corner of his eye he caught a glimpse of Harry Grant who gave him a thumbs-up.

Directly behind Grant was Sandy Sanders. He grinned when he saw her dip her head up and down. *She'll come on Thanksgiving*!

Grant and the President returned to the Oval Office for their standard post-mortem and strategy session. Atkinsen had scanned the room for Sandy after the telecast, but the television crew were scampering around like bees. She was nowhere in sight.

"You did well, Herb," Grant said.

Now it's up to the voters, Atkinsen thought. *Que sera, sera.*

Chapter Fifty One

What the hell does he want? Wagner was reluctant to return the call, but knew it was bad politics to burn bridges. "Missouri is a toss-up and we may need his help," he said to himself.

"Governor Bliss, this is Steve Wagner. I understand you tried to reach me."

"Yes, Steve, thanks for calling back. I haven't seen you out on the campaign trail so I thought I'd give you a call."

"I'm sticking close to the White House these days." He was getting tired of hearing comments about his whereabouts in the midst of a difficult campaign.

"I want to give you some information that may be helpful to the President."

"Really!"

"You don't have to sound so surprised," Bliss said. "I've put aside all the rhetoric during the primary fight as politics as usual. Besides, I have to admire Atkinsen for his choice of VP. It was a gutsy move that has excited a lot of voters in my state, particularly independents. Also, I thought he was sincere and forthcoming on *Sixty Minutes*."

"That's nice of you to say, Governor. So what's the information you have for us?"

"You know we've been working on an inland port in Kansas City at the enlarged Kansas City Southern Railroad terminal and the land on the perimeter of the airport. KC Southern has acquired extensive railroad lines in Mexico. However, there's hot local opposition."

"Well, the President's gave the project concept a thumbs-up. Trade with Mexico has increased and there is great potential for imports and exports with the Asian Pacific Economic Community through Mexico."

"I had spoken to him about it before our debate," Bliss continued. "We agreed it would reduce cargo shipping costs and provide new capacity from the congested California ports. It—"

"We already know that, Governor," Wagner said. "What's your point?"

"I received a call from Congressman Hank Hannigan. Hank represents the district west of town. He's on the Economic sub-committee of the House Commerce Committee. He tells me that a developer has been acquiring land on the cheap in major stops along the route, including in Mexico, and has a substantial interest in the Kansas City SmartPort project."

"Uh huh."

"The name of the company is Development Corp of America," Bliss announced in a lucid tone. "The president is Bruce Robinson."

"Bruce Robinson?"

"He's Senator Robinson's son."

Wagner feigned a so-what reaction. "Governor Bliss, thanks for keeping us informed. I'll look into it first chance I get."

* * *

Wagner opened the file his secretary had left on his desk. He had decided to forego his after-work cocktail and stay late to become more familiar with the scope of the Kansas City SmartPort project.

Clipped to the inside jacket pocket were file references—see North America Free Trade Agreement (NAFTA) and the Safety and Protection Program of North America (SPP).

EXECUTIVE SUMMARY:

--KC project is an inland port solution to the congested ports in California and the east coast. The success of NAFTA has enhanced the project's need.

--KC has the most advantageous transportation infrastructure, including navigable waterways, railroads, and interstate highways. Freight shipping costs are expected to be substantial lower.

--An Intelligent Transportation System (ITS) will be developed by EDS of Dallas (Ross Perot company).

--The expanded KC Southern Railroad (NAFTA Railway) stretches from the Pacific deep water Mexican seaport of Lazaro Cardenas (north of Acapulco) through Laredo, Texas and KC to Canada.

--The settlement of all disputes will be handled by the UN Commission for International Trade Law. This Commission sets rules on the limits on liability of operators of transport terminals.

--A Mexican custom office will be located in Kansas City to speed inspection of cargo for export. State Department approval is required for the facility as Mexican sovereign territory.

CAVEATS:

■   Concern that NAFTA may evolve into a North American Union, similar to the European Union. Immigration, security and cultural issues. Project magnifies AFL-CIO objection to NAFTA.

■   Security concerns that Mexican cargo inspection and regulations are below US standards; Mexican truck drivers in the US??

Wagner pushed away from his desk, threw his head back and closed his eyes. *This thing is like an octopus—the economic and political implications are staggering.*

"This is bigger than just the KC project. I bet the whole thing will hit a trillion dollars," he mouthed to the photograph on the wall of himself shaking hands with President Atkinsen on Inauguration day.

What do I do next?

"Where does Robinson's son fit in ... and Robinson himself?"

He googled on the computer Development Corp of America and read:

Nature of Organization:

The Development Corp of America was formed to acquire land and/or to manage properties and construct malls in Midwest states and Mexico. Several subsidiaries have been formed to comply with local regulations.

Officers:

President—Bruce J. Robinson, MBA, Princeton University

Treasurer—Charles Zeigler, MBA, Princeton University

Secretary---Dorothy Robinson

Capitalization:

The largest investor is the Alpha-Omega Group, a venture capital firm in Minneapolis, Minnesota.

The questions were swirling around in Wagner's brain. He was getting a headache trying to fathom the meaning of everything he had just learned.

Should I tell the President about this?

"No way," he blurted to the empty office. "Atkinsen would accuse me of taking flimsy information to intentionally make the Robinsons look bad."

I'd only get deeper in his doghouse.

Since it was after nine o'clock, Wagner decided he should go home and sleep on it. As he was leaving the office with the file in his briefcase, he turned back to his desk and held the phone for several seconds.

"Director Morgan, its Steve Wagner." He breathed deeply to sound calm.

"Yes Steve, how are you doing? A little late isn't it? My meeting just ended and I'm about to go home?"

"Director, I've received some information that I'd like you to take a look at so I know how to proceed."

"Uh huh. You want me to see the information because you're concerned about a law enforcement issue or situation?"

"That's right, however, I only want your opinion at this time."

"Should I bring my deputy?"

"Not necessary," Wagner answered, almost before the words were out of Morgan's mouth.

There was a pause.

"Suppose I come to your office at seven tomorrow morning. Is that okay?"

"Thank you. I'll see you then."

Wagner locked the file in a lower drawer of his desk. As he left the office, he turned the lights out.

* * *

Steve Wagner finished his second cup of coffee. *I think I only got an hour's sleep last night.*

He checked his wristwatch. "Seven forty-five. What's taking Morgan so long?"

James Morgan was in an adjoining conference room. After being briefed by the Chief of Staff, he had read the file and made one phone call.

"What do you think?" Wagner asked.

Morgan sat in front of Wagner's desk. A frown on his face intimated his confusion. "Well, the Kansas City SmartPort project is public information. Likewise, NAFTA has been in existence since 1994. Although there's been some controversy about the benefits or disadvantages to each country, it did eliminate tariffs that have made trade more efficient and competitive."

"I'm aware of that."

"Am I to tell you a crime has been committed … or corruption is involved?"

"Director Morgan, there is the appearance of a conflict of interest. The company owned by Senator Robinson's son is buying up—"

"Hold it, Steve. All I see in this file and your conversation with Governor Bliss represent legitimate business transactions. There's no evidence of—"

"Isn't that up to the FBI to find the evidence?" Wagner had raised his voice; his face reddened.

"But we have no complaint or third party participation in order to start an investigation." Morgan put his hands on the desk and explained, "If the FBI became active in the probe of a presidential candidate based on this information and it became known, well, you can see the implications."

Wagner sat back in his chair and ran his hands through his hair. *Of course he's right.*

After a brief pause, Morgan continued, "I admit there may be something here that is not kosher or possibly unethical, but, for God's sake, our involvement would jeopardize the President's campaign. His administration would be blamed for influencing the election in his favor on unsubstantiated, or worse, no specific charges."

Wagner felt deflated. "Okay, I agree with you. It was never my intention to get POTUS entangled in this at all."

"Seems to me all you might have is a political issue to deal with," Morgan said, standing to end the discussion.

"Thanks for your time, Director. Have a good day."

Wagner moved papers on his desk to the out box and checked his calendar. "Let's see," he mumbled, "the President is in Houston and Granger's in Boston."

There's only one person who can evaluate the political consequences of Robinson's involvement in these transactions, Wagner concluded.

Chapter Fifty Two

There was no way for Harry Grant to know why the President was sitting on the floor with a forlorn look on his face. Grant had an appointment to meet with POTUS in the living quarters of the White House to discuss the upcoming confrontation with Robinson. Earlier in the day Atkinsen had returned from campaign stops in San Diego and Houston.

"I'm okay, Harry," Atkinsen affirmed, as he held the credenza for assistance to stand. "Really, everything's fine," he said to allay the concern on his advisor's face.

Less than an hour ago, after the President was getting settled following his two day trip, he had been browsing through personal legal papers. He came across a letter from Ellen written one month after the Inauguration almost three years ago. Her father had died and Ellen decided to stay in Savannah after the funeral with her sister.

Atkinsen picked the letter off the floor and reread it.

My dearest Herbert,

What price I must pay to reconnect with my sister. I <u>miss</u> you. While I've enjoyed a delightful time with Lauren, she has been kind to put up with my frequent distractions. There hasn't been a minute go by without you in my thoughts.

I know how busy you must be. Please don't allow the stress to change your values. How could that awful reporter criticize your proposal on social security reform!

Many memories have resurfaced during my stay here. How compassionate and loving you were when I hit rock bottom knowing I was unable to have children.

The good news is I will return to the White House one week earlier than expected. I love you too much to stay away any longer.

Stay well and all my love,

Ellen

p.s. Perhaps we could spend a weekend at the Greenbrier again?

The pained look on the President's face was clear-cut for anyone to recognize. The letter he had read was in plain sight on a coffee table.

"Shall I come back another time, Mr. President?"

"Harry, I'm better now. Just give me a minute."

Atkinsen ran his hands over his face as if he were washing. He bit his lower lip and, in a soft voice, said, "I need you to stay here with me. It's hard to believe that Ellen wrote this letter to me the end of February. By September she was dead."

Grant seemed to stoop, as if his knees had buckled. He moved to the back of couch and rested on it, palms down.

They stood aimlessly for almost a minute until the President divulged, "I would let Ellen down if I didn't do my best to win reelection."

"From what I knew of her, you're absolutely correct, sir," Grant said.

"Then let's get down to business about the debate. Your message indicated you have some new information for me."

"Yes, sir. This may not be for the debate, but we wanted to get your advice on how to proceed."

They sat in arm chairs opposite each other.

"Mr. President, I'm not sure how much you know or recall about the Kansas City SmartPort project."

Atkinsen searched the ceiling and said, "I read a summary file on it … and Governor Bliss gave me key facts about the advantages of Kansas City as a major inland port. Is there something wrong with my support for it?"

"Not at all. I met with Steve Wagner last weekend at his request. Turns out Governor Bliss informed him that Robinson's son has a business that is acquiring land along the route from Kansas City north to Canada, and south to a deep water port in Mexico. The implication is—"

"Oh shit," the President reacted in an instant. "I've told Wagner before that we can't inject innuendos into the campaign against Robinson. It would backfire on us for sure."

"I agree, Mr. President, and so does Wagner." Grant shifted his position and signaled more to come. "We're aware that Bruce Robinson is an astute businessman. Forbes magazine listed him as one of the top young entrepreneurs in the country. The land and real estate transactions all seem to be on the up and up. While there may be an appearance of a conflict of interest for the senator, we're not going to go there for the same reason you have. Director Morgan has hinted it may be a matter for the senate Ethics Committee, but not until after the election."

"Well, what is the issue then?" *Why does he persist to discuss a matter irrelevant to the debate?*

"The issue is Robinson's professed isolationist policy."

The President's look conveyed his feeling. "I don't know what you're talking about."

Grant stood and wet his lips.

"Harry, how about we both have a cold beer?"

"I'd like that, sir."

After a healthy swallow, Grant resumed. "Senator Robinson's career has been based on a fundamental principle of avoiding foreign entanglements. Over the years, he has fought any legislation favorable to Mexican immigration and, of course, voted to deport illegal immigrants."

Atkinsen was absorbed in his advisor's presentation, while Grant paused for a drink.

Where is all this heading? he wondered.

"Senator Lewis informed me about the votes in a recent meeting of the Senate Commerce Committee," Grant said, referring to his prepared notes. "Robinson voted for ceding the Custom Port land to Mexico, which clearly implies his backing of the Kansas City overall project. He also praised the impact NAFTA has had to date."

The President appeared startled. "He must have a political motive for doing so. Both actions are contrary to his prior positions."

"Herb, that's what I'm trying to tell you. He's doing a one-eighty on his principles."

"Do you think he wants to come across as more moderate in the national debate?

Atkinsen scratched his head and downed half his beer. "Why else?"

"I have a theory," Grant said, sitting down.

"Okay, Harry, let me have it."

"Please stick with me on this, sir. After the NAFTA agreement was signed, Vincente Fox, the former President of Mexico, promoted the idea of a North American community. Seems he was enthralled with the concept of the European Union."

"So what happened?"

"Two things. Nine-eleven put a damper on the idea for obvious security concerns. Second, your predecessor, President Washburn, agreed to a Safety and Protection Program with the President of Mexico and the Canadian Prime Minister. We know how effective the coordination against terror threats has been under that initiative."

"Hmm. So where does Robinson fit into this grand design?"

"It's my opinion that the business venture of Robinson's son would benefit handsomely if the Kansas City project received approval at all levels, including the Mexican Custom Port, and when combined with the demonstrated advantages of NAFTA. Furthermore, there are a few congressmen who have indicated they would support a North American Union, a la European Union, which would be worth millions to his son's company year in and year out."

"Let me get this straight," Atkinsen interjected, "You believe that Robinson might abandon what he has stood for all his life for financial gain."

"Yes, as long as it's all legal, and Morgan sees no crime in a legitimate business. So it comes down to a political risk Robinson's willing to take for his son's business."

Atkinsen bit his fingernail, as he labored to make sense of Robinson's motivation. He recalled that George Granger had mentioned there were contradictory statements from the Robinson camp on the campaign trail.

Grant added, "A lot of his supporters would be shocked, that's for sure. It puts the two of you in the odd position of complete agreement on an issue … for divergent reasons."

"Yeah, they would be more than stunned and pissed off at him, but only if your theory makes sense and is accepted," Atkinsen asserted, fascinated with the reasonableness of Grant's speculation. "That's a big if."

They seemed to stare into space, like sea captains peering at the horizon. Finally, the President asked, "Now what do we do? This is all below the radar screen."

"Mr. President, I'll be damned if I know."

"Well you better think of something quick, Harry!"

Jesus Christ, there's only two days before the debate and less than a week to go before Election Day.

Chapter Fifty Three

"Good to see you, George. Would you like some lunch?" Atkinsen continued to eat his Turkey sandwich and drink a diet Coke as he motioned to Granger to sit.

"No thank you, Mr. President," said Granger.

Glancing at his wristwatch, the President added, "There's six hours before the big event so we have plenty of time to talk. Harry Grant will join me later." He signaled to his Chief of Staff and said, "Steve, could you leave us for a few minutes."

Wagner picked up his lunch tray and excused himself, heading to the outer room of their hotel suite.

When they were alone, Granger said, "I know you wanted to see me about a few things." He sat opposite the President, who took one last bite of his lunch and finished off the soda.

"Yes, I do." Atkinsen adjusted his position on the couch. "But first, let me bring you up-to-date on Jackman's efforts with the electors in each state. Most slates of electors have pledged their support for the Atkinsen/Granger ticket, but a few are on the fence. There has been pressure for key appointments in our administration in return for their support. I want you to know right up front there are no deals. I expect them to vote on the merits of the Atkinsen ticket, period. The party chairmen in each state know I'm holding the electors to their pledge."

"I appreciate you telling me," Granger said.

"Now then, I've heard you were a little testy with Governor Hughes. Even lost your cool, didn't you?"

"Mr. President, I suppose I did once," he admitted, avoiding eye contact. "Hughes skirts all the issues. One TV ad suggested I practice Cajun voodoo."

"Sounds like he's getting desperate, but—"

"And he's aggravating. He gets right in your face, as if he's spent too much time in the confessional box."

"That may be, but he's not the worst adversary you'll ever come up against. George, don't get the reputation of a whiner, with a bad temper to boot!"

"You're right, sir," said a timid Granger, shaking his head. "It won't happen again. I'm sorry."

"Okay. The other matter is more significant to our relationship." He studied his running mate's curiosity at what came next. "I watched your last Town Hall meeting on TV and was disturbed with your response to a question about judges' decisions."

"Oh."

"I think you crossed the line on your criticism of judges as a group."

"Wait, sir! I was expressing my opinion on the low bail to sex offenders, and the criminal records of illegal aliens who are not deported by—"

"But you incite—"

"Activist judges are part of the problem." Granger's interruption was strident.

"Now calm down, George!" Atkinsen stood and glared at his running mate, who became rigid in his chair.

"First of all, even judges can make mistakes."

"I realize that, Mr. President, but this also relates to law enforcement and the Corrections system. We reduced the appropriation budget for more jails last year because of your veto threat."

Atkinsen felt the hair on his neck tickle; but it wasn't funny and he wasn't laughing.

Good God, is this the way it's going to be between us in the future?

"Before this goes too far, let's start all over." Sensing he started to hyperventilate, Atkinsen took a deep breath and sat opposite Granger. "The point I was going to make before you interrupted me was concerning the independence of judges. Their rulings, however unpopular, must be made without fear of reprisal. We expect Judiciary review boards and or the voters to weed out any misfits on the bench."

Granger nodded, no longer so stiff. The President's commanding stature seemed to tranquilize his perturbed state.

Atkinsen continued, "The Founding Fathers recognized the joint advantages of free speech and freedom from intimidation. What great wisdom they had! You and I have to avoid inflammatory rhetoric, despite our passion about faulty judicial decisions, especially as national leaders. I'm sure you feel the same way."

"Mr. President, it was never my intention to condemn the whole system or imperil individual judges. I regret that impression and I sincerely apologize to you." Granger's tongue wet his lips, as if he had eaten spicy food.

"George, remember what we said to each other when we became partners months ago. At times we would agree to disagree, but we will always collaborate … and integrate politically, setting national priorities. If I'm elected, we'll have to openly negotiate issues like these without the agenda of a special interest."

"Thank you for your frankness, Mr. President. My intense feelings on this subject just got the best of me. I look forward to an intellectual exchange on strategies with you."

As Granger reached the door to depart, he turned back to Atkinsen and said, "Good luck tonight. I've never told you before that I have immense admiration for the honesty and unselfishness of your actions as president. Your values are universal and go beyond the label of any single political party."

They shook hands; it was more than a casual handshake.

Chapter Fifty Four

"Mr. Vander Meer, please keep this unscheduled meeting brief and to the point," Rickman commanded. "I plan to watch the presidential debate on TV in one hour." He eyed the two visitors with suspicion.

"Mr. Secretary-General, thank you for seeing me on short notice. First, I wish to introduce Mr. Stephen Harris, Director of the United States Secret Service."

They simply nodded at one another.

Klaus Vander Meer was head of the UN Office of Internal Oversight. After a three month investigation, he had documented in meticulous detail several charges and complaints against the office of the Secretary-General.

Rickman was apprehensive about the unforeseen participation of the Secret Service head, as he shifted papers around on his desk. *No need to question his purpose at this point.*

"Mr. Secretary-General, I'm here on official business to bring to your attention charges against you and your conduct in office," Vander Meer said. "You will be given an opportunity to respond, of course."

Rickman's face colored. *What has he discovered?* "Are you acting within your authority?" he asked.

"Absolutely, sir."

"Continue!" He glanced at his watch.

"The Chilean Ambassador informed me you were instrumental in trying to influence Chilean citizens with relatives in the US to vote against President Atkinsen in the election."

"My office did communicate the contents of President Atkinsen's proposals through the Department of Public Information last April." Rickman's quick retort was firm.

"Sir, the distribution to select countries may be a violation of procedure, and it has been referred to the Ethics Committee, which I chair."

"I'm sure you will find we were simply providing information on matters before the UN, and I was carrying out my mandate. Is there anything else?"

"We have a document from a Member state that you sought instructions from another Member, which is a violation of your oath and—"

"What government?"

"Israel."

"I'm sure I will answer the specifics of that charge. While I was stationed in Palestine, it was appropriate for me to consult often with Palestinian and Israeli officials."

As Vander Meer referred to his notes, Rickman felt a burden had been lifted off his back. *Those complaints are easily dismissed as being within my broad responsibilities.* He tapped his fingers on the desk, staring at Vander Meer.

Why does Harris have to hear all this?

"Sir, we also have some questions for Mr. Hitoshi, who is waiting for me in his office. Before I leave, may I ask if you know a Roberto Morales?"

Rickman gripped his chair tight to steady himself.

"I believe I read about him … an incident with a Secret Service agent. He was killed, was he not?"

"Sir, at the request of the Secret Service, I have located telephone calls from your number to Mr. Morales."

Rickman's face turned ashen. "Er, now I remember. I promised support for his organization to save the UN. Purely non-violent protests and—"

"I'll take over now, Vander Meer. You can go meet with Hitoshi." Harris had spoken for the first time, staring at the S-G.

Rickman flinched at the authoritative order from the bookish-looking official. He fidgeted with his shirt cuffs. A drenching rain hitting the windowpane hindered him sighting a needed repose from this confrontation.

"Let me get right to the point," Harris said. He removed a pen and envelope from his suit jacket and stood in front of the forsaken official. "First of all, Mr. Morales is alive and in the custody of the FBI. Second, he confessed to us that you paid him to kill the President of the United States."

Gott in Himmel. "A lie. That's a complete falsehood." Rickman was shouting and waving his arms; his protruding eyes looked transparent. "I want my lawyer!"

"There's no need for a lawyer or for talk of diplomatic immunity either," Harris responded immediately, leaving no room for alternatives. "We have the evidence of your contact with a would-be assassin, as well as serious questions about your conduct in office. At a minimum you have been unscrupulous."

Rickman felt his empire unraveling.

"In addition, we have a statement from the Russian Ambassador of your efforts to discredit the American President." Harris' tone was harsh.

Rickman's diplomatic veneer was unglued, as he bent over holding his head in his hands.

Is there any one I can trust?

"There's only one way to avoid the criminal charges against you," Harris said in rapid fire order. "You must resign and leave the country tonight. We'll keep all the facts confidential."

"How can …" His voice tailed off into mumbles.

"I have a car outside to drive you to your apartment to pack one suitcase. A plane is ready at Kennedy airport to fly you to your home in Vienna."

Harris observed the defeated man and said in a softer tone, "I assure you this is the best solution for you, and I'm acting on behalf of President of the United States." He placed a letter of resignation on the S-G's desk.

With trembling hands, Rickman sobbed, "Is there any other way?"

Chapter Fifty Five

Except for two lecterns twenty-five feet apart, the stage of the auditorium was bare. Only a small crowd was permitted in the Chicago amphitheater to witness the debate. The assemblage was instructed to hold their applause.

Jim Lehrer, of National Public Broadcasting, served as moderator.

"The format tonight is a point-counterpoint discussion of issues presented by each candidate. My role is to keep the forum free-wheeling." He checked his notes and said, "Let's start with foreign policy and with you, President Atkinsen."

"Thank you. It's a pleasure to participate in this American tradition of open democracy. My administration has managed to keep the peace around the world and enjoy the friendship and trust of our allies. A Nuclear Test Ban Treaty is about to be signed. Our military preparedness, however, must remain strong. We are proud of our men and women in the Armed Forces. One last thing. Recently, the Arab League met with Israeli officials on Israel's soil in Jerusalem for the first time ever. A significant step!"

Robinson adjusted his microphone and said, "Thank you all for being here and listening to our policy differences. I don't share the optimism of the President on Israeli-Palestinian relations. The fact is we are over-extended in many countries and we must bring our troops home—from Europe, the Middle East, and Korea—rather than reinstitute the draft. Our military is the best in the world, but they're spread too thin. This administration has made excessive commitments on multiple treaties. The President is deluding himself about our allies following his ill-conceived proposal at the United Nations."

The candidates showed no sign of nervousness, although the President's gaze at notes on his lectern was conspicuous.

Robinson stated, "The President changed his position on mental health insurance coverage. He has acknowledged his own problem, which raises question of his clear thinking and a self-serving motive."

"The Senator avoids coming to grips with a national issue. Yes, my condition, which has been publicized and successfully treated, verified to me how much the medical profession has accomplished in the area of mental illnesses similar to surgeries covered by insurance."

Atkinsen introduced the UN issue next. "The current United Nations structure is bloated and conducive to corrupt practices. My proposals will streamline the organization and achieve meaningful results."

"Your flagrant aspersion toward the UN is dangerous," Robinson said, facing the President. "We must give their meaningful reforms an opportunity to work and not use a surgical incision to destroy the organization whose purpose is to maintain international peace and protect human rights."

Robinson peered around the auditorium as he introduced his next point. "Let me backtrack and say that the US gives up too much in the proposed Test Ban Treaty. Now then, we have lost too many jobs overseas and quality standards of products are lower. The President has not reversed his predecessor's mistakes. The best example is the recall of toxic toys made in China."

Atkinsen shot back, "Free trade has been a boom to our economy and our unemployment rate is below five percent. The reality is we function in a global economy with many trading partners. Chinese representatives have promised action similar to our Consumer Protection agencies."

"I'll stick with the economy on my turn," Atkinsen said without delay. "The US remains the envy of the world in terms of our products and the wages of our workers. I believe Ayn Rand depicted it best in *Atlas Shrugged*—free the entrepreneurs from excessive regulation."

"I wish I could believe the President. In truth his policies belie his words." Robinson heaved his chest forward in a superior gesture.

"Just examine the volume of rules and regulations proposed by his Energy Department and the Environmental Protection Agency. Ayn Rand is turning over in her grave."

Atkinsen faced away from the cameras for the first time to glare at his adversary. Robinson responded in kind.

"Okay, gentlemen, let's move on … and it's the Senator's turn," Lehrer advised.

"I stand on my record of cutting personal and corporate income taxes. The Robinson/Vogel Flat Tax bill is working its way through senate committees as we speak. The bill will simplify the income tax system. Recently, I sponsored a bill to reduce the federal tax on gasoline."

"As the Senator knows, my administration is evaluating the impact and implementation of the Flat Tax as well as the Fair Tax. At least conceptually, I support either of these ideas."

While he sipped some water, the President reviewed his notes on an index card.

"Senator, I believe you have praised the European Union, which includes a common currency and free movement of goods and travelers across borders. Why?"

"I have no problem with treaties among other countries to improve their economies. It's none of our business."

"But, Senator, the EU is much more than an economic body. In fact, it may lead to a single citizenship for the member countries."

Robinson waved his opponent off and said, "My next—"

"I'm not finished on my point," Atkinsen interrupted. "You have flip-flopped on major issues, Senator."

"What do you mean?"

"You have taken lead positions in the past on controlling our borders and deporting illegal aliens. But you voted to permit Mexican sovereignty on US territory. The American Truckers Association made the largest contribution to your campaign because of your support of the Kansas City SmartPort project and, as a *quid pro quo*, you've proposed a reduction of the gasoline tax. You've finally admitted the value of NAFTA, which is an economic step toward easing border crossings for goods and people."

"Er,"

"Senator, I know why I favor these actions. I don't get why you do."

"I can point to many issues where you are guilty of flip-flopping," was Robinson's retort.

"Senator, you are confusing a change of position with legitimate compromise."

"Nevertheless, my positions are based on the economic well-being and advancement of our country. There are no foreign entanglements to concern ourselves with."

"Here's where you and I differ. The full development of the KC project is the completion of the free trade objective from my standpoint. You, sir, want to take it a step further. Similar to a European Union, you desire a North American Union, which—"

"Ridiculous," Robinson shouted, banging his open hand on the lectern. "You're the one confusing practical economic advantages with my fundamental convictions."

"Senator, a North American Union would blur our culture, our borders and monetary system, perhaps even citizenship, with Canada and Mexico and, ultimately, become a single community …a super government if you will. Your historical goal of Fortress America has been expanded to Fortress North America."

Robinson gasped and shook his head. He raised his trembling right hand.

Before his opponent could respond, Atkinsen asked, "Do you state unequivocally you are against the formation of this union?"

Robinson looked to the moderator, who had fixed his gaze on the clock above the stage, as if he were a child just learning to read the time.

The audience seemed to be in a stupor.

"You ought to know that you never say never in politics," Robinson scolded the President. "Your own record is replete with inconsistencies and bad judgment over the years, including the mysterious resignation of your Vice-President and selecting a hypocrite and disloyal figure as your running mate."

The President looked stunned by the personal attack on George Granger.

As the President's unanswered question finally sunk in, Robinson appeared jolted. An awkward silence followed while his head drooped. He whispered to himself, "What have I done?" The private admission duplicated Alec Guinness' performance of Colonel

Nicholson's line and guilt in the movie *The Bridge on the River Kwai*.

He pointed a finger at the President, held it outstretched for a moment, and then let his hand drop to his side in submission. "I would not be in favor of a North American Union."

"Time is up, Mr. President and Senator Robinson. Thank you for a lively debate."

The adversaries left immediately from opposite sides of the stage.

* * *

"To be honest, Harry, my pulse was racing the entire time."

"You certainly didn't show it, Mr. President," Grant said, sipping his scotch in the hotel suite. "Let me give the early reaction from TV commentators and focus groups. You came out ahead with a clear vision and Robinson lost points with his crude reference to George Granger."

"I was astonished at the personal attack. His animosity toward George disclosed a simmering mean streak."

Grant handed Atkinsen a drink and said, "I wondered how you would steer the discussion to the about face on his America First principles without naming his son and their business venture."

Atkinsen grinned and replied, "I took a chance of correlating his view on the European Union with the idea or possibility of a community of Canada, Mexico and us."

"Well I'll tell you, Mr. President, it was a master stroke. The subject of a North American Union is obscure to the general public, but they're repelled by the possible implications. Besides, such a union is a pipe-dream. In fact, the promoters have lost support for the SmartPort." Grant stretched his legs and said, "I can't wait to read tomorrow's editorials."

The President took a long swallow. "That hit the spot." He bit his lower lip, loosened his tie and said, "Harry, my sense is Robinson's base and the party leaders are demoralized by his performance tonight."

"To say the least, Mr. President. Do you think he's figured out the power he has if Granger doesn't get a majority of electoral votes?"

"I bet he's tried his damndest to see that neither of us gets a majority. What a predicament that would be for me."

* * *

Grant awoke earlier then usual, put on a bathrobe and slippers, and shuffled to the computer in the Study. He keyed *The New York Times.*

"Unbelievable!" He flopped back on the chair.

Late Breaking News:

UN SHOCKER: RICKMAM RESIGNS, OFF TO AUSTRIA DEPUTY HITOSHI APPARENT SUICIDE

The right hand column read: *Pres excels over Challenger.*

The last paragraph of the article concluded:

The non-issue of a North American Union was reminiscent of the Kennedy-Nixon overdramatized debate over the islands of Quemoy and Matsu, off mainland China.

Chapter Fifty Six

"Where the hell have you been?" Hugh McGarry looked up from the manuscript on his desk and gestured to Fletcher Jones.

Fletcher flopped into the leather armchair and said, "You'll find out in my expense account."

"The debate was over two days ago and I expected an insightful analysis," McGarry continued, a wry smile strained to reshape his face. "And you missed the hubbub over the turmoil at the UN."

"Well I'm exhausted and I never expected this job would morph me into an investigative reporter."

"Really! Let's have it, Fletcher, and no exaggerations."

"Okay. Sure, I was in Chicago for the debate, which I'll tell you about in a minute, but I made a couple of side trips. Let's just say I was checking out my confidential sources."

"Oh." McGarry picked up his pen and hunted for a legal pad in the bottom drawer.

"First, I traveled to Clark Styles home in Ponte Vedra Beach, Florida, near Jacksonville. He lives in a modest place for a former Vice-President." Fletcher placed both hands behind his neck and slowly rocked.

"What did you find out?"

"We had a nice, brief chat. He didn't come right out and elaborate on his resignation. I asked him did he have his eye on the presidency. Did he want Atkinsen to step aside?"

"And?" McGarry leaned forward, arms folded on the desk.

"Styles laughed and stated, 'unequivocally, no chance.' It was clear to me he has great admiration for the President …even got a little emotional."

"So what's the point?" McGarry seemed to be waiting for the punch line.

"Let me get to my other trip first. The morning following the debate, I flew to Kansas City and visited with local reporters."

"Pray tell, why Kansas City?"

"I wanted to find out for myself just what the KC SmartPort project was all about and—"

"Get to the relevance of all this," McGarry interrupted. He stood and sat on the edge of his desk.

"Curiosity got to me after the exchange about a North American Union, so I arranged to meet a friend in the news business in KC. We met up with reporters and drove around the area under development as well as the existing facilities. Despite the support of the administration and local officials, it's not a done deal by a long-shot."

"Fletcher, I'm really impressed," McGarry said. "You're becoming a real newsman, in addition to being a gadfly."

Fletcher ignored the playful taunt and leaned forward closer to his boss. "I researched the project, including the so-called NAFTA Railway extending south to Mexico and up to Canada. The business opportunities along the route are massive, and one company stands out in the transactions. I got some inside information on the agenda of the Alpha-Omega group. It doesn't take a genius to put two and two together."

McGarry stopped him and said, "I suggest you get it all down for your next column. Give me the draft when you're finished."

"Hugh, this is not a regular column. This political season has been a cathartic experience for me."

McGarry put his hand on his friend's shoulder. "I know. I can see it in your eyes."

"I'm prepared to announce our endorsement for President."

"I'll hold the presses for a special Saturday edition," McGarry said, picking up his phone.

* * *

Westchester Weekly
Political Commentary
By Fletcher Jones

A CONFESSION
AND
AN ENDORSEMENT

As the campaign for president winds down, we are obliged to consider what we have heard and seen, and to deliberate before entering the voting booth.

With regard to what the candidates have said, we can excuse their bragging as white lies. We can take their ubiquitous promises with a grain of salt. We might even accept their flip-flops on issues. History tells us that we should not be shocked that presidents or candidates lie, however noble. But lies have consequences.

We can only surmise what is in their hearts and minds.

Specifically, I am heavy-hearted to perceive the everyday routine untruth of campaigning extends to deception and misinformation. Machiavelli in the twenty-first century!

My experience observing this campaign has caused a sort of mid-life crisis. Earlier judgments of mine on the candidates have come into question. I confess to inadequate deference to a person's character and openness and honesty. Disregarding these virtues, I had placed personal style above substance. I apologize for my disparaging remarks.

One man stands out to possess the traits we respect, and expect, in our leaders. His political instincts are remarkable. My faith in the system is restored.

I confess I bet the farm on Senator Robinson the last time; my loss was a paltry sum.

I almost lost my self-esteem this time, until I saw the light.

We endorse for President and Vice-President of the United States the ticket of Herbert Quinton Atkinsen and George Granger—an honorable alliance.

We urge our readers and all voters to do likewise on Tuesday.

Chapter Fifty Seven

"Gentlemen, I'd like to be alone with the Senator for a few minutes. Thank you."

Bruce Robinson waited as several glum-looking advisors left the sitting area of the hotel suite. He had just arrived to spend the last two nights before the election with his dad. News reports painted a negative picture for Senator Robinson, indicating a seemingly insurmountable lead for the Atkinsen/Granger ticket.

"Dad, I'm sorry things are not looking good right now and—"

"Bruce, that's how it goes in politics. We just have to keep a still upper lip and bear with it."

"Do you know what you're going to do after the election?"

"I intend to finish my term and resist the policies of the administration." He peered out the window at the busy street below and mumbled, within earshot of his son, "Unfortunately, I've made too many enemies in this campaign. Ambitious to a fault."

"I deserve some blame, dad. I botched up the business, and the Alpha-Omega people used me to get to you."

Bruce reached out to touch his dad's shoulder, but the Senator had turned at that moment to sit back on the couch.

"Hell, there's nothing for you to feel bad about. When push came to shove, thanks to Atkinsen's cleverness in the debate, I realized I couldn't dignify the concept of a North American Union." He loosened his tie and wiped his brow. "Bruce, you were a whiz at that business ...a true entrepreneur. I'm proud of you."

Bruce arched his eyebrows. "Do you really mean it?" He was taken by surprise at the fervor in his dad's voice. Bruce stood in front of the couch looking down at his dad, who now seemed old beyond his years.

"Well, of course, I meant ..." The Senator stopped and began to shake.

"What is it, dad?" He clasped his dad's hand; sobs had caused the shaking.

It's the first time I've ever seen him cry.

Partially regaining his composure, the Senator wept, "I've let down a lot of people and I abandoned my principles of a lifetime. Worst of all, I haven't been there for you, son, and I'm truly sorry." He gazed at his son and pleaded, "Please forgive me."

Bruce sat on the couch and put his arms around his dad's shoulders.

"Dad, it's okay."

He pulled back to read his dad's face. Feeling an odd emotion, he had trouble breathing.

"I love you," he whispered. He couldn't recall the lat time he had expressed such affection for his father.

He watched his dad nod gently, while his lips trembled, his eyes misty from tearing.

They sat close, looking at each other through understanding eyes.

"Son, I wasn't serious about completing my term. It's time I resign and return to Kentucky with your mom and ...and you and Dorothy, if you wish."

"I'm all for it. I know there are lots of things we can do together."

"Sure, son."

"We can ride those two young stallions mom told me about. I hear she named one of them Wildcat IV." He looked away at a landscape on the wall. "As a kid I used to love riding with you.

"Your mother will be pleased to have us with her."

They remained seated for a long few seconds.

At last, the Senator said, "I'm going to take a crack at drafting a concession to President Atkinsen for election night. I'd appreciate your view of it."

Thirty minutes later, the Senator handed Bruce a single handwritten page of yellow legal size paper. Writing was on every line.

"Dad, it's very sincere. President Atkinsen will accept it as a new beginning in your relationship with him and Congressman Granger." With esteem for his father, he added. "It's a wonderful example of statesmanship and, at the same time, dedication to your core principles."

Bruce placed the sheet of paper in his father's hand, feeling deep respect.

Chapter Fifty Eight

He had not visited the columbarium since Ellen's death.

"I'm glad we could make this stop," the President said to Grant and Wagner. He stared out the car window and thought, *without question, her confidence and support secured where I am today.*

The motorcade drive from the Savannah/Hilton Head International airport to the Greenwich Cemetery took less than thirty minutes. There was enough time for Atkinsen to spend a few moments at the scenic Wilmington River Bluff site before returning to the airport for the trip to his Atlanta headquarters and the pre-election night rally.

"Too bad we can't take in the sights and see some of the characters from that movie," Grant said, as they neared the cemetery.

"You mean, *Midnight in the Garden of Good and Evil*," Wagner said. "I don't expect we'll hear any voodoo or see the Lady Shablis here."

Atkinsen smiled at the playful exchange, which eased his apprehension.

Once Agent Williams opened the car door upon their arrival, the President said, "If you two don't mind waiting here, I'll only be a few minutes."

As he approached the mausoleum-like structure where Ellen's ashes were interred along with the urns of her parents, he stopped in his tracks as the glow of the late afternoon sun between the trees cast a beam at the columbarium. *All that's missing are angels descending from heaven.*

Ellen's words came back to him. "When the time comes, Herbert, I don't want to be in a casket in the ground. My parents are in a beautiful serene location in the Greenwich Cemetery."

He tried to make light of the subject, but she did him one better.

"You know what the minister says at the wedding ceremony. 'Til death due us part.' That's life's myth," she said. Her face blossomed as she perceived a profound thought. "In what will seem like a flash, we'll be together again in heaven."

There would be no need for somber recollections of Ellen on this occasion. He felt her tenderness as sure as she was physically with him, relishing the view of the opposite shoreline and the placid river below.

He walked around the columbarium as if were conducting a military inspection. *She would like this peaceful place.*

Moving to the shade of a moss draped oak, he trembled at the thought of how she loved children. She wanted to have a family, "one boy and one girl," she had said after their honeymoon. His happiness for his life with her held in check any tears for the moment.

Grant and Wagner were now outside the limo, indicating time was short.

Atkinsen closed his eyes tight and said goodbye to her. He felt tranquil for her presence, today and forever. *Thank you, Lord, for allowing me into Ellen's life.*

Half way down the incline to the limo, he turned his back on the motorcade. He masked his final sobs by pretending a chill from the November air caused him to shiver. Wrapping his arms around his chest, he stated, "I'll always love you, my beautiful Ellen."

"Gentlemen, let's get to Atlanta to thank all our campaign workers. It's party time." Atkinsen had that upbeat spark of old.

"Yes sir," they responded in unison, looking at the enthusiastic President.

After they had exited the cemetery, Wagner said, "Mr. President, there have been a host of unexpected editorial endorsements for the Atkinsen ticket. We received word this morning that Admiral Farrell endorses you and Granger." He continued reviewing his text messages. "Here's something interesting. The *Wall Street Journal* reports the Alpha-Omega Group has discontinued its support for Development Corp of America and—"

Grant interrupted with gusto. "Mr. President, I'll wager they were behind the push for the North American Union. Your direct question put Robinson in an inconsistent position in front of a national audience, so once his political influence went up in smoke, the financial backers pulled out."

"I can't argue with your theories," Atkinsen said, reaching out to pat Grant's shoulder, once again impressed with Grant's intuition. "Later, I wanna give George a call in New Orleans," he added, fully engaged in this climactic time. "He's done a great job winning the endorsement of so many in his party."

"You're correct, Mr. President," said Grant. "And he'll make a fine Vice-President."

"Sir, I have to say you and Granger are a great pair," Wagner admitted. "Harry, do you think the Founding Fathers envisioned a collaborative leadership team running the country?"

"Well, I do believe they put patriotism first for those in authority. On the other hand, they gave us free speech in the First Amendment to openly voice our differences. But, after all, I wasn't there." Grant winked at the President, who contained his amusement and returned the gesture.

"Listen you two, you know what they say about counting your chickens," Atkinsen said grinning. "Save the boasting until tomorrow night, if we're lucky."

Atkinsen leaned back on the headrest. He sensed a burden had been lifted off his back. It gave him goose bumps.

As they drove onto the airport tarmac, the President asked, "Have either of you read *The Reagan Diaries*?"

Wagner replied, "I've just started the book."

"I read a few pages each night before bed," the President continued. "I made a copy of an entry he wrote for Nancy when he was in the hospital recovering from the assassination attempt." He removed a single sheet of paper from his suit jacket.

"Listen to this. 'I pray I never face a day when she isn't there. Of all the ways God has blessed me, giving her to me is the greatest and beyond anything I can ever hope to deserve."

"That's a perfect example why they called him the Great Communicator," Grant said.

There's no way I can express my sentiments as Reagan did, thought Atkinsen.

After they had taken off on Air Force One, Wagner answered a call on his cell phone. His smile went from ear to ear.

"Mr. President, the latest Gallup poll results are in. The Atkinsen/Granger ticket is now leading in most states. Independent voters are picking you by a wide margin. Momentum is on our side and they're predicting a landslide popular vote."

Grant clapped his hands softly at the good news and tossed a sly grin at the President.

Atkinsen looked down from 20,000 feet at the rolling hills and lush meadows. He loved his home state and felt an understandable euphoria.

A sleepy Harry Grant was unaware of the President's gaze. Atkinsen reflected on his friend's indispensable role in the campaign and thought what would I have done without that old codger?

"Steve, did you know a Sanders at your old law firm?"

"Yes, sir, Tom Sanders. He was a partner with me representing several clients. Tragic, though. He had a heart attack right at his desk. A great guy ...very ethical."

"Do you know his wife as well?"

"Sandy Sanders, of course. A wonderful, smart lady. She hosted parties at their home ...and had a special way about her. Made everyone feel at ease without being intrusive. She's rebounded from her husband's death quite well. She is—"

Atkinsen interrupted, "Steve, I've asked her to join me for Thanksgiving dinner at the White House."

Wagner rose up in his seat; his smile looked like a gawk. "Mr. President, that's terrific news."

"I want to send her a formal invitation."

"Yes, sir. I'll take care of the arrangements."

Atkinsen resumed staring out the window. Houses now covered the landscape as the plane descended toward Atlanta.

Who could have anticipated the success of the Atkinsen ticket? What will be the consequences?

"Time to put politics out of my mind for now," he concluded to himself. "January to November has been a lifetime." He began a low whistle to the tune of *But it's a long, long time from May to December.*

My best instincts were to ask Ellen to marry me ... and ask Sandy for a date.